PRAISE FOR THE NOVELS OF ERIKA MARKS

The Guest House

"*The Guest House* is a sweet breath of a Cape Cod summer, redolent with the scents of salt air, old houses, and the burning wood of a beach bonfire. Erika Marks creates an intoxicating blend of love, lost and found, and confronting the ghosts that lurk in our pasts. I highly recommend this beautiful story of growing up, growing older, building up walls, and knocking them down."
—Karen White, *New York Times* bestselling author of
A Long Time Gone

"A deftly woven tapestry of love, loss, and family loyalties. Erika Marks's modern-day *Romeo and Juliet* is pitch-perfect."
—Wendy Wax, author of *While We Were Watching Downton Abbey*

"A satisfying read that evokes the leisurely warmth of long summer days and true connection." —*Kirkus Reviews*

"The plot is heartwarming and engaging, stirring up a depth of emotion that makes this novel the perfect summer read."
—*RT Book Reviews*

continued . . .

Written by today's freshest new talents and selected by New American Library, NAL Accent novels touch on subjects close to a woman's heart, from friendship to family to finding our place in the world. The Conversation Guides included in each book are intended to enrich the individual reading experience, as well as encourage us to explore these topics together—because books, and life, are meant for sharing.

Visit us online at penguin.com.

The Mermaid Collector

"An elegant and enchanting story about rescuing ourselves by saving each other, and a beautiful reminder of the magic and mystery we hold in our hearts."
— Eleanor Brown, *New York Times* bestselling author of
The Weird Sisters

"Marks skillfully navigates a course that wrecks most novels: recounting two stories—one historical, one modern—that are equally moving and compelling." *—RT Book Reviews*

"Magical! *The Mermaid Collector* had me immediately transported to the windswept cove at Cradle Harbor, feeling the mist on my face and the sand under my feet—and looking for mermaids at every turn."
— Sarah Jio, author of *The Violets of March* and *The Bungalow*

Little Gale Gumbo

"Spicy, delicious, and filled with surprises, *Little Gale Gumbo* is a wonderful stew, a debut novel that will fill you with joy. Put it on your reading menu and enjoy!"
— Adriana Trigiani, *New York Times* bestselling author of
Don't Sing at the Table

"A debut like this doesn't come along often—this is women's fiction to be savored . . . a winner."
—Library Journal (starred review)

"Built on a roux of charm, intrigue, and family secrets, Erika Marks delivers a savory blend of romance and suspense, bringing New Orleans to Maine in a delectable debut novel."
— Sally Koslow, author of *With Friends Like These*

"Seamlessly shifting in time to reveal the layers of a mystery, this is a poignant story of an unforgettable family bound by secrets, fierce love, and a dash of voodoo. . . . Erika Marks is a shining new talent, and she has written a novel full of heart and grace."
　　　　　　—Rae Meadows, author of *Mothers & Daughters*

"I loved this novel like crazy. With its irresistible settings—from New Orleans to an island off the coast of Maine—unforgettable characters, and heartfelt exploration of love, family, and secrets, [this] is one of my favorite novels of the year."
　　　　　　—Melissa Senate, author of *The Love Goddess' Cooking School*

"This story is simply sublime. . . . The story itself was gorgeous. The characters are complex and unique, and the sacrifices each one made for the other were heartbreaking."　　—Fresh Fiction

"Dahlia and Josie are rich, complex characters. . . . The plot pulls the reader right along, trying to figure out what really happened between the two men, as well as what might still happen for the sisters and their love interests . . . recommended."
　　　　　　—Devourer of Books

"*Little Gale Gumbo* is written in the spirit of Adriana Trigiani's bighearted family sagas. . . . The relationships are complex, substantial, fraught with complications and uneasy answers, but ultimately satisfying. . . . While food plays a central role in this novel, in the end the strength of the story is in how it portrays the healing love between broken hearts, the power of that love to heal in unexpected ways."　　—Reader Unboxed

It Comes *in* Waves

Erika Marks

NAL
ACCENT

NAL Accent
Published by the Penguin Group
Penguin Group (USA) LLC, 375 Hudson Street,
New York, New York 10014

USA | Canada | UK | Ireland | Australia | New Zealand | India | South Africa | China
penguin.com
A Penguin Random House Company

First published by NAL Accent, an imprint of New American Library, a
division of Penguin Group (USA) LLC

First Printing, July 2014

LIBRARY OF CONGRESS CATALOGING-IN-PUBLICATION DATA:

Marks, Erika.
It comes in waves/Erika Marks.
p. cm.
ISBN 978-0-451-41886-9 (paperback)
1. Middle-aged women—Fiction.   2. Widows—Fiction.   3. Female friendship—
Fiction.   4. Folly Beach (SC)—Fiction.   5. Domestic fiction.   I. Title.
PS3613.A754525I83   2014
813'.6—dc23   2014005365

Printed in the United States of America
10 9 8 7 6 5 4 3 2 1

Set in Cochin
Designed by Spring Hoteling

For Ian, Evie, and Murray
Our story will always be my favorite.

It Comes in Waves

October 18, 1989

Dear Foster,

Right now my brain may be stuck in this library studying the most boring textbook ever written but my heart is with you, up on our boards and about to launch into the perfect wave. I miss you something crazy.

My roommate, Courtney, thinks I made you up because she's of the opinion that there aren't any guys our age who would be okay with a girl who surfs, but she won't even go to the bathroom without lipstick, so I'm not sure she's the best judge about what guys do or don't like. Either way, send me a picture of your gorgeous face—or write me—so I can put this to rest already.

I'm counting the days until Friday. Are the waves still good? Do you think we could get some more of those crab bites with the peachy-colored sauce? I can't stop thinking about those things. (Or you.)

Oh, tell your mom that I looked up Frieda Zamba like she suggested and WOW! She's amazing! Do you suppose she'd ever show up for the Folly Classic? I would die to meet her! Did you know she was the youngest surfing champion ever? Isn't that incredible??? Maybe they'll be saying that about me one day, huh?

Okay, enough daydreaming. I have to get back to back to the zzzzz. . . .

(Sorry. I glanced over at my textbook and immediately nodded off. Ha.)

Say hi to Shep and Jill for me. Did I tell you already that I miss you? I did? Oh well, I'll say it again. Just in case you missed it the first time.

I

miss

you.

And I can't believe how much I love being your,

Pepper

1

GOLDEN, COLORADO

*T*here was a time when Claire Patton looked forward to storms. The kind of crackling skies and wild winds that would send most girls under their covers; those were her very favorites. Because the bigger the storm, the bigger the swells: waves that would quiet those sanctimonious surfers who came from Malibu or Oahu and scoffed at her little Folly Beach tubes. The kind of waves that could hush the world, that reminded her why the ocean was always her master and never her friend.

But today, as she studied the darkening sky from the deck of the town house she shared with her teenage daughter, all that Claire felt was panic. How long did a child have to be missing before a mother could call the police? Hours? Days? Claire should know these things—why didn't she know these things? The minute she found the texts on Lizzie's phone, she should have made it her mission to know how long. A mother could never have enough information. That was going to be Claire's excuse should the truth of her snooping ever come to light: An informed parent was a smart parent. She wouldn't feel guilty for breaking her daughter's trust. After all, Claire paid for the phone and the monthly bill. Lizzie should have known better than to store top-secret escape plans there. Claire had been a far more clever love-struck teenager.

Up until four months ago, Colin Jefferson had been "that boy" Lizzie had known since kindergarten, a squinting, gum-snapping, freckle-faced kid whose upper lip was permanently stained with a red Gatorade mustache. His mother, Deborah, and Claire had been close friends once, eager to coordinate after-school playdates in each other's backyard while they sipped cheap red wine and waited for their husbands to come home from the college. Now Colin was the center of her daughter's universe. No, he *was* Lizzie's universe: a lanky, sullen galaxy of reckless stars that her daughter was hurtling herself into like a rocket. The irony stung Claire hourly; the many times she had pressed to bring them together as children, now all her efforts were in keeping them apart.

Two weeks ago putting away laundry, Claire had found a nearly drained bottle of vodka in the back of Lizzie's drawer and sat down with it on the edge of her daughter's bed, staring at the frosted glass, as if sure it, or she, might burst into flames, but the only thing she'd burst into was tears. When she'd confronted Lizzie about the liquor that night, her daughter had insisted she was merely keeping it for a friend and promptly poured it down the drain as proof.

Some proof. Everything had snowballed after that. Tests had been failed, curfews broken. The stench of secrets clung to everything in the house like the smell of old smoke. Claire had slept poorly, waking at every creak, sure it was Lizzie slipping out into the night like something small and unprepared, a newly hatched butterfly with damp wings. Then today Lizzie had skipped last period—English class. They were reading *Pride and Prejudice*. Lizzie loved *Pride and Prejudice*! And now, at five fifteen, her daughter was still not home, and the plot that Claire had uncovered two days earlier galloped through her thoughts. Grand plans had been made for flight. From what Claire could glean as she'd scrolled madly through Lizzie's text messages, Colin had a friend with an empty RV in Arizona that would be theirs for the taking—and parking—wherever they wished. All they had to do was find a way out there.

In the two days since uncovering their plan, Claire had monitored her daughter like a documentarian, gauging Lizzie's every gesture, every expression, every word. What else could she do? Confessing that she'd snooped was unthinkable. Claire hadn't even admitted the news to Nick, knowing exactly what her ex-husband would say: Their daughter was just showing a bit of independence, pushing boundaries; what could be more normal? His calm would only unravel Claire more. After all, he wasn't the one who'd fled college at eighteen and moved to Folly Beach to surf with the love of his life.

Claire knew better than anyone that the teenage heart—and its power of persuasion—wasn't to be underestimated.

Yet here she was, losing her beloved child to the pull of a boy's moon, and as ill-equipped to fight the gravity of young love as her own parents had been to stop her from falling into the orbit of Foster King.

Thunder popped and growled; Claire watched the sky for streaks of lightning, her pulse as charged as the air. She bunched her blond hair into a messy ponytail and snapped an elastic band around it. Her work clothes pinched; she wanted to change but didn't dare leave her post. She'd taken off her shoes, and the cold tiles offered some relief to her aching heels as she rubbed her toes into the grout. She held up her smartphone to check the time. Five twenty-one. Claire would give Lizzie until six. At six Claire would call the police and report her daughter missing, or kidnapped, whatever designation turned the wheels faster.

She could call Deborah Jefferson.

And say what?

That Deborah's sixteen-year-old son was plotting to take Lizzie to Arizona to live out their lives in a borrowed RV in a mall parking lot?

Or maybe the truth: that she, Claire, had good reason to believe that making poor choices in love was an inherited trait, as genetically predisposed as eye color or fingernail shape, and that Claire had clearly passed down that curse to her daughter?

Her cell rang out, shattering the silence. Claire snapped

her phone off the counter, so sure it was Lizzie that she didn't even look at the caller before she gasped into the phone: "Zee?"

A man answered, "Can I speak with Claire Patton?"

A telemarketer. She could just tell by the cheery tone of his voice. "This is Claire."

"Claire, my name's Adam Williams. I'm from ESPN, the sports network—"

She cut him off. "I know what ESPN is. I appreciate the call, but I already have cable and I'm not interested in any more channels—"

"No, no. This isn't a sales call," the man insisted with a laugh. "I'm a series producer at the network. Are you familiar with the show *To the Extreme*, about pioneering women in sports?"

The sound of a car nearing and slowing sailed through the opened slider; Claire rushed back to the deck and looked down, anticipation fisting around her heart a second time, only to see the mailman's boxy truck sputter past the unit.

She exhaled; the fist uncurled.

"Claire? Hello? Are you still there?"

It was a prank call. It had to be. One of her students had obviously ferreted out her ancient past online and was having fun, pulling her leg. "Come on, who is this *really*?" she said. "Is this Mike? Michael Young, this isn't funny. I need to keep the line clear for my dau—"

"Claire, this isn't a joke." The man's voice deepened. "We're filming an episode on women surfers in Folly Beach and your name was brought up to our production team. We'd really like to interview you."

"Me?" She blinked out at the street, incredulous. "But— I haven't been on a board in years."

"That's fine," he assured her. "This would be more of a retrospective. A kind of where-are-they-now thing. What we'd like is to film you where you got your start in Folly, have you talk a bit about the scene then, how it was for women surfing in those days, why you chose not to join the circuit—that sort of stuff. We're really excited about it and we'd love to have you on board . . . so to speak."

Claire walked slowly down the deck, trying to wedge this strange new thought between the crushing layers of worry she was stacking for Lizzie. Go back to Folly? It was unimaginable to her. She hadn't been to Folly since Foster and Jill had turned everything upside down seventeen years ago. Not even for Foster's funeral. How could she possibly go back for something as trivial as a television show?

"No," she said firmly. "I'm flattered, I really am, but I can't."

"I promise you won't even have to get in the water if you don't want to."

"No, it's not that. I have a daughter. She's fifteen—"

"So bring her with you. We'll gladly pay for her ticket too if that's what it takes to get you involved. I'm sure she'd be thrilled to see where her mom got her big start."

"My daughter doesn't really know about all that. . . ."

"Then what better way to show her?"

Claire frowned, her patience thinning. He had an answer for everything, this guy.

"You don't have to decide right now," Williams said. "Just think about it. We'll compensate you for your time as well as pay for all expenses. It would just be for a few days. If you give me your e-mail, I can forward a contract for you to look over."

Wait—were those sirens? Claire scanned the street as she recited her e-mail address, barely listening as Adam Williams read it back to her to confirm. What difference did it make? She just wanted him off the phone, wanted the line clear for Lizzie to get through. Maybe it wasn't a prank call, but it was certainly a laughable proposition.

"Great," he said. "So we'll be in touch, all right?"

"*Yes*," Claire gasped, but it wasn't in response to him. Through the shimmering curtain of aspens that trimmed her deck, she glimpsed Colin Jefferson's black Mustang crawl up the hill, the car stopping short of what he no doubt thought was the boundary of visibility, but Claire saw it. Then she saw her daughter climb out from the passenger seat, look around, and wave him off. Claire hung up and rushed to the front door, relief obscuring her fury and filling her lungs like a balloon.

When Lizzie reached the walk, she lifted her head and met Claire's waiting eyes in the doorway. Claire stilled, frozen with the agony of motherly duplicity. She knew the importance of this moment, the line she had to draw in the parental quicksand she was in danger of sinking in or forever lose her daughter's respect, yet all she wanted to do was throw her arms around Lizzie as if her daughter had arrived in one of the *Titanic*'s lifeboats, to hold her the way she used to when Lizzie woke from a bad dream or with a fever, like the time Claire had rocked her under the shower's steam when Lizzie was eleven months old and miserable with a cold, her tiny, wet spine shuddering with coughs.

Claire's heart won out. "You came home."

"Of course I came home," Lizzie said as she tromped up the stairs, wrinkling her forehead and nose in tandem the way only teenagers knew how to do. "Why are you looking at me like that?"

Claire blinked. "Like what?"

"Like you weren't sure I would." Lizzie scooted around Claire in the doorway as if she were a lazy summer fly who could be easily swatted. When her daughter continued her march through the apartment, heading for the stairs to her bedroom, Claire felt a spark of frustration and she seized it.

"I called you three times, Zee."

"I had my ringer off. Sorry." Lizzie climbed higher and Claire felt herself shrinking. She wished she'd never taken off her shoes. It seemed inherently impossible to be a parent in bare feet.

"How did you get home?" Claire demanded.

"Moira gave me a ride."

Claire's heart shrank with disappointment, then swelled with hurt. To be lied to as a parent was one thing; to be insulted with a bad lie was another entirely. For weeks, her daughter had been careful with her alibis. This was brazenly sloppy. Lazy and fearless, the way someone gets who is about to leave a marriage or take a new job.

Didn't Lizzie know who she was dealing with? Claire and Foster's plan had been months in the making, crafted as cleverly as a historic heist: da Vincis taken from the Louvre, or millions from a Swiss bank. Her daughter would have to do better than that.

"He's one strike away from being expelled, Zee. Just one."

Almost to the top, Lizzie stopped and turned slowly. The unspoken threat passed between them; Claire watched her daughter's eyes flash with understanding. Such was the tenuous rope bridge of teenage daring. Halfway out, would it still hold?

"You can't say anything, Mom. *Please.*"

Claire folded her arms, feeling taller now. "I will if I have to."

Lizzie just stared at her. Then, still silent, her daughter squared her shoulders, turned forward, and took the final step to the second floor. In the next minute, her bedroom door slammed. Claire's heart raced, panic sizzling through her all over again.

Memories swirled: a tiny, indignant Lizzie in her room, filling a plastic shopping bag with stuffed animals and toys, announcing she was running away and moving to the library where she could sleep on the giant ladybug floor pillows and cook her meals in the plastic play kitchen. Claire and Nick had chuckled; Lizzie had fallen asleep ten minutes after her tantrum, the bag still clutched in her little hand.

Why had she, Claire, not appreciated how lucky she was then, how easy it was to parent someone so small? You could render doorknobs unusable with plastic covers, bolt cabinets with childproof locks. All you had to do to make a house safe was ensure that medicine caps were screwed on tightly and cleaning products stowed out of reach.

But how did you protect a fifteen-year-old from the dangers inside her heart?

*N*ight crawled across the sky, leaving a dusting of stars in its wake. At two a.m., Claire woke with a thumping in her chest, not sure if she'd heard the clap of a closed door or dreamed it. She threw back the sheets and slipped out into the hall, chastising herself with every step, even as her pulse raced, slowing only when she cracked the door enough to see the lump of her daughter's sleeping form outlined against the blue light of a nearly full moon.

Sinking back into bed, Claire couldn't quiet her thoughts. The standoff she and Lizzie had endured played in her mind, then images of Lizzie alone and preparing dinner in a tiny RV kitchen (not much bigger or more real than the library's plastic version!) in a huge, barren parking lot, pitch-black except for the flickering bulb of a single light pole, waiting for Colin to come back.

Claire lunged across the bed for her phone on the night-stand, too undone to feel any remorse for the late hour.

After three rings, a woman muttered, "Hello?"

Oh, the good old days when her ex-husband's girlfriend was instructed to never answer the phone during their separation; now Nina was Nick's answering service.

"Nina, put Nick on the phone."

"You can't just call in the middle of the night anytime you feel—"

"Put Nick on the phone, *please.*"

There was a huff, muffled voices, a rustling of sheets, and then Nick's weary voice arrived. "Claire, don't talk to her that way."

"Lizzie skipped school today."

Nick sighed. "So she skipped. I skipped classes. I survived."

Claire frowned up at the ceiling, skeptical. What had Nick skipped? Gym? Lunch? Tonight Lizzie had looked down from that top step with the fierce determination only a teenager in mad love wears on her face. Nick couldn't understand that kind of devotion, how deep love ran when you were young. It burrowed into bones, drowned itself in arteries and veins, hiding in places where no parent could extract it.

She fell back on her pillow and pulled the covers up to her chest. "It's not just that, Nick. She lied to me. And it was a lazy lie. Like she thinks I'm not paying attention. How could she think that?"

"Is this about that kid she likes? Connor?"

"Colin. She's going to run off with him."

Nick chuckled drowsily. "To where? The movies?"

"Arizona," Claire said, losing her patience. "Colin has a

friend there with an empty RV. They're planning to drive it off into the sunset."

"Good luck to them. Have they seen the price of gas recently?"

"Nick, this isn't a joke."

"And Lizzie told you this?"

"No, I—I overheard her." It wasn't a lie. Reading Lizzie's texts was a form of snooping, wasn't it? No different than catching a conversation in an adjoining room. "Colin took her off campus today. One more unexcused skip, one more and he gets expelled. All I have to do is call it in. He can't very well take her to Arizona if he's expelled, can he?"

"For God's sake, Claire, listen to yourself. You can't do that."

"Of course I can. I'm a teacher and teachers report unexcused absences."

"She'll never forgive you. You do realize that, don't you?"

"She doesn't have to know I was the one to report him."

"Lizzie's not going to Arizona, Claire. It's not in her nature. She's too fearful. She's not like you. We're not your parents. We haven't screwed her up that badly."

Claire reached across the nightstand to turn a frame toward her. It was a photograph of her and Lizzie at a first grade mother-daughter social, cheek to cheek, each wearing the matching macaroni necklaces Lizzie had made for the occasion. Claire still had hers, the paint long since flaked off on nearly all the rigatoni. She turned to see it wound around the base of her vanity lamp, caked in dust.

Tears pooled.

"I promised her we would be different," she whispered.

"What was that?" Nick asked.

"Nothing." Frustration pushed more tears to her eyes. Claire wiped them harshly with the sheet.

"Claire, are you sure you're okay? Did something else happen today?"

"I got this weird . . ." She hesitated, eyeing a hangnail on her thumb. "I got a call tonight," she admitted, worrying the piece of skin. "From some guy at ESPN."

"Did you say ESPN?"

"They want me to come back to Folly Beach and film an interview for a show on women surfers."

"They want you? Seriously?"

Claire pulled roughly on the loose cuticle. It bled; she winced, sucking it clean. "Yes, *seriously.*"

"Don't get defensive. I'm just surprised. You never made a big deal out of all that, so I never knew you were any good, that's all."

"Well, I am. I mean, I *was.*"

"But you wouldn't honestly go, would you?"

Wouldn't she? Until that moment, Claire had talked herself out of accepting the offer. Nick's discouragement was like a flipped switch; determination sparked, hot and fierce. "Maybe I would," she said. "I was even thinking . . ."

"Thinking what?"

She glanced back at the photograph on her nightstand. "That I would bring Lizzie."

"But Lizzie's with us this summer."

Us. Two years after the divorce, a year after Nina

Bolton had moved into Nick's house, and that one pronoun still made Claire want to jump out of her skin.

"It would just be for a few days, Nick. They want me to come as soon as school's out."

"And you think that's the best thing for Lizzie?"

"I think she and I need some time together, away from here. Away from Colin."

"Have you even asked her if she wants to go?"

"Of course she'll want to go." Claire kicked off her blankets and crossed to the window. "She can see what my life used to be like, how good I was at surfing. I think it's important."

"You never wanted her to know about this stuff before."

This stuff. As if Claire's years of champion surfing were a box of knickknacks she'd unearthed for a garage sale.

She stared out at the row of quivering aspens lit under the streetlight, their silvery leaves trembling as furiously as her heart. "Why are you trying to talk me out of this?"

"I'm not trying to talk you out of it, Claire. I'm just trying to calm you down."

"I don't want you to calm me down. I want you to get crazy too. I want you to at least pretend you're scared shitless that we're losing her. I want you to say it's all going to be okay and that I'm a good mother and that she'd still string a macaroni necklace for me."

"A macaroni what?"

Tears escaped again; Claire licked a fat one off her lip and sighed.

"Look, Claire," said Nick. "Don't make any decisions

tonight. Get some sleep. Let Lizzie cool off. We can talk about this in the morning. After you've had some time to think it over. Things never look the same in the morning."

"No," said Claire, "they look worse."

She hung up and walked to the bathroom, flipping on the light and frowning hard at her reflection in an oversized T-shirt. Okay, so she wasn't as fit as she'd been in those days, those sticky, sandy summer days when she'd been Hot Pepper Patton and able to outcarve any surfer in Folly, but it hadn't been *that* long . . . had it? Claire tried to work the math in her head: seventeen years since she'd last been on a wave? That sounded about right: in Florida, the place she'd fled to after being rushed out of Folly, only to discover her rhythm on the board had been lost with her heart.

Claire hadn't been making excuses to Nick; she really *did* want Lizzie to know this part of her. Maybe it would be the glue Claire had been looking for, the thread to sew their relationship back together—or, at least, tighten the weakest seams. Claire had grown up with a mother who was cold, distant, a mother who wasn't interested in building a relationship with her daughter. But not Claire and Lizzie. They would be the mother and daughter that never broke, never hated, never grew apart.

Claire snapped off the bathroom light and walked back to the window, throwing open the sash to draw in a deep breath of fresh air. The night was crisp, heavy with the rich, mossy smell of the woods. Growing up in love with the water, she never would've imagined the air that filled her lungs would lack that unmistakable tang of salt, the ripeness of a receding tide. Now she could barely remember the feeling of paddling out past the white water, the tickle and itch of stowed-away shell chippings in her suit, catching grains of sand under her nails when she'd comb her fingers through her hair.

Why was she so afraid to go back? It was just a few days. And for all she knew, Jill wasn't even living in Folly anymore. And Ivy: dear, sweet Ivy . . . By now Foster's mother would have to be in her late sixties. Had she stayed in Folly after Foster's death, or sold the shop and left? And what of Shep? Surely he'd fled Folly after the betrayal, just as she, Claire, had. How could he have stayed in the same town with the woman who'd left him for his best friend?

There were plenty of reasons why she should say no to Adam Williams, a hundred excuses she could make for why she couldn't go back to Folly Beach, but in this moment, her heart swollen with longing and worry, the only thing Claire could think of was the one reason she should say yes, the one person. Lizzie.

It had been a long while since she'd compared life to surfing, even longer since she'd existed in that sweet spot outside, past the impact zone of the waves, but it seemed fitting tonight. For the middle of the night, Claire decided, was just like riding a perfect wave; time stood still and the world outside was silenced. All that mattered was the moment.

What was it Foster used to say? Whatever your problems, *the curl doesn't care.*

And so Claire sat down on the edge of her bed and searched her e-mail for the attachment from Adam Williams, the contract he'd promised, filled with legal jargon that swam past her eyes as she scrolled the document. She typed back her acceptance without reading it fully, uncaring.

And just like that, she was going back.

2

FOLLY BEACH, SOUTH CAROLINA

*J*ust before she pushed open the door to the beach house and stepped through, Jill King pulled in a long breath of fresh sea air and held it. She'd already seen the recycling bin at the end of the driveway, overflowing with empty liquor bottles and folded pizza boxes. She could only imagine the mess that awaited her.

She spotted the stain on the couch first. Red wine. The vacationers would lose their security deposit for it; the owner of this particular cottage was notoriously unforgiving, but too cheap to use the money to replace the fabric. Instead he'd have Jill scrub at it until her shoulders ached and pocket the deposit as profit. In the years she and Shep had been in the business of cleaning and prepping rental properties, they'd come to know all the landlords in Folly Beach, only some of whom were locals themselves.

Growing up in Folly, Jill had never imagined she'd be making her living picking up after summer people, cleaning their toilets, changing their sheets. But then, there was little of her current life that was as she'd imagined it.

She rewound the tidy knot of her strawberry blond hair and moved into the kitchen, heading for the sink and the tower of dirty dishes beside it. She threw on the tap and waited for the water to grow hot.

"Oh man . . ." Shep appeared in the doorway, his dark eyes scanning the room.

"There's a wine stain the size of a dinner plate on the couch," Jill said over her shoulder. "We'll never get it out."

"I'll get it out," Shep said, crossing to the sink and planting a comforting kiss on the back of her neck. She turned and relaxed against his cheek, grateful for the pleasing scent of his aftershave. "Are the bedrooms just as bad?"

"Worse." Jill could never understand what came over some people when they stayed in a stranger's house. Did they leave their own homes in such disarray? She doubted it.

"Where's Luke?" she asked. "I thought he was coming over with you."

"Ivy asked him over to the shop. Something about a leaky pipe. I told him if he wasn't done by noon, I was going over there to get him."

"Shep, don't," Jill pleaded gently. "It's okay if he wants to stay and help her. Let him have his last summer there." She sank a sponge into the soapy water and sighed. "He's taking the sale so hard."

Shep reached under the sink for the bin of cleaning supplies. "You're surprised?"

She wasn't, of course. Jill had watched her and Foster's son grow up treating his grandmother's surf shop like his second home. Once In the Curl had been the heart of Folly's close-knit surfing community. Then the megastore Fins had opened on Center Street and business at Ivy's shop had practically vanished overnight. Not that Ivy cared either way. Jill knew that Foster's mother maintained In the Curl as a memorial to her son, which was why she, Jill, and Shep had walked the minefield of its inevitable closing for so long. A parent herself, Jill would never have interfered with a mother's grief. But there were logistics to consider, taxes that were draining limited financial resources, not to mention Ivy's advanced age, and outdated wiring that desperately needed to be brought up to code if the shop was to continue operating.

But there was more to it, of course.

Things between Jill and her ex-mother-in-law had never been smooth. Even before Foster had left Claire Patton to be with her, Jill knew Ivy had never been fond of her. For a time, Jill had hoped she could earn the place in Ivy's heart that Claire had always held, but after years of enduring Ivy's dissatisfaction, even after Luke was born, Jill had relinquished her efforts. Foster had left Claire to be with Jill, and still Ivy kept her photographic shrine to Claire on the walls of the shop as if time had stopped. When Luke was small, Jill had tolerated the pictures as best she could, but when her son turned five and acknowledged the pictures in earnest, Jill had finally asked Ivy to remove one of Claire and Foster enjoying a victory kiss after a surfing competition. Foster's mother had balked before she obliged, but Jill had refused to feel badly for her request.

What wife, what *woman*, wouldn't have found a picture like that hard to bear?

As it was, the concession had been a small one. All the other photos of Claire had remained on the shop walls, images of Claire surfing in her trademark red suit, not as many as there once were, but still enough of them that Jill never felt entirely comfortable going back into the store. How could she? The ropes of betrayal and guilt were too tightly braided to ever be unwound. Claire Patton hadn't just been Foster's girlfriend; she'd been Jill's roommate and best friend too. It had been an excruciating slicing of their shared world, for which they were all, in their own ways, to blame.

But for Ivy, the blame had always fallen on Jill.

From the very beginning, only Jill.

"See?"

Shep's husky voice pulled her from her thoughts. Jill turned to find him pointing at the couch, the dark red stain nearly gone.

"Told you I'd get it out," he said proudly.

She smiled, the heat of affection rushing down her limbs. Sometimes her gratitude for him arrived that way, feverish and frightening, so fast it could bring her to tears.

The tender flames of affection set ablaze by guilt, the most powerful igniter of all emotions.

"My hero," she said.

*T*hey finished prepping all six properties with time to spare. At three forty-five, the golf cart loaded down with dirty linens, Jill climbed in beside Shep and headed home down Ashley Avenue, past the line of Jeeps and SUVs parked along the Washout.

The beach was busy. A surprise swell had stirred up the waters, bringing waves to those who'd come looking. Shep greeted familiar faces as they drove past, male surfers changing behind their cars, half-dressed with towels wrapped around their waists and the giddy look of a good day on the water shining on their faces. Jill remembered those looks well.

Shep squinted out at the stretch of uninterrupted beach and the churning surf beyond it. "Some good little barrels out there today. I figured there would be with that system hanging out so long."

It had been years since Shep surfed as regularly as he once did, and yet he still monitored the weather as obsessively as he and Foster used to when they were younger and surfing was everything, when their biggest worry was who would get the better break or the next case of beer.

Jill knew he missed the sport; she could see the longing ride across his tanned face every time they passed the Washout. Unlike Foster, who had wanted to leave the surfing life behind, Shep had remained a faithful follower, his heart still tethered to his board with an invisible surf leash that was no less binding than a real one.

When they turned into the driveway, Jill searched the lawn for Luke's bike, the sign that her son was home, and her heart settled to see it leaned against the side of the house.

"Don't say anything about staying at the shop," Jill pleaded as they climbed the porch stairs.

The sweet, peppery scent of cooking spices was strong as they stepped inside. Her son might not have inherited many of her physical traits, but he had inherited her love of cooking, her desire to bring friends and family joy with food, and it pleased Jill tremendously.

They found him at the stove, shirtless and barefoot.

"Yum," said Jill, slowing as she walked by to catch a fragrant whiff. "What are we having?"

"Fish tacos and jalapeño corn bread," Luke said, shaking a curly lock of white-blond hair out of his eyes. A soft breeze sailed in through the open screens. Jill was grateful for it.

"We really could have used your help today," Shep said.

Jill looked at Shep, wishing for him to go easy.

"Yeah, sorry about that," Luke said, his eyes still on his pan. "I meant to catch up with y'all, but then I got working on this long board I found in the garage. Grams said it was one of Dad's. It needs some TLC, but it's gonna clean up great."

He looked less and less like Foster as he aged, Jill thought, and more like her own father, a fact that at turns relieved her and broke her heart wide open. Sometimes in the car or at the table, she'd search her son's face for reminders of Foster, any hint, however small. The way one side of his mouth rose in a smile before the other, the shape of his ears, the high curve of his eyebrows, as if he were always seconds away from revealing a punch line. Sometimes she'd plead with Luke to keep his hair short, claiming it looked shaggy, when really—and this filled her with immeasurable shame—it was because he looked less like Foster when he wore it too long.

But despite all that, the connection to his father always remained in his eyes—that immediate charge of recognition—and Jill treasured it, the deep blue pools she wanted to swim in, drown in.

"Want me to make a salad?" she asked.

"Sure, Ma. That'd be great."

She walked to the cabinet, pulled down a bowl, and washed a stack of romaine leaves. "You see Amy today?"

"No. I think she's out of town."

"You *think*?" Jill frowned. "Is everything okay with you two?"

Luke shrugged. "Yeah, sure. I just didn't see her today, that's all. No big deal."

"You ever get back to Chuck about that job at the marina?"

"Not yet."

"He said to call him in June. It's June."

"I know," said Luke.

"But you haven't called him," she pressed gently.

"I will."

"When?"

"Ma." He stopped stirring and leveled a look at her, and there, for a fleeting moment, was Foster, staring back at her. Jill shivered. It was as if a bird had landed on her heart. "I said I'll call him and I'll call him, okay?"

She waited a few beats, waited for him to resume his even strokes around the pan, before she moved closer to him, considering her son before she reached out to slide a loose curl behind his ear. It had been reflexive to reach out for him when he was young, to convey her love in touch. Now she hesitated, understanding the boundaries of age.

Shep returned with two bags of laundry over each shoulder and dumped them at the bottom of the stairs.

"I just saw Chris and Ellie walking Pretzel. They said ESPN is coming here to do some kind of documentary on women surfers. You heard anything about that, Luke?"

"ESPN? No way!" Luke spun from the stove, spoon lifted, his eyes huge. "You think they'll come to the store?"

Jill quartered a tomato. Bless his heart, but her beloved son was delusional.

Shep smiled. "Maybe, kiddo," he said gently. "You never know."

"Hey, what about that old friend of yours?" Luke asked. "You know, the one Grams has pictures of all over the shop, Pepper Patton? You think they'd interview her for it?"

Jill stopped her cutting and shifted her gaze to Shep; their eyes locked.

"That was her name, right?" Luke said. "Pepper?"

Shep nodded. "That was her nickname. Her real name was Claire."

"They couldn't do a show about girl surfers in Folly and not show her, right? I mean, she was, like, the best chick surfer in Folly."

Jill and Shep shared another look, modifying Luke's claim in silent agreement: Never mind gender. Girl or guy, Claire had been the best surfer in Folly, period.

"Man, how awesome would that be if she came for it, huh?" Luke said. "Y'all could talk about the old days. I could hear all kinds of stuff about Dad. Wouldn't that be awesome?"

He stared between them, waiting, his eyes shiny with excitement.

Jill swept her gaze back to Shep, wanting to see his expression before offering her son an answer. Shep's smile was steady but far from matching Luke's.

"It would be," she agreed, deciding it was the best reply. Then she set down her knife, wiped her hands on a dish towel, and rescued them all. "Let's eat."

*A*fter they'd scraped off every last flake of blackened fish from the pan and cleared their dishes into the kitchen, when the house had settled into the quiet of night and the sea breeze had picked up, Jill slipped into bed and watched Shep at the sink, shaving after his shower.

At forty-three, he was still every bit as handsome as he'd been at twenty. His red hair—copper in summer, mahogany in winter—was shorter now but still enviably thick, showing only the slightest threads of gray around the ears, his body still muscular and trim. His beauty was of great comfort to her, the part of him she'd first wanted. Something primal had settled inside her when she met him: a hunger to belong to someone so beautiful, that there was a safety and a purpose in becoming Shepherd Craven's girlfriend. In those days, he had been far from ambitious, but he was still young, Jill had told herself, and with enough encouragement and love he would surely take on the responsibilities of age. She wasn't the first woman to think she could change the foundation of a man.

When Shep had taken her back, fourteen months after Foster had died, Shep told her that nothing had changed, that he'd never stopped loving her, not once in all the years she and Foster were married, and Jill knew he meant it. In their years apart, the eight years she and Foster had been married, Shep had had only one serious girlfriend—not that every available woman from Folly to Charleston hadn't thrown her hat into the ring for his heart.

He'd even remained in the same house he and Jill had shared, a cramped two-bedroom rental with chronic roof leaks, but he never sought to move and Jill never judged. Shep had every right to hold on to what he could of their life together, the reminders of the promises she'd made to him. She'd done the same herself in the months after Foster's death. Old surfing magazines, shoe boxes of board wax—after Foster was gone, everything seemed precious and desperately—*deeply*—important to her. It's all for Luke, she'd tell herself when she stood in the middle of the garage or in the doorway of a closet, looking out at a sea of paraphernalia that she might never have missed had someone come along and removed it all for her.

And the days she'd wished for that! Left the house with the door unlocked, just hoping someone might come in and take every last thing, might spare her the impossible chore of having to part with a piece, however small, of Foster.

Eventually she'd confronted it. On a bright and burning Saturday, three years after Foster had drowned, when Shep and Luke had gone to Kiawah, she sat down with her boxes as a defendant sits before a jury, ready to face the inquisition of memory. The trial was a grueling one, but she endured it, and in the end, what remained was a far smaller collection than she might have expected.

Luke had sulked, angry that she'd cast out so much without warning him. Shep had seemed relieved. Foster's mother, Ivy, had been—not surprisingly—furious, calling Jill selfish when she heard, leaving Jill in tears.

"Long, long day."

Shep snapped off the light and climbed into bed, his skin still moist and warm from his shower. Jill curled into him and let the air settle around them. In the quiet, the strange news of ESPN's visit seemed to knock at the dark, pleading like a mewing cat to be let in.

Shep answered the call.

"It really *would* be something if Claire came back, wouldn't it?" he asked.

Jill shifted closer to him. Claire. After all these years.

"I'm not sure she'd want to see me if she did," Jill said.

"It's been seventeen years, Jilly. I'm sure she's over it now."

How could he be sure? It wasn't as if they'd kept in touch with Claire or knew anyone who had. After Foster's funeral, Ivy had received a letter from Claire explaining why Claire had been unable to make the service, that work and family obligations had kept her away, how sorry she was.

Jill reminded him, "She didn't come back for the funeral."

"She told Ivy she couldn't."

"Maybe." Jill pressed her face against his chest. "Or maybe you never move on from that kind of betrayal."

"I did."

Under her cheek, Jill felt Shep's heartbeat hasten and her own heart fluttered too; his claim was not intended to hurt, but it did, if only for a moment.

She raised her head and tried to find his face in the watery dark.

"If she does come, you'll have to talk to Luke," Shep said. "You'll have to tell him the truth."

Jill turned onto her back and stared up at a thread of moonlight that had slipped through the edge of the blinds. It shivered across the ceiling like a kite string. "I'm not sure I can now," she said. "He'll think I'm a terrible person."

Shep rolled toward her. "Baby, he won't even care. I still don't understand why you lied to him in the first place."

How many times had Jill asked herself the same question? Maybe because she'd spent so many years feeling guilty for betraying her best friend, or maybe it was all the years of enduring Ivy's subtle, and not-so-subtle, implications that Foster had only left Claire because Jill had stolen him away from his true love, not to mention convinced him to stop surfing.

Was it so wrong of her, Jill, to want her son to see her differently?

Remarkably, Ivy had played along with Jill's retelling of their shared past, never speaking to Luke of how his father and mother fell in love while his father was living with someone else—the same someone whose pictures still covered the walls of Ivy's shop and the apartment above it, not to mention the walls of her heart.

Jill frowned, suddenly nervous. Earlier that evening, when the possibility of Claire returning to Folly was just a glimmer of excitement in her son's beautiful blue eyes, she wasn't the least bit worried. Now dread crawled along her skin.

"Good night, baby." Shep drew her against him and brushed her temple with his lips, putting the day and all of its strains to sleep.

Jill closed her eyes and rested her palm on his chest as if to draw out the even rhythm of his breathing and force her own heart to fall into the same beat, but her mind seemed frantically awake now.

Truthfully, she rarely thought about Claire anymore. Maybe sometimes, when she'd pass the Washout and see a woman carrying her board into the water, memory would rise, soft and warm, and take Jill back to those early days, the first time she and Claire met, regarding each other with palpable curiosity across a restaurant booth. In the months after the breakup, Jill had sent several letters to Claire, begging her forgiveness, for the chance to repair their friendship. Not a single one had garnered a response.

She'd missed Claire for a long, long time. Then life had stepped in and washed that longing away. Out of sight, out of mind. Out of heart.

For a while, Jill had wondered if Claire had missed her too, if she'd wished things might have been different. If Claire could forgive her. If she could ever forget.

It had been a long time since Jill had considered those possibilities.

Tonight, as the house drifted into slumber around her, wood and plaster settling under the soft, salty breath of the sea, she did again.

3

One week later

Y ou know, Zee, you might actually have fun here."
Despite Claire's suggestion, Lizzie's gaze remained fixed on the view from the passenger window
of the rental car they'd picked up at the Charleston Airport, white earbuds poking out through the strands of her
brown hair. She had her music device turned away; Claire
couldn't be sure if it was on and her daughter couldn't hear
her or if it was off and Lizzie was only faking deafness. It
amazed Claire how someone could be so quiet for so long.
In her own youth, Claire had tried endlessly to win the war
of silence with her father, but muteness was never something she could sustain.

Lizzie, however, was a natural. Her daughter had remained silent from the moment Claire informed her of the
plan to leave Golden for Folly Beach, and Lizzie had stayed

silent for the six days afterward while school came to a close. All the while Claire had waited for Lizzie to inquire, to show interest in this secret life her mother was about to share with her. But car rides to and from school had been quiet, as had dinners. Not once had Lizzie asked what Claire had hoped her daughter would want to know: Why, oh, why, were they going to Folly Beach, and who had her mother been to make them go back?

But Lizzie hadn't asked. And now they were nearly there. A few minutes and they'd be crossing the bridge into Folly. And for the first time since she'd told Adam Williams she'd do the interview, Claire felt the itch of doubt prickle her arms and legs like chigger bites. She didn't dare start to scratch.

Lizzie tugged out her left earbud. "Are we going to see Grandma Maura while we're here?"

The question was unexpected. Claire looked over at Lizzie. "Do you *want* to see Grandma?"

"I guess. Don't you?"

Claire hesitated. What could she say? In all the planning, she'd not given any thought to whether or not she'd visit her mother and stepfather in nearby Charleston. There was enough potential drama to contend with seeing Folly again; a visit with her mother was more emotional baggage than she was prepared to carry. Claire hadn't even shared the news with her mother that she was coming to Folly. Now guilt danced down her neck.

"She'll be pissed if we don't call her," Lizzie said.

"Mad," corrected Claire. "She'll be mad."

"No," insisted Lizzie. "She'll be *pissed*."

Claire sighed, surrendering. There were plenty of battles she would wage this trip. Underage drinking, skipped classes, plots to run away to Arizona. Bad language out of her daughter's mouth was not the hill on which she was going to die. And besides, they were finally talking. Claire would take it.

The last of the commercial strip thinned and the marshland spread out on both sides of the road, the soft tufts of pale green grass. Marsh fur, Claire used to call it, because it warmed her heart. Surely her daughter would perk up to see—to smell—the ocean. *The ocean!* Claire could count on one hand the times Lizzie had faced the sea. But it was clear from the first that Lizzie didn't feel the same pull to the surf that Claire had felt. Visiting California when Lizzie was five, Claire had watched, agog, as her daughter had stationed herself and a plastic shovel at the highest part of the beach, her daughter's big brown eyes shifting nervously to the waves, as if the surf's fingers might stretch far enough to pull her in. "Some kids never take to the water," Nick had said. Claire hadn't agreed.

"Isn't it beautiful?" Claire tilted her head toward the window and pulled in a long breath. "And that smell . . ."

Lizzie scanned the view, frowning. "I thought we were going to the beach."

"We are," said Claire. "This is marsh. The beach is at the end."

"The end of what?"

"The road."

"Oh." Lizzie threaded the loose earbud back through her hair.

They passed Larson's Fish Market. Claire smiled reflexively to see its familiar weathered-shingle siding, its sunbaked blue awning; she smiled again when the car thumped over the bridge at last.

Downtown Folly appeared before her and she steeled herself for her return. Would Center Street have changed in seventeen years or remain startlingly untouched? Claire wasn't sure which possibility she hoped for more.

"*Whoa*—" Lizzie gasped. "What is *that*?"

The Sea Breeze loomed on the horizon, a salmon-stuccoed, six-storied gate to the beach beyond. It was a Folly institution, the shoreline's oldest and most expensive resort.

"That," said Claire proudly, "is our hotel."

"We're staying there?" Lizzie's expression verged on impressed, another tiny victory Claire would gobble up.

"Not too shabby, is it?" Claire asked as she pulled them into the valet parking lane.

The attendant helped them unpack the trunk and directed them to the front door.

"Do I get my own room?" Lizzie asked.

The question startled Claire, slowing her purposeful gait to the entrance. "Did you want your own room?"

"It doesn't matter," Lizzie said, wheeling her luggage around Claire to push through the glass doors. Her own room? Claire had been indulging in fantasies of them staying up late in their matching complimentary bathrobes, ordering room service desserts and watching old movies; Lizzie had been imagining herself alone and free.

God, Claire was dim.

*C*laire knew the Sea Breeze better than most, having worked there as a chambermaid with Jill to make extra money her second year in Folly, but when she stepped through the front doors, she might as well have been a first-time guest. The remodeled interior, colorful mosaic floors and frosted glass walls bathed in pastel lights, bore little resemblance to the hotel of her memory.

At the counter, Lizzie leaned against the tiled facade and let her backpack slide to the floor. "So, where is this ESPN guy anyway?"

Claire searched for her wallet. "I'm meeting him for breakfast tomorrow morning."

A young woman approached them. "Checking in?"

"Yes," Claire said. "Reservation for Patton."

"One minute." The clerk typed into her computer.

Claire glanced around as they waited. "I can't get over it."

The woman looked up from her keyboard. "Excuse me, ma'am?"

"The lobby," said Claire. "It's so different."

"We had a big renovation a few years ago. So you've stayed with us before?"

"I used to work here, actually. A long time ago."

"Oh. Fun." The clerk smiled thinly, all business. "I'll still need to see some ID."

. . .

*I*t was a lovely room, Claire thought as she and Lizzie stepped inside it a few minutes later, larger than she remembered the rooms being, painted in shades of coral and cream, and cozy with plush bedding and upholstered chairs—or maybe it just seemed especially lovely because she wasn't tasked with cleaning it. All those overstuffed satin pillows seemed luxurious when you weren't the one who had to inspect and stack every one just so.

Lizzie dropped her bag on the closest bed and disappeared into the bathroom. Claire moved to the balcony slider and pulled it open, greeting the view of the beach that spread out before her. She stepped into the warm, wet air and leaned over the railing to scan the length of the shore.

"You should see our view, Zee," Claire called over her shoulder. "It's incredible."

She waited for a response, but none came. She leaned into the room and tried again. "Are you hungry? We could go get dinner."

Still nothing, just the spitting of a faucet turned on high.

Claire returned to the view, tempering her disappointment. It had been a long day. With a good night's sleep, Lizzie might see this trip in a more favorable light. In the meantime, Claire would be grateful that they'd arrived.

But God, she was starving. They needed food. Hunger always made for cranky roommates.

Claire stepped back inside the room. "How about I go

out and bring us back something? We could eat on the balcony."

A muffled response came from the other side of the bathroom door. "Okay."

Claire swept up her purse. "Any requests?"

"Anything's fine."

"So I should get us a large order of fried worms and two broccoli shakes?"

It had been a standing joke in their house when Lizzie was little, always eliciting a squeal. Now Claire got only silence.

"Tough crowd," she muttered as she opened the door and stepped out into the hall.

*C*laire walked through the hotel's glass doors into the warm air of evening. The hot, misty scent of the sea blew at her anew, somehow stronger at this time of day, and with its charge came the flashes of memory she had been too distracted to take in when they arrived.

Stopped at the intersection of Ashley Avenue, the whole of Folly's small downtown visible from where she stood, she felt her nerves churning. Though there were only a few places that had survived the years of her absence, it didn't matter; her heart recognized everything. She saw the Crab Trap on the corner and smiled reflexively, the flavor of their crab bites suddenly filling her mouth, the seafood truffles she'd once eaten by the dozen. She'd given up that craving long ago; now it returned. If she ordered some and brought them back to the hotel, would the balls still be as moist, as sinfully rich as the very first time she slid one past her lips and crunched gently on the breaded crust? Maybe, maybe not. Like so many things here in Folly, she'd have to face the truth of time's wear and tear on them, the possibility of change, of disappointment, of deterioration.

Drawing in another deep breath of salt air, Claire crossed at the light and decided of all the reunions she might have to face tonight, this one she would make herself, seeing Folly as she'd first seen it.

Before Foster.

A time that, for all it mattered, didn't really count as living.

*T*he sidewalks on both sides of Center Street were thick with summer traffic, locals and tourists looking for dinner or a drink, probably both. Claire passed the spot where a T-shirt and souvenir store had once resided and now housed a wine bar, the spicy scent of sandalwood incense and the lulling sounds of acoustic jazz wafting out the opened door. How badly she wanted to take a seat on one of the open umbrella tables and order a glass of wine—a drink she never would have ordered in her twenties. Margaritas had always been their drinks of choice then, tart and cold and slightly sweet, rims caked in salt (as if they'd needed more after a day out on the water!), enjoyed on the Masthead's deck or, if they were feeling decadent, at the bar at Pearl's. Claire scanned the other side of the street, trying to locate the sites of their youthful celebrations, but she couldn't find them.

Walking into the Crab Trap, however, was like stepping into a favorite pair of shoes. Everything felt familiar, comfortable. The rich, greasy smell of fried fish blew at her and Claire smiled as she took in a deep breath of it. She might have known nothing could change in here. The restaurant was a fixture in Folly, its nautical décor as precious as its menu. She walked to the register at the end of the restaurant's crowded bar and glanced down the length of the shellacked surface she'd cozied up to a hundred times over the years, taking a quick survey of the patrons but recognizing no one. She did the same with the young waiter who took her to-go order, trying to decide if he resembled anyone she might have known, but her study yielded nothing, only the reminder that seventeen years was a lifetime.

Her gaze traveled to the corkboard beside the register, to the dog-eared business cards of local vendors tacked to it, rental agencies and surf instructors, names she didn't recognize. She looked for one business in particular but didn't see it.

"You wouldn't happen to know if In the Curl is still open?" she asked.

"In the Curl . . ." The young man looked up from his order pad. "Is that the place out near the Washout?"

Claire nodded.

"I think it's for sale," he said. "But if you're looking for the best surf shop in Folly, you can just head across the street. It's the only place anyone goes now." He pointed his pen to the window, leveling it on a glass and turquoise building that had been a hardware store when Claire was here last. Jagged metal letters climbed the facade: FINS. A surfboard burst crudely out of the awning, the torn pieces of fabric flared out to resemble a wave.

Claire eyed the store skeptically, the reflexive burn of loyalty rising in her. Poor Ivy. All the years that In the Curl had ruled the beach, offering nothing but good products for real surfers, now Foster's mother had been put out of business by some generic superstore. Claire bet she knew exactly what kind of poser owned it too. All flash and no clue. Typical.

"That's too bad."

"What is, ma'am?"

"That people would rather support a gimmicky chain than a genuine Folly institution like In the Curl."

The young man looked at her blankly. "On that crab ball plate, did you want a small or large?"

Why had she wasted her breath? "Large," she answered.

"Okay, cool." The waiter tore off the order slip. "Should be just a few minutes."

"Buy you a beer while you wait?"

Claire turned at the man's voice and locked gazes with her neighbor.

"Me?" she asked.

He smiled. "You."

His eyes were a startling shade of gray, pewter: nearly blue but not quite. Claire hadn't noticed him during her first survey of the bar. Had he arrived while she'd ordered? His hair, reddish brown and wavy and overdue for a cut, was threaded with touches of gray at the temples. He wore a plain white T-shirt, jeans and a diver's watch. Though she didn't recognize him, there was something familiar about his appearance, something pure. He was old-school, the kind of surfer who would have been a loyal customer at Ivy's back in the day. She should have saved her tirade for him instead of her waiter.

"Thank you but no," she said, drawing her eyes away from his. "I don't really have time."

"Kipper pours fast." He nodded to the bartender, who looked up and offered her a quick wave.

Claire smiled, waved back. "I'm sure he does."

"By the way, it's not a chain."

"Excuse me?"

"Fins." The man pointed his beer across the street. "I overheard what you said to Bobby just now. It's actually an independently owned shop and it's not as awful as you'd think in there."

"Trust me," said Claire. "Chain or not, I know what kind of phony opens a store like that. That hideous awning. It's like some kind of mouth trying to swallow up the whole street."

The man chuckled, dimples cutting through the sun-tipped whiskers of his short beard. The bartender set down a pint in front of her, the beer's foamy head cascading down the side. Claire waved it away. "No, really," she said. "I can't stay."

"You sure?" he asked.

She met his eyes again, startled to feel the unexpected tug of temptation spark deep down, a forgotten place, the ripples and warmth of immediate sexual attraction.

"Your crab bites, ma'am." The waiter appeared, rescuing her.

The man leaned back and smiled. "Maybe some other time."

"Maybe." Claire took the foam container quickly and thanked the waiter, glancing over her shoulder to give her neighbor a final glance as she rushed for the door.

Lizzie, she told herself. Her daughter would be waiting for her.

4

*S*ome men made love at all hours, some only at night.

Shepherd Craven was a morning lover.

Jill hadn't known this about him until they moved in together. Before those lazy dawns when they'd had the space and privacy to explore each other whenever they wanted, their lovemaking had been dictated by darkness, and wherever they could find an available bed.

Now as the light of morning poured softly into their room alongside the creaks and sighs of a house rising with the sun, she felt his desire against her hip, then his hands around her waist to claim her in a drowsy but purposeful sweep. She shifted to allow him inside her, their bodies joining effortlessly, wordlessly, the silent symmetry of long-time love.

It was a curious thing, starting your sexual life with

one lover, leaving him for a while, then returning to him after making love with someone else for almost a decade. In their early days together, before she'd fallen in love with Foster, she and Shep had struggled to find the balance in their tastes and needs. Shep was a cautious lover—athletic but quiet, agile and controlled. For Jill, comfort with sex had taken time. More than she would have imagined. For too long, she worried about everything she knew a woman wasn't supposed to worry about if she expected to derive pleasure from sex. In fact, it was years before she made love with the lights on. And then it had been with Foster. Which, of course, made perfect sense. For only with Foster had she let herself be seen in full, in ecstasy. Foster had inspired that kind of abandon. He had made love the way he'd lived: passionately, tenderly, and with his whole soul, every time.

Finished, she and Shep lay entwined, daring sleep to swallow them back up, but the day's list of responsibilities blinked in her mind like the flash of a traffic signal. There was too much to do to languish.

"I'm going to load up the cart," Shep said, dropping a warm kiss on her shoulder before sliding out of bed.

Downstairs, Jill found Luke in the kitchen, leaning against the counter and shoveling in cereal with a soupspoon.

She stared at him. "Good Lord, are you even chewing?"

"The ESPN guys got here yesterday," he said through a mouthful of Raisin Bran. "Amy's cousin works at the Breeze and she told me they all checked in, which means they might come by the store, so I gotta get there and tell Grams."

Jill pulled the filter from the coffeemaker and crossed to the trash, a flutter of apprehension traveling with her. So everyone had arrived. Had Claire come too?

In the past few days, while the town had crackled and buzzed over the impending visit from the sports network, Shep had made inquiries with friends about Claire's possible involvement, her potential arrival, but no one had been sure, and the uncertainty unsettled Jill. She didn't know which worried her more: facing Claire again after so many years, or knowing that Claire's return would make her, Jill's, strained relationship with Foster's mother harder than ever. Foster's loyalty to Claire might have faded over time, but Ivy's never did.

"I thought Chuck wanted you to start on the boat today."

Luke gulped down a last mouthful of cereal and set his bowl in the sink. "He said sometime this week."

"Well today *is* sometime this week," Jill informed him, smacking the filter against the side of the can to empty the grinds, harder than she'd intended.

"Ma, are you kidding me?" Luke exclaimed. "This documentary is the coolest thing that's happened to Folly since, like, *ever*, and you want me holed up at the marina mopping slips?"

Jill rolled her lips to hide a smile. Oh, the urgency of everything at seventeen. How she'd forgotten.

"I know you're excited, baby," she said, returning to the sink, "but life can't stop just because of a surf documentary."

"Of course I'm excited. Aren't *you*?"

Jill shrugged, drawing down the can of coffee. "I'm excited for the town, if it means business for everyone. But it's not like I was ever a surfer."

"I don't mean all that," he said. "I mean because you might see her. Your friend."

Jill slowed her scooping and smiled at her son, reminded of how it was to be young and unaware of life's twists and turns, its painful discoveries, its heartbreaks. Everything could be so simple at his age. Once a friend, always a friend. Forever and ever.

Then she remembered, with a sharp pinch of remorse, that Luke didn't know the whole story.

"Gotta go, Ma," he said, snatching his baseball cap off the chair finial and screwing it on his head. "Later!"

He flew out the back door, letting the screen bang behind him.

Shep came into the kitchen. "Where's the fire?"

"Word is the film crew rolled into town yesterday," Jill said, reaching out to tuck in the exposed tag of his T-shirt as he leaned in to kiss her. "Luke's sure they'll be at the shop first thing."

"Of course he is."

Jill met his questioning eyes, knowing they shared the same thought.

"If Claire's coming for this, she's probably here now too, isn't she?" Jill asked.

Shep shrugged. "Maybe so. I'm sure Luke will have a full report when he gets home."

Another flurry of nerves teased her skin; Jill wasn't sure she wanted a full report.

Shep pocketed his keys.

"You're leaving already?" she asked.

"I want to get a few loads in before the crowds show up."

"But the coffee's almost ready."

"It's okay. I'll pick up a cup at Bert's."

She followed Shep out to the porch. "Make sure you get on Luke about this job at the marina. He's supposed to start this week."

"You're the one who said not to rush him," Shep pointed out.

"I know. But you were right. We don't want him to miss this chance with Chuck. I know other kids are waiting in the wings and Luke'll need that money when he starts classes in the fall. I'd hate to see him lose out, that's all."

"I'll talk to him," Shep assured her.

He swung the laundry over his shoulder and pulled Jill in for a quick kiss, leaving her alone on the porch with the comfort of his promise, and a nagging dread she couldn't quiet, or name.

*P*elicans.

Standing at the balcony railing, Claire watched the five big-billed birds sail across the sky. She'd forgotten how wonderful they were, the curious grace in their otherwise clumsy mass. Watching them fly had always filled her with peace and calm, maybe because their expressions and the ease with which they drifted in the air made them appear enviably carefree.

Lizzie should be seeing this.

Claire squinted through the sliding door to see her daughter still in bed, the dark crown of her head the only visible part of her, the rest of her mummified in a tangle of blankets and sheets. She'd hoped Lizzie would wake in time to join her for her meeting with Adam Williams, but it was now ten to nine.

Stepping back into the room, Claire picked up her phone off the dresser and frowned to see the voice mail icon. Had the call come when she was in the shower?

She sat down on her bed and listened to the message.

"Hi, Claire. Adam Williams here. Hey, I'm sorry to have to do this to you at the last minute, but something's come up and I'm going to have to bail on coffee this morning. The good news is one of the show's sponsors, Gus Gallagher, has offered to go in my place. Gus owns the surf shop in Folly, Fins. He was a big deal in Santa Cruz, surfed competitively out there for years, so he knows his stuff. I told him you'd be at Salt's at ten. I've sent him the filming schedule so he can go through it with you. If you have any questions, give me a call. Otherwise, see you on set tomorrow. *Ciao!*"

Ciao? Claire deleted the message, not sure if she was more annoyed to be dining with Adam Williams's stand-in, or that the show she was joining was funded by that god-awful surf shop. Even worse, she'd have to endure a breakfast meeting with the poser who owned the place. Her appetite waned. Maybe it was best that Lizzie *didn't* come.

Claire scribbled a few sentences on the hotel notepad, certain even as she did that her daughter was only pretending to be asleep. So much for her hope that a good night's rest would improve Lizzie's outlook. Still, it was just the first day. She'd bring back something warm and gooey with chocolate and try to sweeten her mood that way.

The crowd at Salt's Café was daunting. Claire squeezed through the bulk of customers that waited at the counter and scanned the tables beyond, hoping her host would have the good sense—not to mention courtesy— to wave her down so she didn't have to stand there looking like a total fool. Why hadn't Adam Williams described his replacement in his voice mail? She cut her gaze from one end of the room to the other, feeling lost. How would she ever find— what was his name again? Gary? Glen? Then, on a second sweep, her gaze landed on a familiar face two tables away: the man from the bar the night before. He sat alone with a coffee, scanning a newspaper. Before she could look away, he glanced up and saw her. Caught, Claire smiled weakly, not sure what else to do. He stood and waved her over.

He was even more attractive than she'd remembered him, Claire thought as she approached his table, or maybe it was just seeing him standing, the length of his body, the confident stance.

And God, *those eyes*.

"Good morning," he said.

She nodded, as if he'd asked a question. "Hello."

"Join me?"

"I can't," she said, looking around. "I'm supposed to be meeting someone here."

"I know." He smiled. "Me."

Claire blinked at him. What had he said?

"You didn't give me a chance to introduce myself last night." He stuck out his hand. "Gus Gallagher. Owner of Fins, and proud sponsor of *To the Extreme*."

Only after Claire had slipped her fingers reflexively into his and accepted his shake did she realize what this meant. Their last exchange, the disparaging comments she'd made about the store that he'd overheard—about the owner. A phony!

Claire yanked her hand free, the heat of embarrassment soaking her cheeks. "You should have said something."

Gus pointed her to the empty seat across from him. "I would have but you rushed off."

She frowned, sitting down. "How much time does it take to keep someone from looking like an idiot?"

He leaned forward. "In my defense, you made it kind of hard for me to come clean. You weren't exactly complimentary."

"And if you think I'm going to apologize now and pretend I didn't mean every word, you can forget it."

"I wouldn't expect you to. You were being honest. I like honest women."

Good Lord. She stared at him. "Are you *flirting* with me?"

He chuckled. "If you have to ask, I must not be doing a very good job at it. Can I get you a coffee?"

Claire moved to stand. "I can get my own."

"Sit," he ordered, already up and stepping around the table. "How do you take it?"

"Cream," she consented, sitting back. "Just cream."

He wove through the crowded tables and Claire watched him, glad for the free moment to cool the rising temperature of her skin. God, what *else* had she said at the bar? She tried to remember and decided it didn't matter anyway. She stood by her opinions. Just watching the way Gus Gallagher smiled and backslapped his way to the front of the line was proof enough that he was more salesman than surfer. On his return, a woman at the table adjacent to theirs reached out to stop him. Gus obliged her request for an embrace, leaning down enough for her to press a kiss against his cheek.

She gave him a flirty shove. "I'm so mad at you!"

Claire rolled her eyes and dug into her purse for her phone, hoping to avoid overhearing their conversation, but the woman's admiration—and volume—was too effusive to be ignored.

"You promised you'd take me out on my new board last week, remember?"

"I know I did," Claire heard Gus say, "and I'm sorry. Things got crazy at the store and I've been flat out with all these side projects."

"How's Margot doing? She get her cast off yet?"

"Another week," Gus answered. "Man, she's ready."

"I'll bet. So, when's my rain check?"

"I'll call you."

"Okay, but I'm leaving for Oahu in two weeks, so promise you'll make it soon."

Claire glanced over to see the woman stroking Gus's arm, her hand lingering longer than Claire suspected Margot-who-was-another-week-in-a-cast would appreciate.

Men.

Gus returned and set down Claire's coffee in front of her. She scooped it up, hungry for the caffeine. "That was Liza back there," he said, nodding over his shoulder as he lowered himself into his seat. "I promised her a surf lesson. And trust me, she needs it." He dropped his voice to a whisper. "She might be *the* worst surfer I've ever seen."

Claire smiled tightly over her cup. "Then she's a lucky woman to have your *expert* instruction."

"I'm sure she'd be just as happy to have *you* give her a lesson."

"No, I'm fairly certain she wouldn't be."

"Speaking of which . . ." Gus sat forward. "What do I have to do to get *you* back on a board while you're here?"

"Forget it. My daughter would be mortified. Besides, it's been too long. I'd wipe out before I ever got up."

"Oh come on. . . ." He grinned. "It's true what they say, you know."

"And what is that?"

"It's just like riding a bike."

Claire set down her coffee. "I haven't been on one of those lately either."

"Then you should prepare yourself. Surfing's a very different sport now than the one you left."

"Shouldn't we talk about the interview?" she said. "Adam said you'd have details for me about tomorrow."

"He'll have a car pick you up at the hotel at a quarter to ten," said Gus. "I'd bring some sunscreen and a good book. I'll bet they'll have you out there most of the day."

Most of the day? "How much do they think I have to say?" she asked.

"Someone with your history and your talent? A lot, I'm sure."

Claire glanced at his travel cup. "You always bring your own mug?"

"Are you kidding?" He snorted. "I bring my own *coffee*. Between you and me, I'm not a big fan of this place. It's trendy and overpriced, but Adam already had this lined up, so I didn't want to rock the boat."

"Overpriced and trendy, huh?" she repeated pointedly. *"Really?"*

"My store isn't trendy."

"Just overpriced?"

Gus met her narrowed gaze, his gray eyes flashing with earnestness. "I'm not a bad guy, Claire. I'm just an ex-surfer who still loves the sport and loves helping people do it right. I won't apologize for that."

"Even if it means putting someone else out of business?"

"Now, hold on. I haven't put anyone out of business."

"Clearly you have. The waiter at the Trap said In the Curl was for sale."

"That wasn't Fins' doing. Business has been slow for Ivy for years. She just felt it was time to retire, that's all."

Claire bristled at the easy way he used Foster's mother's name, as if they were good friends.

"And Ivy told you this?" she asked skeptically.

"In so many words."

Claire stared at him, unconvinced.

"But I'm sure you've been out there already and talked to her yourself," he said.

Shame tightened her throat. It was, of course, damn nervy of her to question his affection for Ivy when she herself hadn't even put in a call to let Ivy know she was here.

"No," Claire admitted quietly. "I haven't had a chance yet."

Gus settled back into his chair and stretched out his legs. "When was the last time you saw it?"

When? God . . . Claire studied her coffee before she took another sip, unsure of her measure. She "saw" the shop long after her last visit there. For years its crowded interior was the constant backdrop of her dreams. Did that count?

She swallowed her coffee. "It's been a while."

"From what I hear, it never changed."

"I'm glad."

"Don't be," said Gus. "Change is crucial when you're trying to compete in a growing market."

"Maybe Ivy didn't want to compete."

"Trust me; everybody wants to compete." Gus reached for his coffee. "You did once, didn't you?"

She met his gaze across the table, startled at the bald challenge in it. What did he know about what she'd wanted?

"Look," Gus said. "I think we got off on the wrong foot."

"You mean the one you let me insert directly into my mouth?"

"I'd like to make it up to you. Let me buy you dinner."

"That's not necessary."

"I didn't say it was necessary. I said I'd like to."

Claire squinted at him. "I'm not sure *Margot* would appreciate you taking me to dinner."

"You'd be surprised." He smiled. "Margot's *very* understanding."

"How nice for you." She pushed out her chair and stood. "My daughter's waiting for me. I promised I'd bring her breakfast."

"Let me order her something from here and put it on the network's tab," he offered. "The huevos are out of this world."

"Thanks, but I'll get her something from the bakery down the road."

"If you mean the Flour Pot, it closed two years ago."

"Oh." Claire stared at him a moment, startled by the news. The Flour Pot, gone? Their apple turnovers had been everyone's hangover cure of choice in the day.

Gus rose. "So I'll see you tomorrow."

"You're coming?"

"The famous Pepper Patton back at the Washout?" He grinned, matching dimples winking back at her. "Hell, I wouldn't miss it."

The mention of her old nickname was as unbalancing as if he'd tipped her over with his hands. She turned to escape the maze of chairs and tables that surrounded them, colliding with several on her mad dash to reach the exit.

*G*od, when had it turned so humid?

Back in the hotel elevator, Claire fanned herself madly with a to-go menu she'd pulled from her purse. Living in Colorado's dry heat all these years had made her soft. She plucked at the front of her blouse, wishing she'd brought lighter clothes. Walking toward the room, she steeled herself for Lizzie's continued silent treatment, sure her daughter would still be in bed, so Claire was pleasantly surprised to open the door to their room and find Lizzie awake and watching TV.

"You're up," she exclaimed, setting down the bakery bag.

"Of course I'm up. It's almost eleven." Lizzie gave her a quizzical look. "Are you okay?"

"I'm fine; why?"

"Your face. It's all red."

"It is?" Claire clapped both palms against her cheeks, feeling heat. "It must be the weather," she insisted, moving into the bathroom to see for herself. Sure enough, her skin was every bit as flushed as she'd feared. She scrambled for a facecloth, dousing it with cold water. "I brought you back a croissant," she called over her shoulder as she mopped her cheeks. She frowned impatiently at her reflection. It had to be the temperature.

And okay, fine. Maybe she *had* been a bit unnerved by Gus Gallagher. The way he had studied her across the table with those relentless gray eyes, the way he'd presumed to know all about her past—who she was and what she'd wanted from her life. Calling her by a name she hadn't been called in nearly twenty years—and with good reason.

Still, he had made her realize one thing: That she'd been in Folly almost twenty-four hours and not yet visited Ivy, or the shop, was downright shameful.

She'd correct that right now.

Giving her face a final splash of cold water, Claire walked out of the bathroom and scooped up her purse. "You can eat that in the car, Zee. There's someone I want you to meet."

5

*I*vy King brushed a long strand of kinky gray hair from her face and scowled down at the smoking slice of charred pumpernickel in the sink, the stench of burned toast already thick inside the apartment, which meant, of course, that within minutes the smell would make its way downstairs into the surf shop.

She'd have to get the stink out before Luke arrived. He'd smell it and have a fit. Or worse, Jill would drop him off, catch a whiff, and imply that Ivy had to be out of her mind to use a toaster in a building with outdated wiring and blah, blah, blah— Oh, that woman! It wasn't bad enough that her daughter-in-law had finally managed to force Ivy into retirement, but Jill was also determined to have her certified as incompetent in the process. Ivy leaned over the sink and threw open the sash. She needed a breeze to rinse out the smoke, but the sea air was petulantly still.

Damn. She rummaged through drawers until she found a box of incense.

This always happened when she was in a hurry. Of all the mornings for Jerry to ask her to come to Edisto! Luke would be crushed. He'd plead for her to stay, but Ivy never dared disappoint Jerry when he had one of his panic attacks. She knew too well how dark episodes could swallow a person whole, and she was all Jerry had. Blood or not, they had worked side by side at In the Curl for twenty years, and if that didn't make them family, Ivy didn't know what did.

She perched the incense stick in its holder, lit the powdery twig, and watched the smoke drift around the kitchen, gently covering the noxious smell as it traveled.

And just in time too. She glanced out the living room window to see Luke sail into the shop's gravel lot. He screeched to a halt at the For Sale sign at the edge of the sidewalk and let his bike drop to the grass. After a quick look around, he gave the sign a hearty yank, pulled it out of the ground, and shoved it under his arm, walking it up to the steps, where Ivy watched him slide it under the stairs, out of sight.

God, how she loved that boy. Not a day—not a minute—passed in his company that she didn't think how proud his father would have been to see the young man he'd become, how caring, how responsible, how loyal. He was a marvel.

No, he was a miracle.

She heard footsteps in the store and then the creak of the door opening to the apartment stairs.

"Grams, you here?"

"Come on up!" she called, rushing to bury the blackened bread in the garbage and clap her hands clean in time to meet him at the door.

She held her breath as he stepped into the apartment, watching to see if he'd detect the odor, but his expression didn't falter. Relief filled her. "Ready for your close-up?" he asked.

"You know it." Ivy gave him a loving pat on the cheek as he passed. "Just waiting for the makeup trailer to pull in any minute."

Luke looked down at the overnight bag she'd left by the door. "What's that for?"

"Jerry's having one of his spells. I have to go."

"What?" His face withered. "But you can't leave today. The film crew's here!"

"And they'll be here for a while," Ivy assured him. "It's just one night, honey. You know how Jerry gets. I have no doubt the big show will go on without me. Want some breakfast?"

"No, thanks." Luke followed Ivy into the kitchen. "I still think it's crap that no one asked you to be a part of it," he said, reaching into the fridge for the orange juice. "Stupid Fins."

"Now, now," Ivy chided gently. "Gus Gallagher is an accomplished surfer who knows his stuff and, more important, knows a hell of a lot more people in the surfing world than I do."

"Bull," said Luke. "He has money, that's all. He bought his way in."

"That is the idea behind being a sponsor, honey. You pay to play."

"Well, I think it stinks and I think they suck for choosing Fins over In the Curl. So there." Luke took a fierce slug of OJ from the carton and shoved it back into the fridge.

"No one wants to see an old lady talk about surfing, sweetie. Trust me."

"You're not old," he said. "And anyway, if Pepper Patton *does* come, I bet she'll make sure they interview you. How could she not?"

Ivy glanced around the apartment walls at her treasured gallery of surfing photos, still a few among them of her beloved Pepper. A rush of hope filled her, the same sort that had been rising and falling in the days since she'd learned of the planned filming. A show about women surfers, set in Folly? Who else would they interview if not Pepper?

"How long's it been since you saw her, Grams?"

Ivy smiled. "Too long."

"You think you'd recognize her?"

What a question! A hundred years from now and she could pick out Pepper from a room of thousands. She had known that girl almost as well as she'd known her own child.

Not that Pepper was that girl anymore. A woman now, a mother!

"I think the better question," said Ivy, "is would Pepper recognize *you*?"

Luke frowned. "But she's never met me."

Ivy's eyes filled. She turned to hide her tears and used her fingers to dry them.

"By the way . . ." She tugged a sheet of paper towel from the roll and wiped her nose. "You better stick that ugly thing back in the ground before your mom and Shep see it missing and raise hell."

"Yeah, I know." Luke gave a sheepish shrug. "I didn't want those ESPN guys driving right by, thinking the place was empty," he defended. "And if the sign just happens to get, I don't know, *lost* under the steps . . ."

"We've been over this, honey. We've had a good run here, but it's time to hang up our boards."

"That's Mom and Shep talking."

Maybe it was, Ivy thought, and maybe it wasn't. Ivy had held on to the shop with both hands for so long. When Foster and Claire had promised to take it over almost twenty years ago, she was ecstatic, relieved. Then when Foster had fallen under Jill's spell and turned his back on Pepper *and* surfing, Ivy was crushed. Luke's birth had given her hope—maybe she'd be able to pass down the legacy of In the Curl after all—but over the years, that plan had gone away too.

Then, just when she'd been feeling as if her fight was gone, the building inspection that spring revealed daunting code violations. Ivy had surrendered. Luke had been devastated.

"Admit it, Grams." Luke stepped closer, his eyes flashing with an earnest hope that always stole her breath. "You know you still love this place."

"I do, and I always will," said Ivy. "But life goes on. Now help me get that bag in the car before Jerry sends out a search party."

*A*s Claire steered down Ashley toward In the Curl, few of the cottages looked familiar. But that shouldn't have surprised her. The night she'd left Folly, there might well have been skyscrapers on either side of her sputtering hatchback; in her anguished flight, she would never have noticed them. Her view had been blurry with tears and her focus of Ashley Avenue, once wide and vast and all-encompassing, had shrunk to that of a pinhole. She'd cared only about the tiny point of light at the end of the road, the one that had signaled escape.

She glanced over at Lizzie. Her daughter picked absently at her croissant.

"Aren't you hungry?" Claire asked.

Lizzie shrugged. "It's kind of stale."

"Then don't eat it."

"It's fine. Whatever."

Whatever. The mantra of a teenager. The most maddening word in the English language.

"Why are you so nervous, Mom?"

"Me?" Startled, Claire glanced across the seat, meeting her daughter's narrowed eyes. "Do I seem nervous?"

"Yeah, you do."

Claire cleared her throat. Of course she was nervous.

Ivy—after all these years. Lizzie couldn't understand; Claire didn't know where to start.

"I think I'm just feeling a little out of my element, that's all. Maybe thinking about tomorrow, what I'm going to say on camera."

Lizzie continued her surgeon-esque peeling of the layers of her croissant. "So, how was your meeting this morning?"

The image of Gus Gallagher's broad smile came rushing back to Claire. She flexed her fingers over the wheel. "It was fine," she said. "The guy thinks he's going to get me back on a surfboard before it's all over."

"Oh my God, you wouldn't." Lizzie's face drained. "Promise me, Mom. Promise me you wouldn't."

"Good grief." Claire reached over to tear off a hunk of Lizzie's croissant, tired of watching it be plucked like a chicken. "It wouldn't be *that* bad."

"Are you kidding? It would be awful. It would be all over school. It would be like when Jenna's mom posted her belly-dancing routine on YouTube."

"Elaine did that?"

Lizzie nodded, eyes rolling.

"Wow." Claire turned back to the road, teasing a smile. "You know, Zee, I think that was the longest conversation we've had in weeks."

"That's not true."

"I think it is."

"Maybe it's because all you ever want to talk about is

how you don't approve of Colin." Lizzie pushed out a frustrated breath, expelling with it any hint of lightness Claire had tried to infuse their car with just seconds earlier. "You used to like him. You used to make me feel bad because I didn't want him coming over and using my toys."

Claire frowned at the reminder, not unlike the ones she'd been making to herself in the past few months. "It's different now. He's different."

"How?"

"You know how, Zee."

"Maybe you're the one who's different," Lizzie muttered, dropping her head against the window.

Claire frowned, having no good reply.

They rode on in quiet again, her daughter's final words hanging in the air between them like a bad smell. Claire lowered her window, hoping to chase it out, but the warm sea air only seemed to force it back in.

Not so long ago, it had been she, Claire, riding silently along this same stretch of shoreline, stealing angry glances at her own parents from the backseat of her father's Cadillac, certain that he could never understand the longing in her own heart for change—and she never knowing that the change she hungered for, the one she couldn't name, only crave, was about to arrive. Collide, really. As all-powerful things eventually do when their point of impact is standing absolutely still.

6

The first moment Claire laid eyes on Foster King was just before noon on a July Saturday with the air still damp from a morning misting, and seconds after her father had nearly run him over.

They'd been in Folly Beach for only a few minutes, her father having rushed them through the small stretch of downtown shops and restaurants as if they were outrunning a tornado. In the backseat, Claire leaned in as close as she could to the window, determined to soak in the scenery Harp Patton was equally determined to deny her. Now as her father steered them down Ashley Avenue, she searched the view for the one stretch of beach she knew would be bare of homes but teeming with waves, and the surfers who would be riding them.

"The speed limit is thirty, Harp," Claire's mother noted evenly.

"I'm aware of the damn speed limit, Maura. I'm also aware of the two pounds of potato salad in the trunk that's rapidly spoiling in this god-awful heat."

Potato salad. Of all the sorry excuses her father could make for hurling them to their destination, ripening potato salad had to be the most pathetic. Claire wished for the sound of sirens to rush up behind them; for a policeman to force her father into the soft, sandy shoulder and keep them there, long enough to let Bibi Danvers's beloved store-bought potato salad bake rancid in the hot sun. It would serve her father right.

"Claire, Bibi tells me Warren will be there. Back from a trip to Bermuda. I'm sure he'll be anxious to share his adventures with you."

Claire kept her gaze fixed on the view of the water and muttered, "Lucky me."

"What was that?"

"When did you talk to Bibi?" her mother asked, turning her head sharply as if she'd been goosed.

"I told you," said Harp. "This morning."

"You said you spoke to *Pierce* this morning," her mother corrected. "You said Bibi was out."

"Pierce, Bibi. Lord, Maura—what difference does it make?" Harp shifted in his seat. "Claire, did you hear what I said about Warren?"

She met her father's fierce study in the rearview mirror. "I heard you."

"Well, you might perk up a bit, young lady. It's great new—"

"*Harp!*"

Her father's eyes snapped back to the road just in time to see the throng of teenagers that had stepped out into the lane. "Shit!" He slammed on the brakes, sending Claire and her mother lurching forward.

A group of golden-skinned, shirtless teenage boys, surfboards at their sides like giant wings, stood in front of the car in a formidable line, all of them but one stretching out a middle finger in outrage. At the very end, the tallest of them and the only one who hadn't given the bird, shouted, "Slow down, old man!"

Red-faced, Harp raised the heel of his hand and slammed it down on the horn.

"Dad!" Claire cried.

"Harp, you *were* speeding," Maura pointed out gently as the group delivered him one last round of scowls before resuming their path across the road.

"I was hardly speeding, Maura. They didn't look. Christ!"

Mortified, Claire sank back in her seat to watch the boys reach the other side of the road. When the young man on the end stopped to send her a huge smile with big teeth as white as his spiky blond hair and a single dimple stretching the length of his jaw, her skin nearly melted off her bones.

Claire pressed her palms against the window. She would have pressed her whole body if she could. *I'm sorry*, she mouthed as her father sent the car forward.

The young man waved at her, but it wasn't a good-bye wave. It was a beckoning "come with us" wave, an unmistakable invitation. Whatever he was offering, Claire wanted to throw open the door and accept it.

"Claire Louise, sit back," her father ordered.

She did, slowly, meeting her mother's gaze in the side mirror.

"See that?" Harp Patton cut his glare to the rearview as he accelerated. "That's *exactly* why I warned Pierce and Bibi not to rent out here. Loafing little shits. You ever come home with one of those, Claire, and you don't bother coming home."

"Oh, Harp, *really*." Maura rolled her eyes to the window.

Claire twisted in her seat to catch one last look, but the road was empty, the surfer with the blinding smile and his chummy crew already disappeared down the dunes.

*O*nly the Danverses could have brought them out to Folly Beach. For as long as Claire could remember, her father had always preferred the quieter coastlines of Kiawah or Isle of Palms for their beach vacations. But this summer he would make an exception.

Claire's father and Bibi Danvers had grown up together, graduated from the College of Charleston together, and always remained close even after marrying their respective high school sweethearts. Though the Danverses now lived in Raleigh, each summer they'd rent a house on the water. It wasn't for lack of money—Pierce Danvers could easily have afforded to buy any waterfront home he wished—but rather for lack of commitment. It was a well-known fact that Bibi Danvers bored easily. After she had tired of three summer homes in as many years, Pierce had decided to save himself the headache and rent.

As her father steered them into the driveway, Claire peered up at the taupe, three-story, flat-roofed house. Like most of the houses along the Carolina coast, it stood on wooden piers to protect against flooding. Tidy porches skirted the first and second floors. Off-white Bahama shutters angled up like drowsy eyelids.

"I'm surprised Bibi agreed to this," her mother said dryly. "It's so plain-looking, so . . . understated."

Claire's father had barely brought the car to a stop before the home's front door swung open and Bibi Danvers sailed out in a strapless sundress, long black hair teased and frothy. She rushed to the railing, waving down at them as if she were a giddy newlywed departing on a honeymoon cruise. Claire was certain she heard a quick puff of air leave her mother's throat as Maura Patton snapped open her compact and gave her makeup a final inspection, efficiently brushing her crisp blond bob with her fingers.

"Harp, darling, don't forget to bring in the pie too."

But Claire's father was already out of the car and up the front steps with the speed of a boy rushing to Santa's lap.

Pierce Danvers, fully gray at forty-five, arrived beside his wife and pointed with his tumbler. "Look who decided to show after all!"

Determined to soak up her last seconds of freedom, Claire took her time emerging from the backseat and

helped her mother empty the trunk of food. "This is a a ridiculous amount of potato salad for six people," Claire
groused. "Why did he have to buy so damn much?"

"Your language, Claire Louise." Her mother reached
for the pecan pie she'd made that morning, visibly wounded
that her husband wanted to buy potato salad instead of letting her make her own. "But you know how Bibi loves the
potato salad at the Blue Moon, Maura," Claire had overheard her father insist the night before. "She has since we
were kids!"

"Watch the cover on that monstrous tub," her mother
warned. "They sometimes forget to snap it on tightly all the
way around."

Claire didn't know why she'd bothered asking. She
knew the answer to her own question; she just wanted to
hear her mother to say it, to admit why her husband had
taken them a half hour out of their way to secure too much
potato salad, why he'd sped to get them here, as if the Danverses' house were a plane he might miss boarding. In the
silent moments as they walked side by side before they
mounted the steps, Claire watched her mother's lips shift
until they settled on a tight smile, like someone making
last-minute alterations to a ball dress, knowing she would
have to wear it long into the night and wanting to be as
comfortable in it as possible.

"Hello, Bibi," Maura said.

"Maura!" Bibi leaned in to accept Claire's mother's
measured kiss, quiet for only a second before she leaped
back and cried, "Oh, y'all, I was frantic!"

"We were about to send out a search party," Pierce said. "I'm not kidding!"

"He's not," Bibi insisted, her lined brown eyes huge. "I had the phone in my hand ready to call the police. Didn't I, Warren?"

Eighteen-year-old Warren Danvers stepped out from the edge of the group and into the receiving line, hands shoved deep into the pockets of his snug khakis, bow tie askew.

"Warren!" Pierce snapped at his son like a hypnotist yanking someone out of a trance. "Be a gentleman and take the food, son."

"Yes, sir." Warren reached out, his dark eyes fixed firmly on Claire as he removed the potato salad from her hands.

"I assure you we were right on schedule when we left," said Harp. "And we would have made it with time to spare if we hadn't suffered a run-in with some local *wildlife*."

"How's that, now?" Pierce looked fiercely intrigued, but Bibi stepped between the two men before they could continue.

"Save it for later, Harpy," she said, sliding her fingers around Claire's father's arm and steering him to the double doors. "We've got just the thing for weary travelers."

*S*ure I can't fix you something stronger than sweet tea, Maura?" Pierce asked from his post behind the wet bar.

"No, this is plenty strong, thank you." Claire's mother

gestured to the glass she'd been nursing since they took seats in the living room to wait for lunch to be served. It was a massive room, surrounded by windows on three sides. Too anxious to sit, Claire wandered the perimeter of it, feeling like a cricket in a lizard's cage as she tried to avoid Warren's repeated attempts at conversation. Each time she slowed at a picture frame or a row of books, she'd sense his advance and resume her pacing. Despite her efforts, he'd managed to trap her by the piano. The Coke he'd poured for himself was so swollen with stolen rum Claire was sure she'd lose consciousness each time he moved his glass.

Outside, the breeze tickled the porch swing into motion, its every short creak causing her mother's gaze to snap to the glass doors.

Pierce laughed. "Leave it to my wife to turn a quick show of the gardens into a grand tour."

From across the room, Claire glared at her mother's profile, willing her to do something, *anything*, but sit there primly and calmly rewinding a napkin around her sweating glass as if it were far more pressing than the bald truth that her husband and Bibi Danvers had been gone for over a half hour to inspect a flower garden that could have been surveyed in less time than it took to swallow a pill.

"They've probably just got to talking to our neighbors," Pierce said. "Nice young couple from Atlanta. Husband's in insurance. Not an ounce of fat on him, the lucky bastard. Runs the beach every morning like he's being chased by a swarm of bees."

Claire stepped forward. "Maybe someone should go look for them."

Warren snickered into his cup. Claire glared at him.

"Oh, no need for a search and rescue just yet." Pierce sent Claire a wide grin as he squeezed a lime wedge over his fresh gin and tonic and dropped it in. "Remember, your father knows how to handle Miss Bibi when she gets like this. He'll catch a whiff of Lottie's Royal Red Alfredo and have my wife corralled before— Aha! What did I tell y'all? I can see them coming up the stairs now."

In the next moment, the high sound of laughter arrived, cracking the awful quiet like a snapped branch, and Bibi Danvers blew through the door as if she'd narrowly escaped a tornado, Claire's father on her heels. The distinctively sweet smell of cigarette smoke floated in with them, creeping across the room like a fart.

Claire saw a pained flicker of recognition cross her mother's tight face.

"Pierce, I may have to take it all back," Harp declared, marching to the wet bar and smacking his palm definitively on the polished wood. "Your wife has shown me the charms of this place."

"Oh, that sea air!" Bibi flounced down beside Maura, throwing her head back and using both hands to tame her blown curls. "It's utterly delicious but *murder* on the hair."

Maura rose. "Maybe I will take a glass of Chardonnay, Pierce."

"Wonderful." Pierce pulled a bottle from the minifridge.

"Now, Harp, what was all this about a run-in with the locals this morning?"

"Surfers!" Claire's father cried. "The lot of them stepped right out into the road as if they owned it. Not a one even looked to see if a car was coming!"

"That's because it's the Washout," Claire announced.

All eyes turned.

Her father squinted at her. "The *what?*"

"The Washout," she repeated evenly. "It's where everyone surfs here."

"Everyone, huh? And how would *you* know that, young lady?"

"Ooo, that's right!" Bibi spun around on the couch. "You're quite the surfer, aren't you, Claire?"

Harp groaned. "Don't encourage her, Beebs."

"Why not?" Bibi flashed a mischievous grin in Claire's direction. "I think it's fabulous she gets on one of those things. Why should the boys have all the fun?"

"She doesn't *get on one of those things*," Claire's father corrected, walking toward the couch and taking a seat beside their hostess. "She got on one *once*. Without my knowledge."

It had been more than once. Many more, but Claire let the details of the previous summer's secret trips slip away.

"Oh, hush," said Bibi, swatting Harp on the knee. "Now, don't you mind him, Claire. I think a girl should ride all the waves she can, as *often* as she can."

Her father wagged a finger at her, close enough to Bibi's face that she lunged, pretending to bite it, then smiling the slow, velvety smile of a cat kneading its claws into a freshly fluffed comforter.

It was too much. Claire rushed for the door.

"Claire?" Her mother leaned forward. "Claire Louise, where are you going?"

"For some fresh air." Her hand shook as she curved it around the doorknob, twisting it harder than necessary and pushing it open. More calls for her to come back followed her out onto the porch and down the steps but Claire didn't slow. The boardwalk stretched out in front of her like a ladder. She kept her eyes forward. She just needed to get to the water.

No matter how many times she took the length of weathered wood, her heart always opened, unzipped like a heavy jacket, letting cool air at hot skin. It was, she imagined, though she had yet to find out, like walking toward a lover, the prickling, dizzying anticipation of knowing what was to come and what wasn't. She kicked out of her sandals in two efficient strides and took off in a run down the last of the walkway.

The moment her bare feet landed on the sand, relief filled her. Sunbathers and swimmers dotted the shore, then farther down, the clumps of surfers, the telltale silhouettes of their boards upright. Had it occurred to her that she might see the same boys again—that she might see *him*? The same craving she'd known in the car hours earlier, instant and hot and whole, flared up inside her again. She walked down the beach toward the surfers like someone in a dream might, her steps decidedly purposeful but having no logical purpose at the same time. And just like in a dream, everything seemed to make perfect sense.

It was one of his friends who pointed his attention to where she stood. The two young men conferred briefly; then the blond began toward her.

It was only then, as he approached, that the dreamlike certainty of her thoughts crumbled and doubt flooded her. He'd beckoned her to join him that morning, but what if he hadn't really meant it?

Deciding it was too late to alter her course or pretend that she had any other reason in the universe to be there except for the implicit desire to see him, Claire crunched her bare toes firmly into the sand and waited for him to arrive.

When he did, he was already smiling. "I know you," he said.

Claire smiled back. "I'm sorry about this morning."

"No apologies needed. It wasn't your fault."

"I know. I'm still sorry."

"It's forgotten." He thrust out his hand, slick with water just like the rest of him. "Foster King."

She took his damp hand, amazed at the heat of his skin, amazed more at how tightly she wove her fingers inside his, as if she were hanging off the edge of a cliff and he'd come to lift her to safety.

"Claire," she said. "I'm Claire."

7

*W*hile it seemed the universe around In the Curl had altered in every way, Ivy's salt-and-sunbaked cottage remained impossibly unchanged. Even the building's color—aquamarine with cantaloupe trim—endured.

"Where are we?" Lizzie asked as Claire steered them into the parking lot and turned off the car.

Home was the answer that rose in Claire's throat, startling her. But no, she couldn't say that. She smiled and said instead, "Just someplace where I used to spend a lot of time."

Lizzie said, "It looks closed."

Was it? Claire squinted up at the shop. How to know? And if it was for sale, where was the sign? She scanned the lawn, then the parking lot, seeing only a van. Since Ivy had never believed in posting the shop's hours, there was no way to be sure until you laid your palm on the handle of the door and pulled.

"It's open," Claire said firmly, climbing out and starting for the steps.

She told herself she wouldn't look through the glass. When her hand landed on the door and she tugged, it gave, with the same shudder and squeak it always had. Claire walked in.

Gus Gallagher was right. The interior hadn't changed. Every shelf, every display, every board was exactly where it had been when she left seventeen years earlier. The only thing unfamiliar was a curious staleness to the air, as if little had moved around within it for days. In her time, the shop was never this quiet. Not even after hours.

Lizzie came up behind her and whispered, "I told you they weren't open."

"Can I help y'all?"

Claire turned to face the voice, meeting the smile of a teenage boy who might have been only a couple of years older than Lizzie. He glowed like someone dipped in gold leaf, every part of him touched by the sun.

"I'm sorry," Claire said. "The door wasn't locked. Are you closed?"

"That's kind of a tricky question," the young man said. "Technically, yeah, we're closed until further notice, but seeing as we haven't gotten around to moving out the inventory, I'd say if you've come looking to buy gear, we're open."

Claire smiled. "No, I'm afraid my days of buying gear are over. I'm actually looking for Ivy King."

"You just missed her. Grams went out of town for the night. Hey, are y'all here with the ESPN guys?"

Grams?

Claire stared at him, the heat of understanding washing over her. Why had it not occurred to her this young man would be Foster and Jill's child? Looking at him now, really seeing him—God, it was so obvious it practically hurt. She took a startled step to one side and knocked into Lizzie.

"Ow. That's my foot."

"Sorry." Claire reached for her daughter, to apologize or maybe just to steady herself. It was then that Claire saw them, lining the wall behind the register, each one slightly tilted, the glass streaked with dust. Photographs of her on her board, doing expert turns and cutbacks to change her direction on the wave. The very same pictures that had hung there the day she left Folly.

Oh, Ivy.

All these years later, Foster's mother had never taken them down.

Claire turned back to the young man, slowly, like someone trying not to look directly into a bright light.

"Hey . . ." It seemed he'd had a revelation too. His eyes— good Lord, *Foster's blue eyes*—rounded and blinked, sliding from her to the wall and back again. "That's you, isn't it? You're Pepper Patton."

"You can call me Claire." She glanced to Lizzie. "And this is my daughter. Lizzie."

"I'm Luke." The young man lunged forward, hand outstretched to each of them, a tribal tattoo riding along the inside of his forearm, a chain of navy swirls. "This is so cool—I *knew* they'd ask you back!"

"Claire?"

The timbre of the man's voice was as familiar as the creak of the door that had preceded it. Claire spun to face both sounds, and there he stood, looking so unchanged, so like the last time they'd seen each other: that empty, endless night they'd shared a final beer on his porch, their eyes stuck to the silhouette of her stuffed hatchback, too afraid to look at each other or sink into tears all over again. She'd never seen the night sky so black.

Shep.

If not for the gentle lines beside his warm brown eyes, or the threads of gray tangled in his pale red hair, she might have believed he'd eluded time's crawl completely.

"Hey, Shep."

"Claire," he said again. "Wow. Look at you."

He leaned in to hug her, his embrace quick, tentative. Unprepared, she was slow to hug him back and had barely lifted her arms over his shoulders before he retreated.

"See?" cried Luke. "Told you she'd be here!"

"We weren't sure you'd come," Shep confessed.

"We?" Claire asked.

"Me and Jill."

Her stomach flip-flopped. Of course. It stood to reason if he was still here in Folly, he probably saw Jill around town. Perhaps they'd run into each other in the past few days and discussed the news of ESPN's project. Surely Claire's name had come up.

"I wasn't sure if I would come at first, if I *should*," Claire said, suddenly filled with guilt for not having called to let

Shep know. She'd not even tried to reach out to him. She'd
been so certain he'd have moved on, moved away. But here
he still was.

"It's good to see you, Claire. You look . . ."

"Pale and ferociously out of shape," she finished for him.

He searched her face and smiled. "I was going to say
exactly the same."

God love him, he had always been a miserable liar.

"I take it you've met . . ." Shep's hand and gaze swung
to Luke, his voice slowing, the implication in the sudden
silence an impossible one, but how else could it have gone?

"Yes," Claire said, rescuing him. "And this"—she turned—
"is my daughter, Lizzie."

Shep waved to Lizzie; Lizzie offered him a short wave
in return.

"So, where are y'all staying?" he asked.

"At the Breeze," she said. "It's all the network's doing. I
wouldn't have picked it." Where *would* she have picked? The
question hung there, foolish and unanswered. It wasn't as if
she could have crashed at the Glasshouse, Foster and Shep's
old place, or as if she could have stayed with Shep wherever
he lived now. Surely he had someone in his life: a wife
maybe, a girlfriend, children?

"How long are you in town for?" he asked.

"A few days." Claire looked at Lizzie to bring her into
their conversation but her daughter's eyes traveled the interior instead.

"You should come over for dinner tonight," Luke exclaimed.

Claire saw the same wary look on Shep's face that she was sure flashed on her own. Go to Jill's house for dinner? She couldn't possibly.

But Luke was determined. "Come on," he said, moving closer. "It would be the coolest thing ever. Y'all could talk about the old days. Tell me the crazy stuff y'all used to do with Dad."

Claire looked briefly at Shep, then away.

"I'm sure those ESPN guys have something flashy already lined up for her tonight, Luke," Shep said.

"Oh God, hardly." Claire waved her hand dismissively. "It's not this big deal."

"Sure it is," Shep insisted. "Pepper Patton on ESPN. That's huge."

"*Now* they want me, right?" she said, matching his measured smile. "Not then, when I actually looked *good* in a suit."

Lizzie turned and pushed through the door, sending the bell at the top jingling madly. Claire watched her leave, feeling powerless again. She looked back at Shep, Luke's dinner invitation still hanging in the air between them like a ripe piece of fruit dangling from a branch, in danger of dropping to the ground and spoiling if someone didn't pluck it soon.

"Will you come?" Luke pressed.

"I don't know," Claire said to Luke, letting the swollen fruit swing another moment. "Maybe you should call your mom first. Just to make sure."

Shep nodded to Luke. "Why don't you finish up what you were doing and we'll figure it out on the ride back?"

The plan seemed acceptable to him. His smile remained bright and hopeful. "It's really great to meet you, Miss Claire, I mean, really great," Luke said, moving for the back door.

"*Miss* Claire . . ." Claire shook her head, reminded of the favored regional address. "This is how I know I've been out of the South a long time."

"It has been a long time," Shep concurred.

Just the two of them now, she and Shep looked at each other. Despite his sturdy smile, there was no way to avoid the confession she needed to make.

"I'm sorry I wasn't here for the service, Shep. I wanted to come back, but everything got so complicated. There was work and my daughter was sick. . . ."

"I wanted to call you myself and let you know what happened," he said. "I should have. I don't know why I didn't."

The sound of steps above shifted their attention: Luke moving around Ivy's apartment. Claire could still visualize the space in her mind: the tiny kitchen under the eaves, the narrow bathroom with the peeling lemon yellow paint, the faded corduroy sofa with the foot that always came loose.

She smiled at the ceiling. "He's so sweet."

"Luke's a good kid."

"He looks so much like him. I almost couldn't breathe." Claire hadn't meant the words to spill out so dramatically. She felt badly for them, foolish, but Shep persevered.

"Is your husband here too?"

"Lizzie's father's still in Colorado," Claire said. "We're divorced."

"Oh. I'm sorry."

"Don't be. Really."

"Okay, I'm not." Shep dug in his pockets, fingering change.

Claire paused to let a beat settle the air around them. "Luke's sweet to offer, but I don't know if it's such a good idea for me to see Jill tonight. I mean, it's been a long time."

"Hey, I totally understand. I mean, if you're still . . . if it's still . . ."

"No, it's not that."

"Then you should come," he said gently. "I think Luke would be disappointed if you didn't."

Claire searched his face, still leery. "It's not Luke I'm worried about."

"Jill would want to see you too."

"You seem so sure. You've stayed in touch with her, then?"

"Well—yeah." Shep looked at her. "I thought you knew."

Claire stared at him blankly.

"Jill and I got back together, Claire."

He could have struck her and Claire wouldn't have felt any more startled.

"Wow." She blinked. "When?"

"About a year after Foss died." Shep studied her face. "You look so surprised."

"I am," she admitted. "I'm—I'm shocked, actually. I mean, after everything that happened . . ."

"Yeah, well." He gave her a small smile. "Life's about moving on, right?"

Claire recalled the two of them on his stoop that final night, his profile in the porch light, his eyes watery and dull.

He'd taken her back.

After the months of lies, after everything she'd done to break his heart, Shep had taken Jill back.

Claire swallowed, suddenly dizzy.

Shep took a step toward her. "Are you okay?"

"I'm fine," she said quickly. "I should check on Lizzie." She moved to the door and pushed it open. Shep followed. They stopped at the front steps and looked out at the parking lot, at Claire's sedan, Lizzie slouched in the passenger seat, sunglasses down, head back.

Claire took in a deep breath, just glad to be outside again, out of the store, freed of the choke hold of memory. God, it had snuck up on her. She'd been unprepared to feel so strange in a place she'd once considered more home than her own home in Charleston. Or maybe it was the impossible news that Shep and Jill were intact again. There was something cosmically inconsistent about it.

No, that wasn't the word.

Unfair.

There was something cosmically *unfair* in it.

Never, not in a million years, would Claire have imagined . . .

She brushed back a loose piece of hair, wanting to shake off the thought. Who was she to begrudge them their reconciliation? Besides, there were bigger concerns. "I was hoping to see Ivy."

"She should be back tomorrow. She's just gone to

Edisto. She never stays more than a night. You remember Jerry, the shop's old shaper?"

The image of a rangy, ponytailed man hunched over an unfinished surfboard flashed through her thoughts. "Sure, I remember Jerry."

"He has these panic attacks. She goes down there to calm him down."

Ivy and her bevy of suitors. "I heard the shop was for sale," Claire said, "but I don't see a sign."

Shep turned to search the lawn, his eyes narrowing on the empty grass, and he sighed wearily. "No, it's definitely for sale."

"So, how is she?"

"Jill?"

"Ivy."

"The same, mostly," said Shep. "Still doing her own thing, still making waves—even if she can't ride 'em anymore. Luke means everything to her. It's helped her having him here."

Claire smiled. "Of course."

"You and your daughter really should come for dinner tonight. Luke'll be crushed if you don't."

Claire squinted out at the street, the invitation somehow harder to accept now knowing Shep and Jill were back together. It shouldn't have mattered. Not after all this time. So why did it?

"The best part," said Shep, "is I won't even have to give you directions to our house. I bet you could still find it blindfolded."

He smiled at her, no doubt waiting for her expression to shift with understanding.

Just when Claire was sure Shep couldn't have shocked her a second time.

"You won't believe it." He beamed. "Jill and I bought the Glasshouse."

8

When Foster had led Claire down to the water to meet the same band of boys her father had nearly flattened earlier, her heart was in her throat. Would they shun her? Ridicule her? She needn't have worried; after Foster's glowing introduction, the young men smiled and waved agreeably. Then Foster ordered them all into the surf and asked Claire if she wanted to watch them ride for a few minutes. She had nearly burst but managed to contain her excitement with an understated nod and dropped down to the sand to watch. He wouldn't believe her—and why should he? Dressed in a stiff, floral sundress, Claire no more looked the part of a surfer than did the shorebirds that skittered around them.

Fifteen minutes later, when Foster came in to check on her, unable to hold it in any longer, she made her confession to him.

"Get the heck out!" he cried. "*You* surf?"

Claire lifted her chin. "I surf."

"Show me," he said.

"Now?"

"Why not now?"

"I don't have a suit," she said.

"No problem. I'll get you one from my shop. Well, technically it's my *mom's* shop," he added sheepishly. "It's where everybody hangs out. It's kind of like our extended family. It's just up the beach."

Ten minutes later, Claire was stepping into a brightly painted cottage packed with customers. Music blared and voices rose to be heard above it. Claire followed Foster as he snaked through the crowds and the cluttered aisles of merchandise, pointing. Up ahead, a loud group of men in their twenties, most of them barefoot and shirtless, flocked around the counter.

"What's up there?" Claire asked.

Foster grinned at her over his shoulder. "My mom."

Sure enough, when they got closer, Claire could see a woman with nearly waist-length kinky blond hair shining through the masses.

Foster shoved his way through the crowd. "Hey, y'all, break it up, break it up!"

Good-natured laughs ensued as the crew slid apart to let him in, taking turns slapping him on the back. The blond woman darted over the counter, arms out, and pulled Foster in for a long hug. When she released him, he turned and motioned for Claire to join them.

"Claire, this is my mom, Ivy. Mom, this is Claire. Claire says she can surf and I'm not letting her go back to her fancy house up the beach until she proves it."

The two things Claire noticed when the woman reached out her hand in greeting were her beautiful cornflower blue eyes, the same shade as her son's, and the tattooed purple and navy vines dotted with richly colored poppy blossoms that ran down the arm she'd extended. "Atta girl! This world needs more of us women blowin' these know-it-all men out of the water. What kind of board do you use?"

Claire looked at Foster, stunned and thrilled at the question. While she knew there was a whole world of sizes and shapes, she'd only ever used one.

"A long board," she answered.

Ivy nodded. "Foss, honey, ask Jerry to give her Mike's. Claire, look on the wall for a suit you like," Ivy said, gesturing behind her. "Take your pick."

Claire reached first for a simple navy one-piece, then stopped, seeing a bright red one behind it. Why not? A little color never hurt anyone. She changed in the stockroom, left her clothes in a tangled pile in the corner, and met Foster outside, where he waited with two boards.

"*Wow.*" His face lit up. "You look totally hot. Like a little spicy red pepper."

She'd ride like one too, Claire decided as they walked down the beach toward the waves. She'd ride as if her life depended on it and make his jaw drop.

At the water's edge, Foster steered them to where the breaks were best.

"Your mom is really cool," Claire said as they walked into the water.

"She's the best. Everybody loves her."

"So, where's your dad?"

"In Hawaii, last we heard." His smile thinned, his eyes squinted harshly against the sun. "He's got this whole new family out there. Like, five kids. I don't hear from him, and I don't want to." Foster turned to her, his smile back again. "You're gonna blow my mind, aren't you, *Pepper*?"

*F*rom the minute she got up on her board, Claire did just that. Whether her talent was a product of luck or the swells or the sun or the thrill of being there with him, Claire didn't know and she didn't care. As soon as she cleared the white water and found herself in the lineup with the same boys who'd crossed in front of her father's car just hours earlier, her rhythm couldn't fail. Every set was hers and she carved better than she'd ever carved the summer before. She saw the boys eye her suspiciously while she sat on her board, bobbing in their company, the wary looks that said, *We think you're just a kook with a crush and ten bucks says you drop in on us the next break.*

After her first wave, they just stared.

But there was only one pair of eyes she hoped to catch and hold.

"Holy crap!" Foster hollered as he paddled over to meet her between sets. "Where'd you learn to surf like that?"

"We spent a month with family and friends at

Wrightsville Beach last summer," Claire said. "I met a group of kids who taught me how to surf and I snuck off to ride with them every chance I got. My parents thought I was at the movies."

"You got that good in a month? That's like some kind of prodigy thing, huh?"

"I guess I just took to it, that's all."

"No kidding. Remind me not to compete against you in a heat."

"I'm not that good," she demurred.

"Yeah, you are," he insisted. "Hey, didn't you see the way these guys shut up as soon as you got up on your board and carved the heck out of that first wave? I think Andy Bosworth pissed himself."

Claire tilted her head to hide her blush.

"Are you hungry?" Foster asked. "We could get changed and grab a bite at the Crab Trap. Shep and Jill are probably there."

Hungry? God, she was ravenous. By now her parents and the Danverses had surely cleaned their plates and were scouring the beach for signs of her. They might even have called the police—Claire wouldn't put it past her father.

Still, she answered, "Okay."

"I hear you just put a half dozen boys to shame out there," Ivy said when they'd returned to the shop. "And I *also* hear I'm to call you Pepper from here on out."

Claire smiled at Foster, his eyes dancing down at her. Pepper. She liked that. "Thanks for letting me borrow everything, Mrs. King. I washed the suit and hung it up in the storeroom. If you tell me how much it costs, I'll send you the money as soon as I get home."

"It's Ivy," she said, "and don't you send a dime. Take it with you. It's yours now."

"Take it," Foster insisted. "You're coming back tomorrow to ride with me again, aren't you?"

Claire smiled, not wanting to break the spell of their magical ride, of this whole universe she'd stepped into barely an hour before.

Ivy turned to Foster. "You make sure she comes back, Fossie. I like her. I might just like her better than you."

*T*hey took a beat-up lime green sedan into town—"We call it the Pea Pod," Foster explained. "It's kind of a communal car"—that smelled of ripe bananas and was filled with squares of board wax that slid across the dashboard every time they hit a bump. He zoomed them right past the Danverses' rented beach house (where Claire's father's Cadillac was still parked) and flew up Ashley. Barefoot, drunk on seawater and sun, her hand out the open window, hot air blowing their hair and voices around the car, Claire felt as carefree as one of the pelicans that flew overhead.

"Ever been here before?" Foster asked as he parked them in the Crab Trap's dirt lot.

Claire stuffed her feet into her sandals and looked up at the restaurant. "Never," she said.

"Their crab bites will make you cry," he promised.

She smiled. "Do they make *you* cry?"

"Every time." He rushed around the front of the car and opened her side before she could. If only her father had been there to see what a gentleman he was. Loafing little shits, huh?

Foster led them through the front door and into the heady scent of fried seafood. Canopies of fishing nets hung from the ceiling; Jimmy Buffett sang through the speakers, barely audible over the din of customers and clinking silverware. Claire felt sure she'd be swallowed up; then Foster's hand slid around hers and squeezed.

"Shep said he'd be here." Foster stretched to scan past the bar to the restaurant beyond. "Wait, I see him." He led them to the very last booth, where his redheaded friend sat in front of a plate of fried oysters and clams. Seeing them approach, Shep greeted them with a smile.

Claire thought he was one of the most handsome boys she'd ever seen. Movie-star handsome.

Foster offered her the bench and slid in after her.

"I saw you ride earlier," Shep said to Claire. "You killed it."

Foster nudged Claire gently with his shoulder. "Told you," he said, picking out a fried oyster and plunging it into a pile of tartar sauce. A waitress arrived and took their order for two Cokes and two fried flounder sandwiches.

"You'll love 'em," Foster assured Claire, scooping up another oyster. "Hey, did Jill come?"

"She just went up to get us more napkins," said Shep. "You know how she is about napkins." He gestured behind them. "Here she comes."

There had been only a handful of times in Claire's life

when she was disappointed in her lack of exotic beauty, when she wished she'd been blessed with long legs and perfect skin. With her shiny, pumpkin blond hair, her thin nose and full lips, Jill Weber was the sort of beautiful that made being good on a board seem totally worthless.

She slipped in beside Shep and smiled at Claire as she set down a pile of napkins between them.

This time, Shep made the introductions. "Jill, this is Claire."

"Nice to meet you, Claire." Claire had been so sure the girl would be aloof, disapproving, the way remarkably pretty girls tended to be toward other girls, especially around their equally remarkably good-looking boyfriends. But Jill's face was warm and open.

The waitress returned with their drinks.

"Claire is an amazing surfer," said Foster. "We just met today. She's from Charleston, but I'm going to convince her to move to Folly next summer so I can get her to compete in the Classic with me and Shep."

"Dude, that reminds me—I saw Biff by the bar," Shep said to Foster. "Maybe we should go talk to him about the house?"

"Let's do it," Foster agreed, giving Claire a quick squeeze on her shoulder and sliding out. "Be right back, Pepper."

"In case you're wondering," Jill said when the boys had gone, "Biff organizes all the surfing competitions on this part of the coast. Foster thinks he walks on water. Biff and Foster's mom were together for a while."

"I met Ivy," Claire said. "She seems really cool."

Jill grinned. "I'll bet she *loved* you."

"Why do you say that?"

"Because you're a real surfer. The first time Ivy met me and I told her I didn't like to surf, I swear she looked at me like I'd sprouted a third eye."

Claire laughed. "I could see that."

"So why does he call you Pepper?"

"Apparently because I wore a red suit today." She shrugged. "It doesn't make a whole lot of sense."

"I think it's sweet," said Jill. Claire did, too. She liked the name, but even more, she liked that Foster had given her one.

"You *should* spend next summer here," Jill said. "We'd have a lot of fun, all of us."

Claire twisted her straw. "I can't. I'm supposed to go abroad for an immersion program. That's when you go live in another country to learn the language."

"I know what it is," Jill said, though far more politely than Claire suspected she deserved.

"Right." Claire smiled contritely. "Sorry."

"That's too bad you already have plans. Summers here are a blast. And next summer I'll be trying to find my own place, so I'll need a roommate."

"What about asking Shep?"

"Are you kidding?" Jill looked at Claire over her Coke. "My parents would never let us live together. Not until we're engaged. Besides, he and Foster are hoping to get this little beach house Biff rents out. That's why they went up to the bar to find him. They're pretty excited about it, and frankly, that's fine by me. My mom moved right in with my dad and she never had her own place. I like the idea of having my own place first. Don't you?"

"I never assumed I wouldn't," said Claire. "I'm not even sure I want to get married."

"You say that now . . ." Jill slid her gaze pointedly behind Claire to the bar where Shep and Foster had disappeared to find Biff.

Claire sipped her soda. How to tell this girl, this complete stranger, that if she, Jill, spent five minutes with Claire's parents she wouldn't want to get married either? Claire would bet Jill's parents were loving and tender, the sort who really *were* fun and freethinking, and didn't just pretend at cocktail parties for the sake of their friends or to annoy the snot out of each other.

"So, what about it?" said Jill. "Want to be roommates?"

Claire smiled. "I don't know."

"I'm a great cook."

"I'm not."

"See," said Jill. "It's perfect! I've had my eye on this little café table set that would be adorable on a deck. And these strings of star-shaped lights we could hang along the railing. And candles. I'm crazy about candles. Especially the scented ones. . . ."

Listening to Jill, Claire had to admit it sounded like fun. Playing house, their own apartment, their own rules. Certainly more fun than being shipped off to another country, miles from any surf. But weren't any of them planning to go to college in the fall?

The boys swung back into the booth.

"Good news, babe," Shep announced to Jill. "Biff says the Glasshouse is ours."

Claire looked between them. "Do y'all call it that because it's made of glass?"

"No, glasshouse is a surfing term for being inside a big wave," Foster explained. "You know, like the green room."

"It has one of those too," Shep added. "A green room, I mean. One of the bedrooms, painted bright green. And it's got this huge deck for parties. And plenty of couches for people to crash on."

"It's not nearly as disgusting as it sounds," Jill whispered to Claire, leaning in. "I've seen it and it's really very cute."

"Aw, babe, come on," Shep whined. "You don't call a surf house *cute*."

Foster chuckled into his soda. Jill shrugged sheepishly and delivered Claire a conspiratorial smile. "Oops."

*A*n hour later, all four spilled out of the Crab Trap into the afternoon air.

The sun was lower, signaling the afternoon's passing to evening. Claire knew she'd pushed her luck far enough.

"I should really get back," she said.

Shep hooked his arm around Jill's waist. "We can give you a ride," she offered.

"It's okay, I have the Pod," Foster said, reaching for Claire's hand and threading their fingers.

"It was great meeting you, Claire," Jill said. "Make

sure Foster gives you my number in case you change your mind about next summer."

Foster steered them toward the parking lot. "What about next summer?"

"Jill said she'll be looking for a roommate." Claire smiled. "She wasn't serious."

"Jill's always serious, believe me," said Foster. "Too serious sometimes."

"She seems nice."

"She is. She's can't surf, but no one holds it against her."

Your mother does, apparently, Claire wanted to say but didn't. The urge to defend Jill was strangely reflexive. "Most girls can't surf."

"I know, why do you think I'm so excited to find *you*?"

To find you. Claire flushed appreciatively as Foster opened the passenger door and closed it behind her. She loved the phrase, that she was a treasure to be held on to.

He slid the key into the ignition but didn't start the car. "So . . . ," he began, twisting in his seat to face her. "I guess it's all set."

"What is?"

"Next summer," he said, matter-of-factly. "You can room with Jill and work with me and my mom at the surf shop."

Claire stared at him. He *was* kidding, wasn't he? He had to know she couldn't possibly spend the summer after her first year of college working at a surf shop. Even if she wasn't already set to go abroad, her father would never agree to it.

"I'm serious." Foster's eyes danced feverishly. "We always

need extra help teaching surfing classes—and I bet we'd get a ton more girls trying to carve if they saw you on your board."

"I don't know."

"I do. Us meeting like this, your dad almost crashing into all of us—don't you see? It's fate."

Fate. A glorious word. Staring into his eyes, a person could believe in almost anything, Claire decided. Even fate. *Especially* fate.

"Say yes. Say you'll come back next summer." Foster leaned in, his arm a barricade. "Say it, or I won't let you leave this car and a week from now they'll find us in our seats, all shriveled up like two strips of bacon."

When she laughed, he swooped in and kissed her hard enough to steal her breath. He tasted of soda and tartar sauce and salt water. She swallowed, as if she could draw the flavors inside her lungs and exhale the memory of him all night.

He released her mouth but didn't move back. Claire looked up at him, their faces so close that she could see the crisp rings of turquoise around his pupils. She reared up and kissed him back.

"You'll forget me tomorrow," she whispered against his lips. "You'll forget this plan."

He smiled that big smile she'd wanted to crawl into that morning.

"I don't forget things," he said. "Not things like this."

"Like what?"

"Like you. Like us."

Us. He said it as if they were already joined, dovetailed after just one hour on the water, one meal in a fish shack.

"I can't come back next summer," she said. "It's not possible."

"Everything's possible, Pepper. Heck, if a dude can fly to the moon, you can figure out a way to spend next summer here with me."

Claire stared up at him, lost in his infectious smile; he might as well have drawn up the ends of her mouth with his thumbs.

Was it true? Could it be that easy?

Maybe. Plans changed, deposits were reimbursed.

Claire looked out and saw Shep and Jill nearly at the end of the sidewalk, Shep's arm draped over Jill's shoulder with a certainty that Claire craved. She looked back at Foster, one arm resting on the wheel, the other slung across the back of her seat; how easily she could imagine them fitting around her, his shoulders the hinges that would hold her in, his arms the doors, his fingers the lock.

Claire's pulse raced with possibility, even more than she'd felt during her talk with Jill. Only a few hours in Foster's company, and she'd fallen into a whole new world. His mom, pulling her into their circle without hesitation. Ivy was so independent, so bold. What would it be like to have a mother with that kind of energy, that kind of carefree joy? Claire wanted to know. She hadn't felt this certain about anything in her life, least of all which was enrolling in college, and she was about to devote four years to that endeavor.

All of her life, she'd been given orders, not choices. This was her time to choose.

Foster traced the collar of her dress, sliding just his thumb beneath the seam. "You and me, and Shep and Jill. We'll be unstoppable. We'd be perfect."

And just like that, Claire felt the natural sliding of their places into formation, like pieces on a chessboard, settings on a table. They were four people, but they could be like two, the way couples who were destined might become. Not vicious or sad like her parents or the Danverses, not people who had no business being bound, but kind and loving partners who fit into one another seamlessly, permanently. Beautifully.

That afternoon they became what they would surely always be.

Foster and Claire.

Shep and Jill.

How could the math of the universe have so miscounted?

9

For the next year, Claire wrote Foster every week. Long, luscious letters meant to be fondled and smelled, paper like flesh. When Claire could catch a ride off campus, she'd meet Foster in Folly and they'd spend the afternoon surfing or visiting Ivy at the shop, then a final hour lying on the sand, rolling toward each other for sticky, lazy kisses with salted breath and reciting the details of their precious plan for the coming summer when Claire would share an apartment with Jill and work at In the Curl. It was like living dual lives: one of her going to lectures and study sessions while the other one of her, the one that was alone in her bed or walking to classes or meeting her parents for church and brunch every Sunday, would live with the promise of a new world on the shore, kept in constant company with Foster King. She plotted in secret, knowing all the while that one morning she'd have to get out her knife and cut the other life loose, set it adrift, and hold fast to the one she wanted.

*Y*ou're not working at some sleazy surf shop and that's final."

Claire had managed to get two sentences into her plea before her father had cropped her proposal short with the snap of his napkin over his lap, the sound as definitive as the crack of a whip.

But this horse, Claire had decided months earlier, would not go.

"You haven't even let me tell you all of it," she said firmly.

"Lord help us, there's *more*?"

Their waiter arrived with a fresh carafe of coffee. Her mother thumped a pair of sugar packets and tore them open.

Claire took a breath to find her balance. The many times she'd rehearsed this speech, all the ways she'd imagined her father derailing her, bullying her. For every possible dismissal, she had an answer waiting.

"I'll be giving lessons too," she continued, and the unabashed way she spoke of it as fact, not a possibility but a certainty, made her father's scowl deepen.

"Eat, Claire Louise." Her mother tapped Claire's plate with her fork. "Before everything's cold."

Claire pushed her plate away, wanting the space to plead her case. She leaned forward, her fingers laced in what she hoped her father might take as a gesture of prayer.

"I want to earn my own money, Daddy. I would think you'd be proud of that."

"I'm very proud. I just don't want you earning it around a bunch of thugs who nearly took out my windshield."

"You mean the ones you almost ran over?"

Her mother cut Claire a fierce look over her coffee.

"We're not sending you to school to be a beach bum, young lady," said her father. "You don't need a degree to be lazy."

Claire glared. "Not going to college doesn't make someone lazy."

"If you don't want to go abroad, then you can stay here." Her father gestured for the waiter to bring more cream. "But I'll not have you commuting out there every day in summer traffic. It's out of the question."

"I know," Claire said quickly, "which is why I'd be living with a friend."

Her mother's eyes lifted. "What friend?"

"A girl I know. Her name's Jill. Jill Weber."

Her father eyed her cautiously. "This is someone from your dorm?"

"Not my dorm, no."

"But she's a student?"

"Yes," Claire lied, deciding it wasn't entirely untrue. Surely Jill had been a student somewhere, at some point in time?

"And this girl's family is from Folly, you say?" Her father swung his gaze to her mother. "Then Bibi and Pierce probably know them."

Claire kept her expression even, not wanting to complicate things any further. The mention of Bibi Danvers had improved her father's opinion of the proposal considerably.

"I *could* give Pierce a call, I suppose," her father said, wiping his mouth. "But I'm not agreeing to anything, understand?"

Claire speared the soft center of her egg, biting back a smile and thinking that the sunny filling that ran out was the most beautiful yellow she'd ever seen.

*C*laire would never know if it was the mention of Bibi Danvers that turned the tide, or simply her father's dogged belief that indulging his daughter this one request would eliminate the need for any others, but she didn't care. Three days after their brunch debate, he consented to Claire's plan.

Two months later, she arrived in Folly Beach in the same car that had first carried her to Foster, this time with three bags and a heart that beat so fast Claire didn't dare open her mouth for fear it would fly right up and out her throat.

Jill Weber had found a garden apartment with a tiny deck a few blocks from Center Street and a few more from the beach.

Jill met Claire and her mother at the door, looking as flawless as the interior behind her. Claire stepped inside and smiled. Her new home.

"Isn't your father coming in?" Jill asked, looking behind them.

"He's moving the car," Claire said.

"He doesn't have to do that. There's plenty of parking."

"It's fine, dear. He likes doing it," Claire's mother said absently, scanning the room. "It's quite small, isn't it?"

"There's only two of us, Mom."

Her mother wandered into the kitchen. "So, how do you like school, Jill?"

Jill looked at Claire, her eyes flashing with confusion. Claire widened her eyes, hoping Jill would catch the signal. "Oh, it's fine, Mrs. Patton," Jill said. "I've got some sweet tea made up if you'd like some."

"None for me," said Maura. "What sort of phone do y'all have here?"

"Excuse me?" said Jill.

"Is it cordless?"

Jill smiled politely. "I think it's on the wall, Mrs. Patton."

"Then it's not cordless. Claire, I can come back next week with one of your father's old phones."

"That's not necessary, Mom."

"How will you answer if you're on the deck?"

"I'm sure we'll hear it, ma'am," said Jill. "It has a very loud ring."

Thirty endless minutes later, after an exhaustive tour of the bathroom and the kitchen appliances, Claire's mother gave the apartment a final disparaging look from the doorway, and left.

"Lord," Jill said, joining Claire at the window to wave the car off. "No wonder you wanted to live in another country."

"And she's not nearly as bad as my father."

"I can't imagine."

"I'm sorry about all that with school," Claire said. "I just figured they'd be more agreeable if they believed we met at college."

"I thought it was something like that," said Jill. "But you should know I'm a terrible liar, so if you want me to keep this up, you'll have to remind me before we see them again."

Claire collapsed on the couch. "If we're lucky, we *won't*."

"Speaking of luck . . ." Jill reached into the fridge and pulled out a bottle of white Zinfandel, the soft pink of the wine nearly matching her lipstick. "One of the bartenders at the Trap snuck it out for me. Want some?"

Claire drained her first glass quickly, probably too quickly, and took a second to her room to unpack, but she didn't get further than stuffing a handful of underwear into one drawer. She felt like a spun top, unable to sit still. Jill made them sandwiches, possibly the most exquisite-looking sandwiches Claire had ever seen outside a restaurant, thick slices of baked ham stacked between creamy chunks of Brie cheese and crisp wedges of pear, but when Claire joined Jill at their café table to eat, Claire couldn't manage more than a bite before she gently pushed the plate away.

Instead of being insulted, Jill just laughed.

"Come on," she said. "We can take my car."

The Glasshouse was everything—and nothing— like Claire had imagined. Squat but wide and painted sloppily in shades of green and taupe like an anole lizard caught between dirt and leaf, its skin not sure which color to commit to. Music spilled out every open window, the bass so loud that Claire swore her bones shuddered when they reached the porch.

"Just a word of advice," Jill said as she opened the door. "Breathe through your mouth."

Claire laughed, but the house could have stunk with the smell of a burst sewer pipe and she wouldn't have cared. Inside, Shep and Foster flew across the living room floor, skidding through piles of clothes and towels, to greet them.

Foster kissed her without warning, hard and fierce. "Ready for the grand tour?"

Jill disappeared with Shep around one corner and Foster pulled Claire around the other. The tour was a brief one, kitchen, bathroom, porch, deck, and Claire took it all in like water, a necessary substance but utterly tasteless, until he stopped them in front of a closed door.

"And now," he said, "the most important room of all." He gave the door a quick shove and it creaked open, revealing a wide swath of dark. Foster felt the wall for a switch, and with a snap, the room bloomed into full light, the walls and ceiling painted a shocking turquoise green.

"Behold . . ." He smiled proudly. "The Green Room."

Claire looked around, startled at the bleakness of it. A bed hugged one wall, unmade and covered in only a wrinkled sheet. On the opposite wall, a dresser held a lamp and a scattering of loose change, crumpled receipts, and other indiscernible items that would find themselves stuck in a nineteen-year-old's pocket. The walls were bare, the floors too. Even the ceiling fixture had been removed, leaving a naked bulb.

"Where's all your stuff?" she asked.

Foster shrugged. "Like what? I keep my suit and board and all that out in the shed and under the house."

"But . . ." Her eyes drifted back to the bed. "You don't have any blankets."

"I don't need any. I'm like a furnace all the time. You'll see."

The suggestion of his rising body temperature under that wrinkled sheet ignited the air around them. Foster came toward her. Ten months of letters and plans and secret meetings and now they were here, together at last.

Her new life had arrived.

Foster took her cheeks in his hands, tilting her face gently as if trying to decide where to kiss her first.

"Are you hungry?" he asked.

Claire shook her head.

"Tired?"

Again she shook her head.

Her searched her eyes. "What, then?"

She smiled up at him, knowing exactly what she was. She was *ready*.

10

*I*n the minutes before Foster drowned, those minutes when Jill had been coming back from the
Piggly Wiggly with Luke's football-shaped birthday cake,
the plastic goalposts sinking into the green frosting Astro-
Turf, she'd felt something shift, something shudder under
her skin, like fingers drifting across her scalp. It wasn't the
sort of wall-shaking, fainting-spell-inducing alarm that
people often reported in the seconds before they lose
someone they know. She'd heard about those moments,
known neighbors and friends, deeply spiritual people, who
swore they had sensed the passing of their loved one in the
seconds before it had happened. Some had fainted; some
had grown so dizzy they'd had to sit down; some had bolted
awake from a deep sleep. For Jill, she'd blinked and pulled
her car to the side of the road.

This was how she knew Claire had come to Folly. Jill had felt the same flutter around her heart that she'd felt the day Foster died; not once, but consistently, that whole morning as she'd dried and folded piles of guest towels and ironed pillowcases and sheets in their bedroom, a makeshift office and linen closet in the busy season. She heard Shep's footsteps ascend the stairs and watched the doorway, waiting for him to fill it. When he finally did, he wore a resigned smile.

"She's here, isn't she?" Jill said. "Claire's here in Folly?"

Shep nodded. "She came with her daughter. She's about Luke's age."

"You saw her?"

"She was at the shop when I dropped by."

At the shop? Jill drew in a quick breath. "So Ivy's already seen her too?"

"Not yet," Shep said. "Ivy took off this morning for Edisto before Claire got there."

"Oh." The thrum of panic slowed; relief ebbed in. Jill sat down on the edge of the bed. "How did she seem?"

"The same, I guess. More put together, maybe. Her hair's not quite as blond. A little shorter. It was hard to tell; she had it pulled back."

But that wasn't what Jill had asked and they both knew it.

She searched his face, waiting.

Shep leaned into the doorjamb and sighed. "She didn't pull out a strawberry blond voodoo doll and start sticking pins in it, if that's what you're worried about."

"Maybe she didn't want to upset her daughter."

"You can decide for yourself. Luke invited her over for dinner tonight."

"He *did*?" Jill stood, jostling the edge of the bed in her haste and sending a pile of towels on the edge tumbling to the floor. She dropped to pick them up. Shep arrived to help her.

"He just blurted it out, Jill. What could I do?"

"And Claire said yes?"

Shep nodded, but Jill pressed, not yet convinced. "Yes, like she really wanted to come, or yes, like she didn't know how to say no?"

"Jill." Shep smiled knowingly. "When did you ever know Claire not to say what she really felt?"

Never. And that was exactly what Jill was afraid of.

She turned back to face the bed, where she'd organized the next week's rental linens, each stack topped with a numbered note card. She stared out at the piles, another burst of relief blooming in her stomach: Ivy gone meant that Foster's mother wouldn't join them for dinner. A small blessing, but Jill would take it. At least their unexpected reunion could be uncomplicated.

Well.

Not *as* complicated anyway.

"What about Luke?" Jill asked. "Did he like her?"

"He only met her for a few minutes, babe."

Jill folded her arms, not sure why she'd even asked.

"He took down the sign again," Shep said gravely. "He

was worried the film crew would pass them by if they saw it."

She sighed. "Of course he was."

Shep turned to go, turned back. "Also, he wants to make dinner for her. Paella."

Jill blinked. Paella was fancy, expensive. Special.

But what could she say?

"Great." She nodded, turning back to her work. "That sounds great."

When Claire Patton stepped into the apartment they would share, Jill wanted everything to be perfect. It wasn't out of character for her—she'd always taken great pains to keep her space tidy and decorated with care, which surprised no one who knew the home she'd grown up in.

Jill also knew what girls like Claire thought of girls like her. All her life she'd watched the summer kids from Charleston, carefree and fun-loving, arriving in their expensive cars, trunks and bumpers covered with edgy stickers in an attempt to hide their conservative pedigrees.

But in many ways—maybe the most important ways— Claire Patton was different. For one thing, she surfed— *well!*—and she didn't flaunt her family money the way so many visitors did in Folly.

Jill believed they could be friends. Maybe even good friends.

Foster believed it too.

Shep wasn't yet certain.

"You've cleaned that stove three times since I've been sitting here," Shep said the morning before Claire was to arrive, he and Foster keeping Jill company in the kitchen. "She's not the queen, you know."

"She is too," Foster defended. "She's going to be my queen."

Shep balked. "I don't care what your last name is, bucko—her daddy won't let you be *her* king."

In spite of their teasing, Jill would be grateful for her obsessive cleaning when Claire finally arrived. Claire's mother's inspection of the interior rattled Jill terribly and the strange absence of Claire's father was equally unsettling. Close with her own parents, Jill found the strained relationship hard to understand. When pressed afterward, Claire was tight-lipped.

A few weeks later, clarity came.

She and Claire had been walking back from the market, each carrying bags of groceries, when Claire came to an abrupt halt in the middle of the sidewalk, her eyes locking on something in the distance. Traffic had stopped for the light. Jill scanned the row of cars trying to decide which one had caused Claire to freeze in place.

It was the Cadillac, Jill decided. A man at the wheel, a woman with her head leaned against his arm. Then the driver's eyes locked with Claire's too. He was an older man, but his study wasn't one of interest.

Jill looked between the man and Claire several times before she asked, "Is that someone you know?"

"Yes," Claire said, staring into the car. "My father."

Jill looked back at the Cadillac and this time took in a longer study of the woman in the passenger seat. Jill had met Claire's mother. The woman who sat beside Claire's father, the woman who had been stroking his jaw only moments earlier, was most definitely *not* Claire's mother.

Jill turned to Claire. Her cheeks were nearly as scarlet as the woman's painted nails.

Surely he would pull over and park, Jill thought. Surely he wouldn't pretend he hadn't even seen his own daughter?

But when the light changed, the man's eyes swung forward and the car followed, lunging to join the traffic as it filed down the road.

For a moment, wanting to spare Claire's feelings, Jill wondered if she should make believe that he hadn't seen them, that his flagrant rejection was misunderstood, but how could she?

"Oh, Claire." She turned slowly, her heart in her throat. "I'm so sorry."

"Don't be," Claire said, drawing in a sharp breath and marching them forward. Jill resumed her steps.

"You want to know the craziest part?" Claire asked, her gaze still fixed on the Cadillac as it sped away. "They were friends once, that woman and my mom. Good friends, supposedly."

Jill shook her head. "I don't care how great a man is. Men should never come between friends. No man is worth that."

They walked on in thoughtful silence.

It seemed like such an obvious thing to say, Jill almost felt badly for it.

*J*ill forced an agreeable smile as she walked with Luke through the grocery store, thinking that every time he took an ingredient off the shelf and dropped it in their cart, she should tell him the truth about Claire and Foster and get it over with. All day, ever since Shep had arrived with the news that Claire would be coming for dinner, Jill had felt the seed of dread sprout and grow inside her, twisting around her ribs. She moved through the day with a tightness she couldn't loosen. She felt like a giant fist, a tightened lid.

Shep had assured her that there could be no hard feelings anymore, that with Foster gone and so much time having passed, Claire would arrive at the house fresh and forgiving. But as Jill watched her son fret over brands of rice and saffron threads, watched his beautiful face flush with innocent anticipation, her heart ached with worry.

Of course Shep would think it all water under the bridge—men weren't like women that way. They raged and they cursed. They purged their anger on front lawns or football fields, letting it spill out completely, draining their hearts of whatever hurt had entered there. But for women, betrayal took root. There was no quick way to cast it out.

Jill envied men their process.

She kept silent all the way through the checkout line and then to the van, their groceries unloaded and nestled safely in the back, but when Luke slid the key into the ignition, she laid her hand on his.

"Baby, I have to talk to you about something."

He leaned back against the seat and blew out a frustrated breath. "If this is about me taking down the stupid For Sale sign, I told Shep I'd put it back up first thing tomorrow."

"It's not that." Jill cleared her throat and reached out to wipe dust off the top of the dash. "This is about Claire Patton. About her and me and your father. And Shep too, I guess. It's about all of us."

"What about it?"

She looked around the busy parking lot, regret filling her. Why was she doing this here? She should have waited until they were home.

Too late now.

She folded her hands in her lap and started again. "You know we were all friends."

"Yeah, I know. And I know Dad and Claire dated a little bit and then she broke up with him and you guys fell in love."

"Well, that's not exactly what happened. . . ."

Luke frowned at her.

"Your dad left Claire," Jill said. "He left her to be with me."

Luke swerved his gaze to the window, considered an abandoned shopping cart for a moment, then turned back to her. "Dad did that?"

"We both did it. It wasn't your dad's fault. It wasn't anyone's fault."

"Grams never told me that."

"That's because I asked her not to."

"Why?"

Jill shrugged. "It wasn't something you needed to know."

"But I need to know now?" It wasn't a question as much as an accusation.

"I thought you should know since Claire's coming over. In case it all feels strange."

"Then why *is* she coming over?"

Jill smiled weakly. "Because you asked her. And who can resist you?" She reached out to touch his face; Luke moved back, his gaze fierce.

"Is that why you guys never kept in touch?" he said. "Because she's still pissed off?"

Jill stared at her hands, wishing she'd never opened this sealed box. "It's hard to explain, Luke."

"You should have told me. Now I feel stupid asking her to come over. She must have thought I was a jerk. Or just really thick."

"No. She would never think that."

He turned to her. "You're mad at me, aren't you?"

"About what?"

"Because I asked her to come over."

"No," Jill said. "Oh, baby, *no*. It's been a long time. We're all grown-ups. It's really not a big deal."

"If it's not a big deal," Luke said, "then why are you telling me?"

Jill met his deep blue eyes, at a loss for an answer. She feared she'd failed him somehow, disappointed him.

Luke looked away from her, back to the parking lot. His expression shifted. In his profile she saw a fresh realization. "So you got pregnant when Dad was still with her?"

"It's a lot, I know."

"I just don't understand why you lied about it."

Words failed her again. She was right to doubt her decision. It was too much for him. All the pieces, all the layers she herself struggled most days to peel through—she at forty-two. Her son, not even eighteen.

Luke turned on the van. "We should go. Before stuff spoils."

Jill nodded, but she feared it already had.

11

A soft sea breeze pushed gently through the screens, blending the smells of sautéed garlic and saffron into a heady stew. Jill walked past the kitchen and smiled to see Luke at the stove. He'd changed into a clean T-shirt and shorts, his curly hair brushed behind his ears. Pride swelled.

Too nervous to sit still, she moved through the house, tidying, checking; fluffing sofa pillows, straightening pictures.

She's not the queen, you know.

Shep found her in the living room and wrapped his arms around her waist to quiet her relentless fussing.

"You look beautiful," he said.

She'd debated over her meager wardrobe options for far too long before deciding on a simple sheath dress, a bold print of bone and coral, and twisted up her hair in a sleek knot, beaded earrings brushing the sides of her bared neck, matching bracelets covering one wrist.

She laid her cheek against his chest, drawing in the faint scent of cut grass.

"The place looks great," he said. "I doubt Claire'll recognize it."

She will, Jill thought.

Shep leaned back to study her face. "Are you nervous?"

"A little," she admitted.

"It was another lifetime, Jilly. We're all different people. She agreed to come, didn't she?"

"What if it's only to finally let me have it?"

Shep stroked her cheek. "Is that what you want?"

Jill frowned at the question even as a part of her considered saying yes. The guilt had been unbearable for so long. "And she knows we bought the Glasshouse?"

"I had to give her an address for dinner, didn't I?"

She nodded, feeling dim.

"You should have seen how Luke stared at me when I told him the truth. Like he had no idea who I was all of a sudden. My heart stopped, Shep, I swear."

"You're making too big a deal out of this. This isn't shattering his world. It's just him needing a little while to digest it, that's all."

The sound of clanging dishes broke out from the kitchen; Jill glanced to the doorway.

Shep smiled. "He makes paella for us all the time."

"Not with fresh royal reds."

Shep kissed her softly on the mouth, tasting of beer. For the first time, Jill considered what Claire would think to know Shep had taken her back. Would Claire be angry? Jealous? Shep had told her, Jill, that Claire was divorced. Raising a teenager alone couldn't be easy; Jill was grateful she hadn't been forced to do it.

Nearly, yes. But then Shep had come back.

She took his hands in hers, stroking his knuckles, the weathered, chapped skin. "Thank you."

He searched her face, confused. "For what?"

She touched his cheek.

"Everything," she said. "Just everything."

$\mathcal{S}$o, who are these people anyway?"

Lizzie waited until they were in the rental car and on their way to Jill's to finally ask the question Claire had been waiting days to hear. Now that it had come, Claire hesitated in her answer; the layers she had hoped to convey—rehearsed, even—seemed burdensome to someone Lizzie's age, even if her daughter was only a few years younger than Claire herself had been when she moved to Folly. Or maybe it was simply geography: they'd arrive in a matter of minutes; not nearly enough time to dig deep.

"They're just old friends," Claire said finally, deciding it was the best answer for the moment.

"They must have been more than that. You changed your outfit seven times."

Claire frowned. Had Lizzie actually *counted*?

"They were *good* friends, Zee. They meant a lot to me once."

"If they meant so much to you, then how come I've never heard of them before now?"

"It's complicated."

Lizzie eyed her and muttered, "That's exactly what Dad said when you guys were getting a divorce."

"That's because divorce *is* complicated."

A lie. What had happened between her and Foster and Jill and Shep was far more complicated than anything Claire had endured during the end of her marriage to Nick. What had lived and breathed between the four of them, bloomed and wilted, soared and sunk, had made her divorce look no more complicated than drawing the blinds. Which was what she had done.

Only with Nick, it had been a quick cutting off of the light.

*C*laire wasn't going to be one of those women.

If she had gleaned anything from growing up with a cheating father and a mother who lived in willful denial, she'd learned the signs of infidelity in a marriage. If she ever caught a whiff of deceit in her own, she'd run.

In the months after she'd left Folly, after she'd tried, and failed, to resume her surfing career in Florida and moved out to Colorado, Claire learned to forgive herself for being blind to Foster and Jill's affair, for breaking the one rule she'd set for herself. It would not, she decided firmly, happen twice. So by the time she met Nick Matheson at a party for mutual friends, she'd believed herself reformed, wiser. He was charming and smart, and totally bald—by choice, he clarified, having decided thirty was too young for a comb-over. He got her a glass of wine and made her laugh almost immediately. When he invited her to hike Chief Mountain with him the following Saturday, she agreed, and when they reached the top and looked out at the view, her first thought was how much the mountains looked like waves, and she burst into tears. He asked her what was wrong. Not knowing where to start, Claire just kissed him instead and that was that.

She would never get back to answering his question. Two months later, she was living in his bungalow and going back to school for her degree. Her muscles no longer ached to paddle out, to duck-dive, to launch. She watched, with some strange relief, as her body softened slightly with every passing day. A lover would never notice the change, but she did. When she learned she was pregnant, she felt absolved, as if she was granting her body a purpose she'd taken away from it when she stopped surfing. Holding Lizzie for the first time made everything else—eating, breathing, sleeping—seem singularly purposed. Not since surfing, not since Foster, had she known such complete direction. This, Claire thought, as Nick drove the three of them home from the hospital, this was who she was meant to be. *Elizabeth's mother.* And with every sleepless night, every laundered onesie, every new tooth that pushed through velvet

gums, Claire's devotion grew firmer, denser, like ice form-
ing on a lake. The thicker it became, the less anything
underneath would matter.

*Y*ears later, when Nick surprised her with dinner
in the middle of the week, making reservations
at their favorite restaurant, it was a perfect mountain
evening, crisp and cool, and Claire had carried a sweater
just in case. They'd seen little of each other in the past few
weeks. Her work teaching history at the high school was
always demanding around exam time, and she looked forward to catching up, to filling him in on Lizzie's latest suc-
cesses. It had been a flawless year for their daughter. She
loved her teachers and they loved her. Claire had been relieved that middle school was kinder to her daughter than
it had been to her. Tonight Lizzie was at a friend's house,
baking brownies for a fund-raiser for the no-kill shelter.
Claire had requested a call when Lizzie arrived, but her
phone had been silent.

"What are we celebrating?" Claire asked when the
waiter brought a bottle of Sauvignon Blanc.

Nick tasted the sample pour and nodded for the waiter
to fill both glasses. "You'll like this," he said. Claire picked
up her wine and studied her husband as she sipped. He
looked tired, she thought. The kind of tired that would nor-
mally find him on the couch, drifting off to a Rockies game.
Instead he'd wanted to take her out to dinner.

She ordered first—peppercorn medallions with fingerling

potatoes—and while Nick chose, she reached down to pull her phone from her purse. Just a peek.

"She's fine, Claire."

She looked up to see her husband's chastising gaze. She smiled, caught. "I know."

"Then stop checking the phone every five seconds."

She would. She pushed her purse under the table with her foot.

"You didn't answer my question," she said.

Nick drew a poppy seed roll from the breadbasket and eased it apart. "Which was?"

"What exactly are we celebrating?"

"Who says we have to be celebrating anything?" He buttered the roll. "Maybe I just thought it would be a nice place for us to talk."

So they did. Sipping and talking, buttering and talking. About work, about the house, about plans for the holiday. When their salads arrived, Nick emptied the last of the wine into his own glass and motioned for the waiter. Claire didn't say anything as he ordered them another bottle, but her expression must have revealed her surprise. In thirteen years of marriage, she could count the times Nick had allowed himself more than one glass of wine with dinner.

"What?" he defended. "It's not like we have to drive home." True, their house was just up the hill. "Besides." He refilled her glass with a generous pour. "Since when do you say no to more wine?"

The edge of anger in his tone startled her almost as much as the additional bottle. He was stressed, Claire could see that now. But he always was at this time of year. Exams and papers, panicked students e-mailing him around the clock. Compassion sparked inside her, turning quickly to longing. She admired his jaw, the crisp green of his eyes. They could make love later. She'd been missing him.

The new bottle came with their entrées; a red this time. Nick filled their glasses.

"How is it?" he asked after she'd taken a few bites of her dish.

"It's not as tender as it usually is. But the potatoes are perfect. How's the fish?"

Claire looked at his plate, surprised to see he'd barely touched his salmon.

He set down his fork and folded his hands. "Okay, here's the thing . . ."

She frowned at him, confused. "The thing about what?" she asked.

He took a long sip of wine before answering, enough to drain his glass, then poured more into his and hers.

"You're probably going to hear things," he said.

"Things? What things?" Now Claire set down her fork. "Nick, what's going on?"

"I may have done something . . . something pretty stupid." He met her eyes over his laced hands. He no longer looked tired; he looked nauseated. "No, I did," he said. "I definitely did something really, *really* stupid, Claire."

The possibilities flooded her mind. There were lots of stupid things people could do. They could forget to pay a bill. They could get a speeding ticket. They could leave a pen in their shirt pocket and ruin a load of laundry.

But a married person . . .

There was only one really stupid thing a married person could do.

She swallowed. "Oh God, Nick."

"It was just one time, Claire. I need you to understand that. It was one damn time, but one of her friends talked about it and it got back to Brad and now the department knows—"

"Are you saying you slept with a *student?*"

The table beside theirs quieted, the diners shifting with interest. Nick offered them a nervous smile, then cut his gaze back to Claire and whispered, "She's not a current student."

"And that's supposed to make me feel better?" Claire cried.

More heads turned. Nick leaned in. "Keep your voice down."

"Maybe you shouldn't have chosen a crowded restaurant to tell me you're screwing your student."

"I just thought it would help if you were around other people."

"Help *you*, you mean. Because you thought if you told me here that I wouldn't make a scene, right?"

"No," Nick said calmly. "That's not at all what I—"

The wine in her glass landed with remarkable symmetry, drenching his shirt, his lap, and equal parts of his sleeves. Who would have known she'd have such good aim under duress?

Walking home, shaking with bewilderment and panic, Claire kept thinking, *Not again, not again.* When Nick called an hour later, Claire refused to pick up. Instead she woke Lizzie and wooed her downstairs with Rocky Road ice cream and a movie of her choice. When midnight arrived and Nick had yet to appear, Lizzie asked what was keeping her father. Claire said he was staying late at school and that he might be gone all night.

If Lizzie knew even then that her mother was lying, she'd never let on. And Claire was too grateful to worry.

*C*laire didn't want to remember the way to the Glass-house. She didn't want to flick the turn signal when they passed Ocean Street, but she did. When she'd steered them into the driveway, she didn't want to recognize it. The patchwork of paint colors had been covered with a flawless coat of burgundy, the windows and trim a beautiful sand. Gone was the peeling porch swing that groaned when anyone dropped into it and shrieked when anyone forced it to move. In its place was a pair of tidy wicker chairs and a potted gardenia.

Only as she and Lizzie began toward the front steps and the glow of the porch lights that flanked the door did it occur to Claire that she'd come empty-handed. Her mother's chastising voice rang out; the sleight of etiquette was unforgivable. Even to the home of the woman who was having an affair with her husband, Maura Patton had arrived with a still-warm pie and a gracious smile.

Claire tried to swallow the knot in her throat, but it wouldn't budge. The last time she'd stood on this porch, the door was unlocked and she walked right in.

She raised her knuckles and knocked.

"How long do we have to stay?" Lizzie asked.

"I don't know," Claire whispered, fixing her eyes on the door, trying to imagine who would answer. She was certain it wouldn't be Jill.

Or maybe she just hoped.

The door opened and Shep appeared. Behind him lay the house she'd stepped into a thousand times, the interior she could find her way around in in her sleep. What would it be like now?

The scent of lemon and saffron was dizzying when they came inside. Claire glanced around the entry; quick, safe looks.

She caught Lizzie watching her and gave her daughter a reassuring smile.

"Luke's making dinner," Shep said, leading them down the hall. "I hope y'all are hungry."

"Starving," said Claire.

Lizzie trailing her, Claire followed Shep through the living room and into the kitchen, and there was Jill, standing in front of the table, hands clasped, her expression almost as warm and welcoming as it had been the first time they met across the booth at the Crab Trap.

Almost.

"Hi, Claire."

Stopped on the threshold, Claire took in her old friend in the brief moments before Jill crossed to greet her. The women hugged, then stepped back, forcing a wider gap between them than they'd had at the start.

"It's great to see you again, Miss Claire," Luke said. "You too, Lizzie. I hope y'all like paella."

Tension filled the room like smoke.

Claire smiled, just glad for something to do.

"We love it," she said.

12

ake yourself comfortable in the living room," Shep said. "I'll open a bottle of wine. Is white okay?"

"White's great," Claire said, feeling bad again for having arrived without a gift. Jill had retreated to the kitchen to keep an eye on the paella. Luke had poured Lizzie a Coke and told her that there were chips and salsa on the deck; they'd disappeared through the sliding doors soon after.

Now Claire sat alone in the living room, trying not to catalog all the memories hidden beneath the fresh décor as she looked around. Just as she'd always vowed, Jill had made the Glasshouse warm and cozy and wholly respectable. The transformation was remarkable. They'd replaced the missing floorboards by the door; they'd fixed the stretch of loose crown molding that had dangled precariously for so long. They'd even covered the gash beside the window where Foster had accidentally punctured the wall with the tip of his board.

They'd removed so much. And yet . . .

"Here you go." Shep arrived with a glass of Chardonnay; Claire took it and downed a long, grateful sip.

He chose a seat across from her. "Jill'll be right in. Everything's mostly done; it just has to simmer some, I think." He squinted. "Is that the right word, *simmer*? What do I know, right? We never were the cooks, were we?"

The sound of shuffled silverware sailed in from the kitchen: Jill setting the table. Shep tapped his fingers against his bottle of beer. It was like their last night together, Claire thought as she swallowed her wine. Neither one wanted to meet the other's eyes, steering their gazes to every other point around them, feigning deep interest in floorboards and rug patterns.

She took a second, longer sip. Where was Lizzie? Still on the deck? What could she and Luke be talking about?

"Looks a little different in here, doesn't it?" Shep asked, gesturing around them.

Not different enough, Claire wanted to say but didn't. It would take more than a fresh coat of paint and new furniture to make her forget her years in this house.

"We did a bunch of work on it when we moved in. It needed it. The backside was totally rotted out. Remember how the shower wall collapsed after that bad storm?"

She shook her head. "That must have been after I left."

"Oh. Right." Shep slugged his beer. "So . . . Tomorrow's the big day, huh?"

"I don't know how big it will be," Claire said.

"Oh, come on. They flew you all the way over here, put you up at the Breeze. I wouldn't be surprised if they turn it into a documentary about just you."

The song on the CD ended; in the brief quiet before another began, Lizzie's and Luke's voices sailed in from the deck. Claire looked toward the sound, grateful for its interruption.

"They're about the same age, aren't they?" Shep asked.

"Lizzie's fifteen."

There was, of course, no need to specify Luke's age.

Claire took another sip.

"Sorry that took so long." Jill came in and sat beside Shep, putting her hand on his knee. "Shep said they put you up at the Breeze?"

"I barely recognized it."

"It's very different," Jill said. "I've only been in the lobby once since they redid it."

"Get you some more wine, Claire?" Shep asked.

Claire glanced down at her glass, startled to see she'd nearly drained it. No wonder she was feeling more relaxed. More would be good. "Sure, thanks."

"I can get it," Jill said.

"No, you relax," Shep ordered gently, squeezing her hand. He rose and stepped around the couch for the kitchen. Claire waited until she heard the refrigerator door creak open before she said, "I want you to   know I asked Shep to call you first about this. About me coming over tonight. I didn't want you to feel put on the spot."

"Don't be silly. Of course we want you here. It would be so weird to think you were in Folly again and we didn't see each other, have our kids meet." Jill recrossed her legs, folded and unfolded her hands. When had she stopped painting her nails? "Especially since we didn't see you at the funeral."

The funeral. Claire looked reflexively for her glass, forgetting Shep had taken it. "I wanted to come," she said. "I really did, but my daughter was sick and my husband—ex-husband—had this conference he was speaking at—"

"I understand. I do," Jill said. "Thank you for your note."

God, how Claire had labored over that one short letter. Moving between stationery and a card, afraid to write too little, afraid to write too much. In the end, she'd compromised on five sentences that she'd rewritten and reread a dozen times before finally sealing the envelope.

Jill took a short, quick sip of her wine. Claire had always felt like a lush in Jill's company. The disparity between their sipping styles had been something they'd laughed over in those early days. Now it made Claire feel badly about herself.

Jill looked around the room. "I always said I'd make it sweet, didn't I?"

"You did." Claire let her eyes travel the space too. They'd burned through whole nights in this room, gossiping and complaining, crying and laughing. They'd shared dreams; they'd shared secrets. Now they sat across from each other like strangers trapped in a stalled train, desperate for someone to come in and relieve them of the impossible quiet.

"How are your parents?" Jill asked.

"My mom's fine; she's still in Charleston. My dad passed away."

"Oh, I'm sorry. I didn't know."

"Are yours still in Folly?" Claire asked.

"No, they moved over to Kiawah." Jill smiled. "Shep said you stopped by the shop. It's like a time capsule, isn't it? I'm sure you were surprised to see everything was still there."

"Honestly, I was more surprised to find it for sale."

"Really?" Jill looked surprised. "But you were there. You saw for yourself how badly the shop is showing its age."

"Funny," said Claire, "I thought it looked great. Aside from all the dust."

"Oh." Jill twisted her bracelet and shifted her gaze to the kitchen, searching the doorway. In the next moment, Shep returned with Claire's glass. Jill's face bloomed with relief.

Shep moved to take his seat, but Jill stood before he could.

"I think dinner's ready," she announced. "We should eat."

The paella arrived in a fragrant halo of steam: parsley, lemon, and saffron.

When they'd all been served, Claire took a good scoop, catching a royal red shrimp in her spoonful. "It's wonderful," she said to Luke. "You're quite the cook."

Luke shrugged, smiled. "I try."

"You must do better than that if your mom lets you in her kitchen." Claire glanced at Jill. "She never used to let anyone in her kitchen."

Luke looked at his mother. Jill smiled thinly. "You always said you hated to cook, Claire."

Shep thrust out his hand. "Luke, pass the bread, will you?"

He handed Shep the basket, but his gaze remained intent on Claire. "You must be superstoked to get back on a board."

Lizzie's head snapped up, her expression stricken.

Claire smiled. "I'm afraid that's not part of the deal."

"Really?" Luke's face fell. "I just figured you'd want to surf again. Being back here and all. At least a little bit."

Did she? Claire wasn't even sure. In all the activity surrounding her trip, all the worrying about Lizzie, about returning and seeing Shep and Jill, Claire hadn't had time to consider the part of this return that had given her pleasure. Once surfing had been her release, her place of peace. Truthfully, right now she would have given anything for fifteen minutes in that sweet spot of calm, sitting on her board, legs dangling in the water, waiting for a wave, when nothing else mattered and nothing could touch her.

"Miss Claire, if it's not too much trouble," said Luke, "I was hoping maybe you could put in a good word for Grams tomorrow and get the ESPN guys to film something at the shop. I know it would mean a lot to her."

Claire stared at Luke. "They haven't interviewed Ivy yet?"

"Nope." Luke speared a shrimp with his fork. "They never even contacted her."

Claire blinked around the table, stunned.

"I don't see how someone could film a documentary on surfing in Folly and not include Ivy or In the Curl. It's outrageous." Claire looked between Shep and Jill, waiting for their agreement, but all they did was exchange a short, wary look with each other. Surely they believed it was an unforgivable oversight too? "Maybe they saw the For Sale sign and assumed it was empty?"

"The sign had nothing to do with it," said Shep. "The shop's not really on the public's radar anymore, Claire. Well . . ." He glanced at Jill before adding, "Except for the building inspector's."

"There are some issues," said Jill. "Things not up to code."

"If it's just a matter of a few repairs, then make them," said Claire.

Jill smiled tightly. "That's not really the point. No one was shopping there anymore. Why invest the money?"

"Because it's Ivy's home," Claire said.

"Don't worry about Ivy." Shep reached for Jill's hand and held it. "We found her a great apartment. They just built a new condo development on the other side of the bridge. She'll be very happy there."

Ivy, happy living in a condominium? Shep and Jill didn't really believe that, did they?

"I still think it's shameful that no one invited her to be

a part of this documentary," Claire said. "But you can bet that I'll make sure they get to the shop to film it. *And* Ivy."

Jill lifted the pan of paella. "More, anyone?"

Luke smiled gratefully at Claire. She smiled back.

*T*he night air was cool and tangy on their ride back to the hotel. Claire lowered the windows and let the wind fill the interior and the quiet. The last two hours had been everything and nothing like what she'd expected. There'd been no uproars, no tears. But what had Claire expected? An apology? Of course not. But at least some acknowledgment that their reunion had arrived with rough edges that no amount of wine or paella would smooth over. Then there was the casual way Shep and Jill had spoken of moving Ivy to a condo. A condo! They might as well have reserved her a bed at Waveland Retirement Home and been done with it, Claire thought as she stared out at the road. And the way Jill had given her that placating smile as soon as Claire had challenged their plan, the smile that said—politely but firmly—You, Claire, don't have the foggiest idea what Ivy needs anymore.

Bull. Claire might have been away from Folly for almost two decades, but people didn't change. Ivy belonged in that shop. No matter what some building inspector said.

Claire glanced over at Lizzie, her irritation shifting focus. Her daughter had been sullen at dinner. She'd tolerated Lizzie's silent treatment at the outset of this trip, but enough was enough.

"You might have said more than five words tonight, you know. It's considered good manners to make conversation when someone invites you to their table."

"Even if it's someone who stole your boyfriend?"

"What?" Claire looked over at Lizzie. "Who told you that?"

"Luke. He told me everything. He told me how you and his dad were together and how you were going to get married but then he left you for his mom after he got her pregnant."

Claire gripped the wheel. "Luke said that? Those exact words?"

"I can't believe you went to her house and ate her food. Aren't you still mad at her?"

Claire raised her window several inches, chilled suddenly. "It was a long time ago, Zee."

"Then why were you so touchy at dinner?"

"I wasn't touchy." She frowned. "Why are you being so rude?"

Lizzie dropped her cheek against the window. "I just wish . . ."

Claire looked over at her daughter expectantly. "You wish what?"

"Never mind."

"Damn it, don't do that, Zee. If you want to say something, say it."

"Fine. You really want to know?"

God, did she? Claire stared at the road, unsure now. Still, she said, "Of course I do."

"I just wish you'd let me live my life by myself for once. I wish you'd let me breathe."

"What? I let you breathe."

Lizzie closed her eyes and turned into the door.

Claire felt the gap between them grow again, an urgency to reach out and pull Lizzie close, to hold her and bury her nose into her daughter's soft hair the way she used to do when Lizzie was little and wanted a hug every minute, when she made Claire promise she would never, ever let go.

Why hadn't Claire demanded the same promise from Lizzie?

*J*ill waited until Luke had tromped upstairs to bed before she walked out to the deck. Shep was nursing a beer and watching the fireflies that hovered above the grass. She dropped to the empty chair beside him and relaxed into the soft plastic weave.

All evening she'd clung to his side, catching his gaze and holding it like a guardrail. Not until Claire and her daughter had backed out of the driveway and slipped away down Ashley had Jill finally felt safe enough to be left on her own. It was over; she'd survived dinner and the relief was immediate, like someone who'd managed to steer a possible intruder off her doorstep without incident, or a driver who'd avoided a crash.

Then there was the guilt from the relief. What right had she to rush Claire and her daughter out of her house, to be glad to see them go?

"Hey." Shep reached for her hand. "You okay?"

"I don't know." Jill laced her fingers through his. "I can't decide how it went."

"I think it went all right. All things considered."

All things considered? The fact that she and Claire hadn't spoken a word since the night Foster broke Claire's heart? That was hardly a small detail to overcome.

"She was surprised about the shop." Jill plucked at her dress. "And she obviously doesn't approve of us moving Ivy. She made it sound like we were shipping her off to a nursing home." Jill looked over at Shep, suddenly worried. "That isn't what we're doing, is it?"

"Of course it isn't. Babe, it's easy for Claire to see it that way. She hasn't been here or been around Ivy in a long, long time. She has no idea how much everything's changed since she left."

Had it? Jill wasn't so sure. With her sitting across from Claire tonight, the tangy sea breeze slipping through the screens and curing the air around them, it might have been twenty years earlier. It might have been any night the four of them had dined together, emptied a bottle of wine together, or a bucket of crab legs.

Except, of course, no Foster.

Jill turned back to the yard and followed a firefly as it flickered across the lawn. "She's obviously still angry, Shep. I'm not saying I'm surprised, or I even blame her, but she's definitely *not* over it." She felt tears well, not sure where they'd come from, and wiped at them before they could fall. "I don't know what I expected. I guess I just *hoped* . . ."

Shep reached for her hand again and gave it a gentle squeeze this time. "It is what it is, baby. It was good you saw her while she was here. You welcomed her and her daughter and that's as much as you could do. Don't beat yourself up for something you can't change now."

She offered him a grateful smile.

The sound of TV floated down from the second floor: Luke's room.

Shep glanced up. "I thought I'd take him over to the Washout for the filming tomorrow morning."

Jill nodded. "Ivy will be crushed to miss it."

"Luke's already called her."

"Oh." Jill looked up at Luke's window, the shimmer of the television screen illuminating the ceiling. "He wants to surf with Claire."

"Of course he would."

"Do you?"

Shep frowned. "Why would you ask me that?"

Jill shrugged. "You and Claire and Foster always surfed together."

"I surfed with a lot of people, babe. Anyway, Claire made it pretty clear she didn't want to get back on a board. With me or anyone."

"I'm sure she'd do it for Luke. I'm sure she'd at least *try*."

"Would that upset you?"

Jill looked at Shep, startled by the suggestion. "Of course not. Why would you think that?"

"I don't know. Because it might be hard. Seeing them together. Out there."

She continued to stare at him, not sure what he wanted her to say.

He smiled, absolving her. "Forget I even asked," he said. "I'll see you upstairs."

But even as he rose and dropped a kiss on her temple before disappearing back into the house, Jill felt the question settle over her like a shawl. She squared her shoulders as she climbed out of her chair, as if to abandon it before she returned inside too, but still it hung on, dangling, unfinished, neither on nor off.

13

*S*unshine burned an outline around the curtains; Claire blinked against the shaft of morning sun and let her eyes fall closed again. She wasn't in any rush to rise. The Washout was a five-minute drive from the hotel, and she wasn't due to meet Adam Williams until ten.

The day of her interview was here, the true reason for her coming back to Folly, and all Claire wanted to do was pull the covers over her head, just as her daughter was no doubt doing a few feet away.

She'd slept fitfully, trying to digest the moods of her meal. Shep and Jill had appeared so calm—why had she, Claire, felt so unwound?

Why had she stayed so long? Why had she gone in the first place? She'd wanted to prove that it was all in the past, that she'd moved on. Instead she'd guzzled wine like a college freshman and inhaled paella like a lifeboat survivor.

Then the subject of Ivy's move, and that had only exacerbated her nerves further. The methodical way Jill and Shep had talked about relocating Ivy, as if they were transplanting a bush from one side of the yard to the other. It had galled her—Claire wouldn't lie. And she knew her outrage hadn't been lost on either Jill or Shep.

Or Lizzie.

Claire turned over to face her daughter's bed, blinked into the light, and saw it empty. Where was Lizzie? She shot up and searched the room, and her heart settled to see Lizzie through the sliding door.

Claire climbed out of bed and walked out to the balcony. Lizzie sat with her eyes fixed on the iPad in her lap.

"You're up?" Claire said.

"Of course," said Lizzie. "It's your big interview, isn't it? The whole reason we're here?"

"I wasn't sure you would still want to come. After last night . . ." Claire stopped, seeing the screen. It was a photograph of her, Claire, nailing a roundhouse turn on a wave.

"Oh my God . . ." Claire pulled the other chair over and sat down, still eyeing the picture. "Where did you find that?"

"It's online. There're lots of pictures of you, actually. I just Googled Pepper Patton and there you were." Lizzie squinted at her. "Why didn't you tell me all this before?"

"I—I didn't think you'd want to know." Claire stared at her daughter's bent head as if Lizzie were a mirage. This girl who twelve hours ago had gone to bed angry and distant was now doing an online search for Pepper Patton and scrolling through surfing photos? Had something happened in the night? An alien abduction, her daughter's body exchanged with that of another teenager?

Lizzie pointed at the screen. "How old were you in this one?"

Claire leaned closer and frowned at the grainy picture. She'd competed in so many heats over the years, and always in her trademark red one-piece; there was no way to know.

"Seriously, though, Mom—that *suit*." Lizzie gave her an admonishing eye flutter. "Didn't y'all ever hear of bikinis?"

"No one surfed in bikinis back then," Claire defended. "I don't know why anyone would *want* to." She caught the time on the corner of the tablet. "I should get dressed."

Lizzie closed the cover to her iPad. "I'll get dressed too."

"No, you take your time. Enjoy the morning. Have breakfast." Her daughter wanted breathing room; how was this for a start? "Tell you what," Claire said. "I'll take the rental and you can catch the car they're sending for us. Just make sure to be down in the lobby by nine forty-five. I'll tell the front desk to expect you. Then call me when they drop you off at the Washout and I'll find you, okay?"

Now it was Lizzie's turn to stare at her mother as if someone had been switched in the night.

Claire dressed quickly in jeans and a T-shirt, packing her on-camera clothes, a terra-cotta shell, and white slacks, in a separate bag to change into. One last good-bye to Lizzie, and then she stepped out into the hall, pausing a moment on the other side of the door, feeling strange and needing a moment to identify the sensation.

She exhaled, tension spilling out with her breath. No wonder she hadn't recognized the feeling. It was utterly unexpected.

It was joy.

*T*he Washout was a circus.

After announcing herself to the orange-vested cop who was directing parking and steering her rental into a special lot, Claire secured her bag over her shoulder and mounted the walkway to the beach, navigating through the caravan of buses and trailers that lined the shoulder. She wondered which one they would point her to for wardrobe changes, who would do her makeup, her hair. She'd worn it down to dry after her shower and now regretted it, the breeze hefty enough to lash it across her face and into her mouth.

Ushered past a clump of security guards, she reached the beach at last and paused a moment to look out at the water. Several surfers, mostly women in tiny bikinis, twisted and turned in the lineup. Claire watched, awed, as they rose and arched their bodies and boards above the waves, landing effortlessly every time. Gus Gallagher was right. The sport *had* changed since she was part of it.

"Claire?" A thin man with a mop of shoulder-length black ringlets marched up the beach toward her. "Adam Williams," he said as he arrived, thrusting out his hand. Claire smiled to keep the shock off her face. He looked barely older than Lizzie. "It's great to meet you face-to-face. Sorry again for having to bail on our meeting yesterday—Gus said you guys had a great time talking shop. I figured you would. He's something, isn't he?

"Oh, he's something, all right." Claire smiled politely. "I have to say, I'm really honored that y'all asked me to—"

"Hold that thought— Hey, Moe!" Williams yelled over her head, silencing her. "Tell Eileen to put Pammy in the *other* red bikini." He directed Claire's gaze to the water. "That's Pammy Ridgeway," he explained, pointing to a blond woman who was expertly maneuvering the surf. "She's a total phenom. She's going to be your body double."

Claire blinked at him. "My *what*?"

"It's this really cool concept Fletch—he's our director— came up with. It's all about contrast. Old you, young her. You sitting on the beach while she's out there killing it. It's like you're looking back on how much things have changed, how far these girls have come. Powerful stuff."

Old you? Claire swallowed, the words sticking in her throat like a too-big bite of food.

"I thought this was a retrospective piece," she said carefully. "I thought it was about the early days of surfing here, the old times. How much fun we had."

"It is, sure, but we can't have *too* much of the old folks. This is a show for young people. They want to see other hot, young people."

"Of course." Claire nodded tightly, but keeping her smile polite was getting harder and harder with each word out of Adam Williams's big, young mouth. "You *are* planning to film over at In the Curl at some point, aren't you?" she asked.

"You mean the place for sale down the road?"

"It's an institution," Claire defended. "And you have to interview the owner, Ivy King—"

"Yeah, well, we decided against filming there. Young people don't want to see all that, the out-of-business angle. It's depressing, know what I mean?"

"But Ivy King was a huge part of the surfing culture here. You can't do a piece on Folly and not—"

"Yo, Adam—Fletch is ready to go in ten." A round-faced, sunburned man darted between them to make his announcement, then slipped out again.

"On our way." Williams steered Claire toward the water and she let him, the wind still whipping her hair in all directions, try as she did to corral it behind her ears.

When they arrived at the edge of the surf, the blond woman Williams had pointed out waved to them from her board, a tiny red bikini barely covering her.

"That's supposed to be me?" Claire asked.

"That's the idea," said Williams.

"But I never wore a bikini."

Williams chuckled. "No offense, but no one wants to see a hot chick in a one-piece nowadays. This isn't *Baywatch*." He gestured to a man in a baseball cap standing behind a camera. "That's Fletch Connor, our director. He'll be over in just a sec and then we can get started."

"But I haven't had a chance to change or do my makeup yet. I brought other clothes—"

"Don't worry about it. This is just to get the levels right. You'll do fine," Williams insisted, already walking away. "Just relax."

*J*ust relax."

Bumpy with gooseflesh from her scalp to her toes, Claire had looked up at Foster and swallowed hard. "I think I'm going to throw up."

"You're not going to throw up," he said, rubbing her arms to warm her. "Everyone thinks that before a heat."

Claire peeked around his shoulder at the crowd of surfers scattered across the beach, mostly men and a few women. "Look at all of them," she whispered.

"It's a big competition. People come from all over for it."

Claire gave him a woeful look. "I'm going to fall on my ass," she decided. "I'm so nervous I can't think straight."

"So *don't* think," he said. "Remember, the curl doesn't care what's going on in your head. It's all about the wave."

The curl doesn't care. She liked that. She would try to remember that.

"What if I don't get into the semifinals?" she asked.

"Do you want to?"

"Of course not." She looked up at him and smirked. "I want to win the whole damn thing."

Foster grinned. "That's my girl."

Claire paddled out hearing nothing but the thumping of her heartbeat in her ears. There were a few girls outside, a few who'd made it through the white water as she had.

They looked at her as she sat up on her board, letting her feet dangle over the rails as they did, waiting for the next break too. They looked at her and she looked right back.

That was the beauty of the outside, the space beyond the waves. Fear was long gone. Once you'd cleared the crush of the impact zone where the surf hit, nothing could touch you. Nothing and no one. She'd heard the stories of surfers who'd bully their neighbors while they waited, who'd bring their board right next to yours, crowd you, and claim, "I'm on you," so you'd never catch a break.

They might have been her father, suggesting with a glance that she had no business being there, that good Southern girls didn't hurl themselves into waves.

When the break came, she paddled to meet it, threw her feet under her chest, got up, and carved her heart out. Somewhere on the beach, Foster hollered and cheered, but Claire couldn't hear anything over the roar of the wave.

She slid toward the shore.

And then, miraculously, it was over as soon as it started.

*I*t was over before she knew it. Claire had shared the story of her first heat, how she'd made it to the finals a virtual unknown, and was just getting warmed up when Fletch Connor raised a hand, called the cameras to cut, and excused himself to confer with his crew.

Claire stood in place, boiling and itchy in her jeans, waiting for Connor to return and give her direction, but it was Adam Williams who arrived instead.

"That was awesome, Claire. You nailed it."

She wiped sweat from her hairline. Was he kidding? They'd stuck her in the sand like an empty beer bottle! "I just think when we do the real take, I'd like to be *walking*—"

"Actually what we got was great." Williams patted her shoulder. "We're all set."

"Wait—what?" Claire blinked at him through the sticky curtain of her blown hair. "But—but you said that was just a test. My daughter's on her way to see me."

"Hey, I'm sorry about that—it happens in filming. You just gotta go with it." He took Claire's hand and gave it a quick shake. "We really appreciate you being here—and don't feel like you have to rush off the set. Stick around. Lucy Furness just got here. She's barely nineteen and taking the surfing world by storm. You should see her aerials. The girl is *sick*."

That makes two of us, Claire thought, her hand going numb as Adam Williams shook it. In the next minute, he was down the beach and enveloped in the throng of young women who'd just emerged from the waves, their bodies gleaming and tanned.

She thought they'd asked her here to honor her, to marvel at the pioneer she'd been in women's surfing. She'd imagined a lengthy tribute to her accomplishments, an exhaustive series of questions given by a moderator, eyes shiny with admiration for all she'd done. Shep had suggested they'd point the entire documentary around her. Claire had balked, but deep down, it had seemed a reasonable possibility. Now embarrassment flooded her skin. She felt duped, cuckolded—*furious*! She hadn't come all this way to be made old and irrelevant. She never would have agreed to this if she'd known their plan! She touched her throat, her cheeks, hoping to hide the rash of pink she was sure had spread there. Making matters worse, the change in schedule meant that Lizzie had missed her interview. Claire scanned the crowd for her daughter but couldn't see her.

Well, so what? she decided hotly. All that mattered in this moment was that her daughter had finally raised the white flag. Maybe not necessarily *waved* it, but she'd certainly put it on the table. Lizzie's willingness to talk, to listen, to bond, was the real reason for this trip, Claire reminded herself as she marched up the sand toward the road—not some phony tribute. Adam Williams and Fletch Connor and all the other big shots could jump off a bridge for all she cared. She just wanted to get out of these hot jeans and into a shower. At least now she and Lizzie were free to enjoy the rest of this trip together. They could go into Charleston. Splurge on a fancy dinner at High Cotton. Tour the homes in the Historic District.

Claire was feeling better already.

When her cell chimed, she pulled it from her bag, sure it would be Lizzie looking for her, but her ex-husband's name flashed on the screen instead.

"Nick, this really isn't a good time."

"Claire, I just got a furious call from Lizzie. Colin's been expelled. Did you report him to the school?"

"What?" Claire stopped, letting her bag slide down her arm to the sand. "No," she insisted. "Of course not."

"Well, Lizzie is sure you did. Colin's *claiming* you did."

"Nick, I am telling you, I never said a word."

"All I know is that Lizzie is hysterical and she wants to come home. I've booked a flight out of Charleston for her this afternoon."

"You what?" Claire stared out at the line of trailers. "But she's here with me until tomorrow. Our flight leaves in the morning. We're coming back together!"

"Believe me, Claire; you want Lizzie on the plane today. She's devastated about this. She thinks you lied to her. She's out-of-her-mind angry."

Angry? Was this a joke? "Nick, she can't leave today. You have to change it back."

"Claire, calm down. It's just one day. Lizzie wanted to leave an hour ago, but I told her she needed to wait for you to get back to the hotel before she le—"

Claire ended the call, hiked her bag over her shoulder, and rushed up the beach barefoot, her shoes clutched in one hand. She tore out of the parking lot and sped down Ashley. Surely she could make Lizzie see this wasn't true, that Colin was lying, that she hadn't broken her promise. Oh God, why did it have to be now? After they'd made such progress that morning! Finally, they were connecting, joking, enjoying each other, just the way Claire had hoped they would on this trip—the way they *used* to—and now this?

When she flew through the front doors of the hotel, she slowed to see Lizzie sitting stiffly in one of the lobby's plump love seats, her luggage beside her.

Claire's heart sank. "Zee."

Lizzie shot to her feet, grabbed the handle of her bag, yanked it into position, and wheeled it around Claire, heading for the sliding front doors. "I promised Dad I'd wait for you, so I did. Now I'm going."

"Zee, I don't know what Colin told you, but I never reported him."

"I don't want to talk about it, Mom. I just want to go home, okay?"

At the doors, Claire reached for Lizzie's elbow to slow her.

Lizzie spun, her eyes filling with tears. "Why did you have to report him?"

"Baby, it wasn't me."

"He says it was."

"That's the proof right there! The school would never disclose their source."

"That's what you were counting on, isn't it?" Lizzie resumed her march, giving the glass a shove with her hip before leading them both out into the hot midday air. Her luggage bounced over the pavers, unbearably loud.

Claire caught up to her. "Zee, it's just one more day. You said you wanted to know more about who I was here, so let me show you. We have all afternoon."

Lizzie dragged her wrist across her wet eyes and sniffed. Her shoulders sagged. "Why couldn't you have been happy for me?"

"Baby, all I want is for you to be happy," said Claire. "It's all I've ever wanted. I just don't understand why you think it has to be him or me."

"Because it does."

"Why?"

"Because you suffocate me!"

Claire reared back as if her daughter had screamed the words. "I *suffocate* you?"

"You have no friends. You have no one. Just me."

"That's not—"

"Do you have any idea how stressful that is?" Lizzie cried. "To think that I have to be my mother's best friend? Well, I can't be your whole world. I can't!"

Claire watched, frozen, as Lizzie yanked the handle of the taxi's backseat door, tossed her luggage inside, and slid in beside it. Claire held on to the door after Lizzie pulled it closed, her legs barely keeping her upright, and stared back into her daughter's eyes through the open window, but Lizzie's expression remained unforgiving. "I'll call you when I get to Dad's," she said, turning away.

Claire felt sure her bones crumbled under her skin, that if she let go of the cab's door she would slide to the sidewalk. She watched the taxi as it thumped over the curb and continued down Center Street. Any minute, the brake lights would shine and Lizzie would rush out and run back to her, realizing her mistake, and they'd go inside together.

Any minute.

But the car never slowed.

Claire waited until it slipped over the bridge and out of sight before she finally turned and walked slowly back through the hotel doors.

Alone.

14

From the time she was a little girl, Jill had always believed that love, like luck, came into a person's life in a variety of forms. Some loves arrived in an instant; others crept in gently, surprisingly. Those loves took their time, attaching themselves around your heart so that by the time you realized they were there, the roots of their devotion had grown too deep and too entwined to be plucked out. She had grown up believing the first kind was the sort of love to be afraid of, the violent attractions, like the one she had for Shep, an immediate love based on lust and admiration of physical beauty, which wasn't really love at all.

Her love for Foster was the slow, creeping kind. Sometimes she likened it to a commute; how a person can take the same road to and from a job every day, for years, and then one day an accident causes traffic to stop and for the first time the driver sees a remarkable house or a flowering bush she has never noticed before because she was too busy driving—but that house, that bush had been there, that re-markable, the entire time.

For Jill, the accident that stopped her car—though she wouldn't recognize it as such for months and months to come—was a romantic dinner she'd made for Shep, only to have Foster step in as her date instead.

They'd had hard weeks, all of them, and Jill knew Shep's grind had been particularly rough. Tourist season had started in earnest, and the housekeeping business that Shep had recently joined was working overtime to meet the demands of the busy rental market. Jill knew it was just a temporary job, something to tide Shep over until the marina could afford to bring him back on, but the schedule had been grueling. Tonight she was going to surprise him with a decadent meal: she-crab soup, seafood pasta with a Creole butter sauce, and for dessert, his favorite, lemon icebox pie. She'd read up on the best wine to pair with their meal, the best dressing for their salad. With a day off from work, she'd holed herself in the apartment cooking and setting an immaculate table. When five o'clock arrived and Shep had yet to show, Jill didn't worry. Five turned to five thirty, and then to six. No Shep. Had something happened? Then, at six fifteen, footsteps on the stairs and a hearty knock. Taking a second to light the candles and snap on the stereo, Jill rushed to the door only to find Foster and his huge smile there instead.

"Sorry to bother you," he said. "I told Pep I'd swing by

and pick her up a sweater. She wants to go to the bonfire tonight."

"Oh." Jill searched the stairwell behind him, sure Shep would be on his heels, but no one followed. She stepped back to let him inside. "Shep isn't with you?"

"No, he's with Larry catching some good waves. They were headed down to the Washout when I drove past—Oh crap." Foster stopped, seeing the spread on the table. He looked back at Jill, his eyes soft with sympathy. "He didn't call you?"

She shook her head. "I guess this makes me a surf widow, huh?"

"Man, I'm sorry." He smiled tenderly. "It smells great."

"Have you eaten? We could call Claire," Jill offered. "There's plenty."

"Claire's giving lessons until seven. Do you think it could wait?" But Jill could see Foster knew the answer before the question had come out of his mouth.

"I'd hate for it all to go to waste," she said.

She watched his eyes scan the table, then the apartment around them.

When he looked back at her, his eyes flashed with anticipation. "Give me a second."

He disappeared into Claire's room and closed the door. While he was gone, Jill opened the bottle of wine and poured herself a glass. Did they have any beer in the house? She searched the fridge but couldn't find one. What would he drink? She was still trying to think of something when

Foster returned in a fresh-looking blue T-shirt. He'd even dragged a brush through his hair.

"Claire washed one of my shirts by mistake," he explained. "Lucky break, huh?"

Jill smiled, touched. "You didn't have to change."

"Sure I did. A meal this beautiful deserves a nice shirt. Not that a T-shirt is a nice shirt, but at least it's clean. Besides . . ." Foster gestured to her outfit. "You look too nice to have to stare across a table at a bum."

"Stop. You're not a bum. You look very handsome."

And he did, Jill decided as they took their seats. More handsome than she might have admitted. Although Foster didn't possess Shep's striking good looks (how many men did?), there was something undeniably appealing about his face. Maybe it was his oversized smile, which wasn't of course a bad thing; having a smile too big, too warm, too genuine. Or maybe it was his singular dimple, scaled to suit his large grin.

"I'm sorry," she said. "I don't have any beer."

"I'll take some wine."

She got him a glass and he suggested a toast.

"You and Claire still like this place?" he asked as she served the soup.

"Better yet, we still like each other. I think any place is fine so long as you like your roommate."

"She likes you, too."

Jill knew he was only being polite, that he didn't care what she thought of the woman he loved. Why should he?

Foster took a spoonful of the creamy bisque and moaned

with approval. "Man, who needs to know how to surf when you can cook like *this*?"

Jill laughed. "We all have things we're good at."

"No wonder Shep never wants to eat out. I could get used to this, Foster said, raising his wine before taking a healthy sip, candle flames flickering in the reflection of the glass.

Jill had never seen him drink wine. It suited him. She enjoyed the way he held it, not sure why it struck her as anything to see him cradle the bowl in his palm as he drank, the easy way he tipped the glass to his lips.

Jill stirred her soup, trying to catch the flakes of crabmeat. "You should probably call Claire so she doesn't worry."

"She's not worried. The bonfire doesn't start for hours. Anyway, I'm sure she and my mom ordered in a pizza at the shop."

"They get along well, don't they, Claire and your mom?"

"You know, sometimes I think Pep's just with me because of her."

Jill eyed him over her spoon. "You don't really think that?"

He grinned. "I'm kidding. But I wouldn't blame her. Pepper's mom is seriously uptight. Have you met her?"

Jill nodded but didn't elaborate. It felt unkind, traitorous somehow, to speak of Claire's relationship with her parents when Claire wasn't there.

"You and your folks get along?" Foster asked.

"They're pretty normal as far as parents go," Jill said. "I know I'm lucky."

"You are. I love my mom like crazy, but some days I

used to wish I could come home from school like the rest of my friends and find my mom waiting there for me with a plate of cookies and a glass of milk."

"She wasn't?"

He shook his head. "My mom was always out on the water. I never had this growing up."

Jill frowned. "What do you mean?"

"*This*," he said again, gesturing to their meal. "Dinner at a table. Food that didn't come out of a to-go box. All these little touches. Candles and real napkins, salt and pepper in shakers." He lifted his gaze to meet hers. "It's nice."

She had never really looked at his eyes before. They were beautiful. A whitish blue that on anyone else would seem cold. But there was warmth in his. Heat.

They finished their soup and filled their plates with pasta.

Foster poured more wine. "You know, I think this is the first time we've ever had a real conversation, you and me."

It was true, Jill thought. She'd been with Shep for years now and yet she and Foster had spent hardly any time alone. Not surprising, of course.

"I know you think I'm too straight for him," Jill said.

"I don't."

She smiled knowingly.

"Okay, maybe a little," Foster confessed.

"I know he wishes I liked to surf more than I do."

"He doesn't say that. He shouldn't," Foster added. "He's lucky to have you."

They looked at each other, their gazes holding a beat

longer than necessary, long enough that Jill lowered her eyes to the bowl of pasta and offered him more. He declined.

"Maybe I *should* go," he said, pushing out his chair.

"Thanks for keeping me company," Jill said.

"I'm the one who should be thanking you. At least let me help you clear everything before I go," Foster offered, sweeping up his plate.

Jill took it from him. "Go. I don't want you to be late to meet Claire. She'll be missing you."

"You can come with us, you know. It's going to be a full moon."

"I think I want to stay in tonight."

When he'd gone, Jill cleaned the table, put away the leftovers, and dressed for bed. If there had been even the slightest tear in the smooth coating of her heart, she didn't feel it then. It was one dinner, one night, one conversation with one friend. She brushed her teeth as she always did, folded her clothes, and why not? Nothing had changed.

But the next morning, when she found Claire in the kitchen having coffee, Jill had hesitated—just the span of a breath—before she'd explained her evening, and why Foster had been so satisfied and full when he came to pick up Claire at the shop. Jill had paused without knowing why. And when Claire had laughed about it and assured Jill that Foster had arrived giddy from the meal, Jill felt a pang of guilt, large enough that she wasn't angry at Shep when he came to apologize for not calling.

She hadn't known it then, and she wouldn't know it for many more years, but the seed of her and Foster's love had been planted that night. Tiny and fragile, and she never intending to water it, it shouldn't have had a chance to grow. But it did.

The next time she and Foster saw each other, they shared the smile of a remembered exchange, two people who'd imagined they had nothing in common but their partners. An unexpected connection. And it was nice.

It would be another few years yet before she would feel the squeeze of those roots, and by then, it was like the sculptor of Mount Rushmore deciding to move Thomas Jefferson halfway through his carving. The stones had been set; it should have been too late to change their positions.

*N*ow, staring out the bedroom window, watching the driveway for the van to arrive and bring Shep and Luke home from the filming, Jill felt as if someone had unzipped her heart and let those memories and those moments—both heavenly and hellish—spill out.

She wondered how the interview had gone, whether or not Ivy had made it back in time, what Claire had said on-camera about those raw and tender years. Turning from her useless vigil, Jill tried to lose the flood of questions in a fresh pile of laundry, but her gaze kept drifting to her dresser, the tickle of temptation rising along her skin like gooseflesh.

It made sense that she should want to see the letter. Ever since Claire had arrived—*no, tell the truth:* Ever since the rumor of her arrival had entered their house—Jill was tempted to unearth the letter, maybe even finally open it. Now she walked slowly to her bureau, pulled the drawer out, dug through the careful layers of scarves and slips she kept stacked in the very back corner, and there it was, tucked between a velvet wrap and a camisole, as if it were just another article of clothing.

When the envelope had arrived in the mail, nearly three weeks after Foster had drowned, it came in a plastic bag. Its journey—according to the U.S. Postal Service's form letter, which was also included in the bag—had been grueling and ultimately fruitless, resulting in tears and rips and accordion pleats in one corner. The damning stamp of Undeliverable/No Longer at Address had been wet at some point, maybe from rain, causing the *No* and the *L* to bleed. Jill knew all this because she had scrutinized every inch of its exterior—it was the contents inside that she had yet to view.

It would have been an easy investigation. The end of the envelope flap had risen with wear, then a little more with age; not enough to break the seal, just enough to tease the possibility. A few times—three, to be exact—Jill had pulled the shade off the lamp in the bedroom and raised the letter to the naked bulb, thinking that if she could only pick out a few blurry words, it might be enough. But the envelope was always too thick, or maybe she just feared looking too long. As she held it now, the paper seemed like tissue, in danger of wilting under her fingers. A part of her thought that today was the perfect day to finally tear it open—when Claire's arrival had already opened every other part of her past, why not rupture this final seal too?

As Jill did every time she held the letter, she weighed the possibilities of its contents. Had Foster sent it to Claire in apology, or had he sent it in remorse? Had he told Claire he'd made a terrible mistake, or had he shared with her the certainty of his decision? Affirmations or doubts? The answer was inside, and uncovering it would have been as quick as a bee sting—one tear, one tug—and in the ten years that Jill had possessed it, she'd yet to reveal its truth. She'd buried Foster believing he had married her, had *loved* her, without regret. Then this letter had arrived.

The rumble of tires sailed in through the screens; Shep and Luke were home.

Jill tucked the envelope back under her scarves and slips. Not knowing was penance, she told herself as she shut the drawer.

Not knowing was still better.

15

*N*ot since she'd come down with mono in sixth grade and been quarantined inside her home for a week had Claire felt so abhorrent. After Lizzie's escape—what else could she call it?—Claire had slunk back up to her room, peeled off her shoes, and raided the minibar with vengeful speed. After they'd cast her as the lead in *The Old Woman and the Sea*, the least the network could do was buy her a twelve-dollar tin of cashews, a five-dollar bag of peanut M&Ms, and three tiny bottles of Kahlúa, which did nothing but make her sleepy and collapse on the bed. Three hours later, she'd barely moved. A few times the rhythm of the surf blew in through the opened balcony door and lulled her into short sleeps, just long enough to leave her feeling disoriented when she woke. Now it was almost five and the fact that she'd been without a decent meal all day was finally causing her stomach to sound the alarm. She rose drowsily, considering her possibilities for food, but the thought of leaving the safety of her room made all prospects unappetizing.

Where could she go? Her flight didn't leave until noon the next day.

It was hard to believe—this town she'd once called home, this town she'd planned to live out her whole life in—and she couldn't think of a single place to go within its borders.

She dragged herself to the sliders and stared out at the swath of blue sky beyond her balcony. Maybe she didn't need a destination so much as a direction.

Shoving her feet into her sandals, she grabbed her phone, her room key, and a twenty-dollar bill. Bare bones for bared bones, she thought as she opened the door and shut it behind her.

What did it matter where she went?

*S*he started walking down the one road that had never led her wrong: the road she took in, the road she took out. It seemed that during all of her life in Folly, Ashley Avenue had been her compass. She scanned the houses as she passed, wanting to lose herself in the study, but her mind continued to flash with thoughts of Lizzie. Claire touched the pocket of her denim skirt where she'd stashed her phone, wanting to check it, wanting to send another text.

She was almost to Eighth Street when she sensed a car slowing beside her to match her pace. She glanced over and recognized the driver of the navy blue truck at once.

"Hitchhikers usually hold out their thumb," Gus Gallagher called through the open passenger window.

"I'm not hitchhiking," Claire said, turning her gaze
back to the road and hastening her march.

"You are now. Get in. I'll give you a lift."

She rolled her lips together, her eyes still fixed firmly
ahead. "I'd rather walk."

He leaned over. "Look, if you don't get in, I'll just keep
following you at five miles an hour and pretty soon the
traffic will build up behind me and there'll be horns and
flipped birds and who knows what else."

"I'm actually feeling very sorry for myself right now,"
she informed him, "so unless you've got some pity to add to
my pile, I'm not interested."

"I've got something better than pity." He held up a six-
pack. "Beer."

"I don't need a beer."

"No, I'd say you need about *five*."

She stopped. The truck lurched to a stop too.

Gus reached over and opened the door. "Come on," he
said. "Get in."

Claire felt all her resolve puddle. Why not? The day was
already an unmitigated disaster. With her luck if she kept
walking she'd be run over by a golf cart or pooped on by a
pelican.

It was only when she climbed inside that she saw the
dog in the backseat, a black Lab with hopeful brown eyes
and a pink cast wrapped halfway up her right front leg.

"Let me guess," she said. *"Margot."*

Gus pulled them back onto the road; a grin teasing his mouth.

"You liked me thinking you were a scoundrel, didn't you?" Claire asked.

"Who says I'm not?" He turned his head and called over his shoulder, "Margot, am I a scoundrel?"

The Lab rose and wobbled to the edge of the seat to nuzzle his whiskered jaw. Gus reached back to knead the dog's ears until she was content and retreated, curling up on the seat.

"What's this pity party in honor of anyway?" Gus asked, reaching down for the beer can that had been teetering in a cup holder between them.

Claire sighed. "It's a long list."

"So start at the top."

"My daughter."

"Let me guess, you don't like her boyfriend."

Claire turned, startled. "How did you know that?"

"You had that I-could-kill-him look on your face just now. I used to see that all the time."

"Wonderful. Is that supposed to make me feel better?"

He yanked a beer free from the six-pack, then snapped the tab with one hand, hard enough to make the can hiss loudly, and held it out to her. "Drink."

She downed a long sip, the cold, spicy beer prickling her throat, so refreshing that she gasped after she'd swallowed.

God, he was right. She did need a drink.

"She also says I suffocate her."

"Do you?" Gus asked.

Claire frowned at him. "Whose side are you on?"

"Easy. It was just a question. So, where is she now?"

"Back in Colorado with her father. She's angry with me because she thinks I got her boyfriend expelled from school—which I *didn't*."

"But you wanted to."

"Of course I did. But it doesn't matter, because she doesn't believe me. She begged her father to buy her a plane ticket so she could leave a day early." Claire looked over at him. "Should I keep going?"

He grinned. "On second thought, we might need more beer."

She turned back to the road to see they'd arrived at the Washout. Gus steered them into the shoulder behind a short line of parked cars, the earlier chaos of the filming crew and their trailers and trucks now gone, the beach quiet again.

He killed the engine and sat back, lifting his arm to rest on the top of the seat, his hand dangling, his fingers nearly brushing her shoulder. Margot sat up and scanned the back window.

Claire sipped her beer and stared out at the water. "I'm sure you already heard about my big film debut today," she said. "I felt like one of those ancient widows they wheel out of the nursing home for five minutes to cut a ribbon. I was waiting for one of them to hand me a walker."

"I never would have pushed to get you down here if I'd have known they were planning something so damn dumb. You have to believe that."

"Wait . . . *you* pushed for me?"

"The producers asked if I knew of any female surfers from the area and I gave them your name."

She stared at him. "Why me?"

Gus smiled. "Because I'd never seen anyone own a heat the way you did the day I saw you out here."

"You saw me?" Claire blinked at him as he took a swig of beer. "When?"

"It was the Folly Classic. Nineteen eighty-eight, maybe 'eighty-nine. You couldn't have been more than nineteen." Gus looked out at the surf. "My friend Dale and I came through on an East Coast tour and we just stood there with our mouths hanging open. I'd been all over the world and I'd never seen a girl carve that hard." He dragged his gaze back to hers, his eyes flashing with admiration. "You were *fierce*."

Fierce. A flush of appreciation rippled under Claire's skin.

She faced forward and rolled her shoulders back, the pleasure of his compliment quickly fading.

"It's my own fault." She took a testy sip and swallowed hard. "I never should have said yes to Adam Williams in the first place. I only did it for my daughter. I thought maybe if she saw me here, if she knew a little about who I was back then, maybe it would bring us closer." She looked over at him. "You have kids?"

"Nope." Gus drained his beer and shoved the empty can into the cup holder.

"Did you want them?"

"Sure I did. I wanted lots of things. But then I got a lot of them too, so I can't complain."

Claire turned back to the view. A pair of surfers waited beyond the white water, sitting on their boards. "You were right," she said. "About surfing being so different now. I had no idea."

"This is nothing. When I left California, the stunts were crazy. In the old days, we were happy to launch with one turn. These new guys do full-rotation flips, they land aerials."

"So I saw."

"And it's not just the moves either," Gus said. "It's everything. Used to be if you wanted to know where the best breaks were, when to catch the best swells, you had to watch the forecast or ask your buddies. Now they've got *apps* for it. One click and you can see what the swells are like at Pipeline or Jaws. You want to see how big the barrels are at Mavericks? Hell, don't even bother going; just scroll through YouTube and watch a damn video."

"Listen to you. . . ." Claire smirked. "You sound like a grumpy old man, you know that?"

"In this business, that's exactly what I am. But it's okay. I see the kids around today and I wouldn't want to deal with all the crap they have to deal with. All the gadgets of modern love. Online dating. Texting. No, thanks. I prefer having sex with someone in bed with me, not on the other end of a phone or a computer screen." He grinned at her. "Not everything is better with technology."

Claire gave him a small smile in return. "I'm not going to sleep with you, you know."

He laughed, a hot, rough sound, making a dent in his beard, a sexy dimple that she told herself was only sexy because she was growing drunk. It was the same with his eyes. It was the beer she'd nearly drained that was turning them a stainless steel and making them go right through her; only the beer. He still needed a haircut. And a shave.

She shifted her gaze to a safer spot, to the waves, seeing the breaks the way she used to see them, the shifting patterns of the swells, the ones that promised height, the ones that would never grow.

"So, why *did* you leave California?" she asked him.

"It got too crazy," he said. "Too crowded. The promoters became kings. It was all about getting the contracts, getting the sponsors. It stopped being fun."

"So you decided if you can't beat 'em, join 'em, right?"

"No, I still want to beat 'em," he said. "I just want to do it on my own terms. The only thing you'll see Fins sponsoring is the chance for some kid to see the sport the way it used to be."

"Or maybe you wanted to be a big fish in a small pond?"

He smiled. "Maybe."

Claire looked back at the water and sighed. "After today I don't think there's a pond small enough to make me feel like a big fish again." And just like that, her buzz started to slip away, bringing life back into sharp focus, and all the disappointments she'd hoped to run from when she marched out of the hotel earlier.

She set her can in the cup holder.

"I should go," she said. "I have an early flight."

"Seems a shame to waste your last night in Folly

packing," Gus said. "I can think of a much better way for two people to spend a beautiful evening."

Claire turned to meet his gray eyes and felt her skin warm. This time she let him hold her gaze, and her thoughts began to soften again.

Maybe it was the beer, maybe it was the night; who knew and what difference did it make? A wild and furious rush of recklessness tore through her at the thought of being wanted by this man. The day—the whole trip!—had been a total disaster. If Gus Gallagher wanted to take her back to his house, carry her up a flight of stairs Rhett Butler–style, and make crazy love to her, why not?

Claire let her head fall against the seat. "I'm game if you are."

His hand was already on the gearshift to steer them back onto the road.

A quarter mile past the Washout, Gus pulled them into a beach house, all glass and metal. Open decking ran around the perimeter. Margot hopped up the steps and scoured the length, disappearing through a dog door before Gus ushered Claire inside.

"I should warn you—the maid quit."

She laughed, but the minute she stepped inside, she stopped laughing.

"Have a seat," he said, pointing her to a brown sectional. At least Claire thought it was brown, what little of it she could see under the piles of wet suits. "Shit. Sorry," he muttered, sweeping it clean and moving the piles to the floor.

Claire bit back a smile and sat down, watching as he raced around the room, relocating more piles on his way to the kitchen. "I keep meaning to get someone in here to clean up, but I'm afraid they'd report me and Margot to the health department. I'm thinking I'd probably be better off just renting a backhoe and a Dumpster. Get you a beer?"

"Sure."

He returned with a pair of bottles, handing her one and knocking the necks in toast. "Cheers."

"Cheers," she repeated.

"Give me a minute to get everything together and I'll be right back. Make yourself at home."

She frowned as he disappeared down a set of stairs. Get everything together? Did he mean to light candles, turn on music?

A bang, and then a series of crashes came from below. Margot bolted upright from her slumber and gave Claire a quizzical look. A few moments later Gus bounded up the steps, wearing a smile, and beckoned her to join him. Halfway down the stairs, Claire slowed. Understanding washed over her, seeing his intentions—and a pair of boards leaned against the wall.

He'd never meant to seduce her. This wasn't about sex. It was about surfing.

Embarrassment swerved quickly to indignation. "Absolutely not," she said firmly as she watched him attach leashes to both boards. "I already told you I can't."

"You told me you promised your daughter she wouldn't see you on a board," Gus clarified. "Your daughter's back in Colorado. Seems to me your excuse just expired."

"It wasn't an excuse."

"Good. This one's yours."

She stared at the thick surfboard he was handing her, then at him. "I said I needed a little refresher. I didn't say I had *amnesia*." She shoved it back at him. "I want a real board."

"That *is* a real board."

"For a beginner. I want a short board."

"Long boards are more stable and easier to paddle. You haven't been on a board in twenty years—why make it tough on yourself your first time back in?"

"*Seventeen* years," she clarified hotly.

"Like I said, it's been a while."

Claire glared at him, bristling with indecision, a part of her wanting to tell him where he could stick his damn long board, another part of her wanting to catch a killer ride that would douse the smug smile right off his handsome face.

She'd have thought whatever was left of her ego had been buried in the sand that morning at the interview. She was wrong.

"Fine." She pulled the board against her side. "But I don't have a suit."

"You don't need one." He pointed to a basket of brightly

colored fabrics. "Everyone wears rash guards and trunks now. Take a look through those floor samples and pick out what you want."

*M*inutes later, down to her bra and panties, Claire stared at herself in Gus Gallagher's bathroom mirror and couldn't decide whether to laugh or cry. What was she doing here? She'd never intended to get back on a board, and certainly not in the company of a stranger. What if Shep or Jill happened by and saw her out there, after she'd insisted on no interest in surfing again at dinner?

Claire frowned at her reflection. And so what if they did? Tonight all bets were off. She'd come on this trip to get closer to Lizzie and now they were farther apart than ever. Not to mention that the interview that was supposed to lionize her had made her feel older than dirt. Every part of this visit, a total disappointment.

Tomorrow she would be headed back to Colorado with her tail between her legs. All that remained was this final night. And this man who, to his credit, seemed genuinely reverential about her skills—ancient history though they might be. It had felt good to be reminded how hard she had carved, to be told she was—what was the word Gus had used—fierce?

Fierce.

Defiance returned, bolstering her. Why shouldn't she try to surf? She was forty-two, not eighty-two. Plenty of people surfed into their fifties and sixties. And anyway, wasn't forty the new twenty?

She took off the last of her clothes and stretched the purple rash guard over her breasts, pulling it down her stomach. The board shorts rode up her rear; she tugged at them, trying to force the cropped seat as far down her thighs as she could. She turned, surveying her body in profile. As strange as the new surfing uniform was, she had to admit it flattered. Even her breasts, never full to begin with and far less so after nursing, looked good, drawn up by the rash guard's tight fit. She slowed her pirouette in the mirror, feeling foolish. Back in the day, she would never have wasted a moment with this sort of review. Then she had pulled on and off her bathing suit without a thought of how the fabric clung to her body. No doubt those girls at the filming today were just as blissfully oblivious of their own perfect figures. Such was the luxury of youth.

She allowed herself one last survey in the mirror.

"Now or never," she whispered to her reflection.

The day was waning. The sun's most unforgiving rays were long gone. Dusk was the kindest light. Everyone knew that.

And anyway, the curl didn't care.

16

*I*t would be just like riding a bike.

As she followed Gus Gallagher down the wooden walkway, her board against her side, Claire told herself that the minute she threw her feet under her chest and got up, it would all come back to her.

Gus had changed into a sleeveless rash vest and shorts.

"I thought all you West Coast guys loved your wet suits," she said as they walked.

"We do . . . when we're on the West Coast," he said with a grin. "But this is *bathwater* compared to where I'm from. I wear trunks almost year-round here." At the top of the beach, they slowed and lowered their boards to the sand. "They're not much to look at right now," he said, nodding toward the low swells, "but I thought they'd be a good place to start again." He held out his hand. "Give me your board. I'll get you waxed up."

"Excuse me?" Claire set her hand on her hip. "I can still wax my own board, thank you very much."

"My apologies." He handed her a bar and stepped back to take care of his. They dropped down to the sand, side by side, and got to work. The motion came back to her at once, the even strokes, rail to rail, nose and tail, then the bumpy tack of the topcoat. She glanced over at Gus, warming at the sight of his tanned arm firmly guiding the bar of wax up and down, the movement rhythmic, sexual. He was fit, lean enough to impress but not bulked up: clearly a man who'd stayed active on the water. She wondered if Foster had kept in shape the same way; had he stayed agile on a board as he aged? She certainly hadn't. Doubt began to trickle in again. Just because she remembered how to wax a board didn't mean her muscles remembered how to surf. There was no faking strength and endurance. Years off the water would show the minute she tried to paddle out, and Claire knew it.

Waxed and ready, they walked down to the edge of the surf and stopped. Gus scanned the water, watching the breaks, searching for the best place to paddle out. He pointed them to the left where the surf was calm, where they'd face the least opposition for getting through the impact zone to the outside.

"Make sure to pace yourself," he said as they attached their leashes. "There's not much white water to get through right now, but you'll still be surprised at how tired you get after a few duck dives. Especially with a long board. Remember, you can always paddle around it. Or turtle-roll."

She nodded, grateful there wasn't a lineup; only the

two of them in the water. Even with the tether of a surf leash, the last thing she wanted to worry about was having locals think her a reckless, clueless beginner—a kook— because she couldn't control her board.

The sea hugged her body as she walked in, the faint flavor of salt already on her mouth when she licked her lips. At chest deep, they climbed on their boards, and began to paddle out. *Rhythm and flow, rhythm and flow.* The mantra she'd used in her youth returned as soon as her hands cut through the water, her heart already racing with anticipation. Gus paddled out in front of her, his closed-fingered hands moving effortlessly through the water.

He glanced over his shoulder at her. "You okay?"

She nodded, too focused on her strokes to speak, her back arched, her head raised. Movements she used to do in her sleep, she now rehearsed in her head. Where to grip the rails, when to pop up. Her head swam with uncertainty.

When they neared the first break of whitewash, she watched Gus send the nose of his board under the wave in an expert duck dive. She gripped the rails, knowing she would have to do the same, but her timing and force were off and the wave thrashed her enough to send her sputtering backward, her board jettisoned.

She pushed to the surface and reclaimed her board, managing to scurry back on before the next break came over her, but she wouldn't have enough time. As the wave hit, she rolled her board with her body underneath it, turtling in the hopes of avoiding another pushback, but her strength wasn't sufficient. Her spin was incomplete and the force of the wave hit her fully.

Again, she pushed to the surface.

Gus called to her, "You sure you don't want to go back in and wait it out for a lull?"

She shook her head fiercely. Dammit, she could do this! She lay down on her board and began her strokes again, harder now. Her neck and shoulders burned, her muscles screamed, but pride screamed louder. She used to duck-dive through white water ten times heavier than this without stopping, and now she couldn't even get to the out-side zone. Exhausted, she tried another roll, but her rotation still lacked and once again, the break thrashed her back into shallow water, bouncing her board off the bottom. When it popped to the surface, she felt a sting on her heel and winced. Jellyfish? She searched the water around her, seeing nothing, but the pain intensified. She grabbed her board and began back to the beach for a better look at her foot.

As soon as she could see the wound, she knew the weapon at once. It was a clean slice, just above her ankle, the cut nearly two inches in length.

Gus arrived, striding through the water with his board under his arm. "What happened?"

"The fin," she said. "It must have cut my heel on that last wave. It's just a little nick."

He pushed her fingers away from her heel and gave it a quick survey. "It's deep enough to quit." He motioned up the beach. "No more surfing for you, hot stuff. We need to clean you up."

By the time they reached the deck steps to his house, the sharp pain had shifted to a dull ache. Claire groaned with each tread. Inside at last, Gus ordered her to wait on the couch while he disappeared into the bathroom. Margot hopped up beside her and burrowed into a pile of towels, the Lab's soft brown eyes flashing with concern before she turned her head toward the sound of closing cabinets down the hall.

Gus returned with a handful of supplies and crouched down on one knee.

"I see my prep nurse is already here," he said, grinning at Margot as he tore open a Band-Aid with his teeth.

"Her couch-side manner is stellar," Claire said.

Gus took her foot into his hands and gently turned it. Claire cried out.

"Does it hurt?"

"Everything hurts," she said.

"Just wait till tomorrow." He reached for a soapy wash-cloth. "You'll be sore in places you forgot you had muscles."

Claire watched him as he slid the Band-Aid carefully over her heel, rubbing the ends of the bandage flat with his thumbs before setting her foot back down. This close, she could see the flecks of gold in his beard, even more threaded through his brown hair. It would be nothing to reach out and run her fingers through one perfect, touchable—

"I think you'll live."

She blinked, startled from her thoughts. "Good. Thanks."

Gus laid a hand on her damp thigh; a tiny, hopeful sound escaped her throat.

He smiled. "I'll take you home."

17

*J*ill saw the headlights swing across the kitchen wall just as she was putting water on the stove for tea.

The side door opened; Ivy appeared in a floor-length sundress, her long gray hair loosely knotted in a side ponytail, and searched the room, her expression stricken. "She's not here?"

Jill and Shep exchanged a confused look.

"Who?" asked Jill.

"Who do you think? Pepper!"

"Claire's not here, Ivy," said Shep. "She's probably at the hotel."

"Well, crap, I just assumed she would be here." Ivy continued to look between them, her gaze demanding. "Aren't y'all planning to see her before she leaves?"

"We *did* see her," Jill said calmly. "She came for dinner last night. We had a lovely meal."

"That's all you've seen her?"

Jill pulled down a mug from the cabinet. "She's here for this film, Ivy. It's not a social visit—we respect that. We're just glad we got to see her at all."

"There hasn't been that much time," Shep added, reaching into the fridge for a beer. "She's leaving first thing tomorrow."

"Tomorrow?" The kitchen crackled with Ivy's intensity. Five minutes ago, Jill and Shep had been quietly winding down for the night. Now Ivy had blown in and infused every inch of peace with frantic energy. It was a trend Jill had learned to expect in her years of being married to Foster.

But tonight Jill was determined to settle things back down. "Can I fix you some tea, Ivy?"

"God, if I have any more tea, I'll float away. Where's Luke?"

"Out with Amy," said Shep.

Ivy sighed. "I don't see the connection there, I really don't. And she never comes with him to the store. I don't even think she knows how to surf."

"Why does that matter?" Jill demanded. "Luke cares for her. You should be happy he's found someone."

"I didn't say I wasn't. I just wish she had a little more spunk in her, that's all."

Jill closed the cabinet door, unnecessarily hard. "Not everyone wants *spunk*."

"Clearly."

The teapot blew out a soft whistle and a ribbon of steam. Jill moved to turn off the flame, feeling the heat of Ivy's gaze as she poured water into her mug.

Ivy shook her head. "I still can't believe you only saw her once this whole time I was gone."

Jill squeezed her tea bag and set it in the sink, twisting to face her ex-mother-in-law. "It's not like Claire reached out to us, Ivy. I'm not sure we would have seen her at all if Shep hadn't run into her."

"Don't be ridiculous," Ivy snorted. "Of course Pepper would have called you."

Pepper. It bothered Jill that Ivy continued to use Claire's old nickname. As if they were still nineteen. As if they were still best friends.

Jill spooned honey into her tea, choosing not to argue.

*H*er hand out the open window and her fingers feathering the wind, Claire leaned back into the passenger seat of Gus Gallagher's truck and watched the soft lights of the waterfront cottages sail by.

She sighed. "I didn't think I could feel any more embarrassed today than I already did."

"You had some bad luck with the board," said Gus. "It happens to everyone."

"Not to me. Bad luck with men, definitely, but never with the board." She rolled her head toward him. "Still glad you pushed to get me here?"

"You bet. And for the record," he said, "I'm only taking it easy on you because it's late. If you weren't leaving tomorrow, I'd have your back on that board so fast your head would spin. Cut or no cut." He grinned.

There were those dimples again, and those eyes. God, she was a mess. She'd lost some blood, not to mention every bit of her dignity, and all she wanted was for Gus Gallagher to pull off to the side of the road, take her face in his hands, and kiss her hard enough to hurt.

Who was she kidding to think he had wanted to sleep with her? All those perky, eager young women around him all day, pleading for surf lessons and whatever else he was teaching—and he'd want *her*? She rolled her head back to the window, regret coursing through her.

When they reached the intersection of Ashley and Center streets, she said, "Just let me off at the light. I can walk from there."

"No way; you're injured. I'll take you to the front."

"Fine." Claire smiled at him. "But if you pull into the handicapped parking, I'll *kill* you."

The light changed and he turned them into the hotel, taking the truck up to the door and shoving it into park. She tugged on the door handle, but he'd already climbed out and come around to help her.

"I thought only Southern men held doors for women," she said.

"California men hold doors for women who surf. It's a little-known distinction."

"Lucky me, then."

"I still owe you dinner, you know."

"Yes, you do. I guess I'll just have to come back to collect."

"I guess you will."

They smiled at each other for a long moment; then Gus stuck out his hand. "Claire Patton, it's been my true pleasure."

She slipped her hand into his. "Mine too."

"Take care of that heel," he said. "And the next time you're in Folly, I expect a call."

"I promise." But they both knew she wouldn't be back anytime soon.

She waited for him to pull out of the parking lot before she turned for the glass doors. She clicked her phone to illuminate the screen, hoping for a missed call from Lizzie or Nick. Nothing. She typed a text to her ex-husband, uncaring if her words were harsh or accusatory: *Did Zee get there all right? She said she'd let me know and she hasn't. Text or call me as soon as you get this.* She considered the demands and added a *PLEASE* before sending it.

Riding the elevator, she reached up to smooth her ragged ponytail, startled at the thickened, chalky feel of her hair after just a few minutes in the water. She held out her arms, seeing the powdery dryness of her skin. The weight and taste of the sea; she'd forgotten so much more than just how to ride. The water had thrashed her soundly and now her whole body ached, but it was a delicious ache.

She smiled. She'd forgotten that too.

The elevator doors opened and she stepped out, startled

to find a man in the hallway, crouched against the wall beside her room door.

Déjà vu charged through her. It could have been Foster. "Luke?"

Seeing her approach, Foster's son climbed to his feet. He shoved the hair from his eyes and smiled weakly. "I know I should have tried to call first, but I didn't have your number."

"Is everything okay?"

"It's fine. I just thought we could talk."

"Sure." Claire fumbled through her purse for her room card. "Come on in."

"We can stay out here," he said, "if your daughter's sleeping."

"She's not here." Finding it, Claire slid her key card in and out of its slot and snapped the handle down. "She went back to Colorado." They stepped inside the room. She flipped on the lights. "You want a soda or something?" she asked, tugging open the door to the minibar.

"No, I'm good, thanks." Luke took a seat on the bed and pointed to her foot. "You okay?"

She waved her hand. "It's nothing. Just my penance for getting on a surfboard and thinking I was still twenty. Trust me, my ego was hurt far worse than my heel."

His face lit up. "You were *surfing*?"

Claire laughed. "I think it would be illegal to call what I did surfing. I'm as rusty as an old plow. It was embarrassing. Two duck dives and I was wrecked."

"Another day on the water and I'm sure it'd come back to you. That's what my dad always used to say anyway."

The mention of Foster spread across the room like the smell of baking bread, instantly comforting.

She smiled tenderly. "Your dad was amazing on the water. He taught me a lot."

Luke studied his hands on his knees. Claire sat down on Lizzie's bed, facing him.

"What is it you wanted to talk about, Luke?"

"My dad, mostly. I guess I just wanted to know about the way he was before I was born. I only knew him for eight years. I'd kinda like to add whatever I can to that, you know?"

He looked so much like Foster. A few times at dinner the night before, Claire had lost her train of thought when she glanced up and saw him across the table: a ghost chewing on bread and shrimp. Now, alone with him, the subject of Foster moving between them as gently as the tide, she found it hard to look him square in the face for too long.

"Does your mom know you're here?"

"She thinks I'm with my girlfriend," Luke said, lowering his gaze. "It's not that I think she'd mind. It's just . . ."

Claire smiled, understanding. "I was sorry to hear about the store. But I can understand if Ivy's ready to let it go."

"Are you kidding?" Luke blinked at her. "It wasn't Grams's idea. She'd keep that place open until they carried her out in a pine box. It's my mom and Shep who've been after her to sell it, saying it's run-down and not worth fixing. It's true, the place is kind of a mess. You saw it in there."

"It *could* stand a little updating. . . ."

Luke snorted. "It could stand *a lot*. She's got this one room, crammed with all of Dad's stuff. She has no idea what's even in there. I've tried to get her to go through it, but she puts me off every time. And the only people who come around are guys from the old days. Mooches who just want stuff for free and she gives it to 'em. Pisses me off." He glanced up, his expression repentant. "Sorry."

Claire smiled. "It would piss me off too."

His gaze deepened. "Are you still angry at my mom? Because it's okay if you are. I'd understand, you know."

Claire held herself, chilled suddenly. His question was unexpected, uncomfortable. "Luke, I really don't think we should be having this conversation. I'm sure your mom wouldn't appreciate me talking to you about all this."

"What does she expect? It's not like she tells me anything. She didn't even tell me the truth about you and my dad until a few days ago. She said *you* left *him*."

Jill had said that? Claire rose from the bed and walked to the dresser, absorbing the news. Seventeen years later and Jill still hadn't taken responsibility for the pain she'd caused?

And what about Ivy? Why hadn't she dispelled Jill's lie? If Ivy hadn't, she'd only done so out of love for Luke, Claire was sure. Or maybe Ivy and Jill had finally mended the broken rails of their fences.

Claire looked back at Luke, willing him to rise, to understand the impossibility of his presence in her room and excuse himself, but he seemed stuck to the edge of the bed as if it were a life raft.

She could tell he would gladly have stayed there all night if she let him.

But she couldn't let him.

"It's late," she said, gently but firmly. "You should get home. Let me drive you back."

"That's okay. I have my bike."

"But it's dark."

"I'm used to it. It's not far."

"No." Claire swept up her purse. "I'm driving you home and that's that."

*B*efore they turned onto East Ashley, Claire decided she would only pull into the driveway of Jill and Shep's home. It was too late for a visit, and with her leaving tomorrow, what was the point? There was nothing left to say, and now with this added news of the real reason for Ivy selling the shop—not to mention Jill's bald-faced lie about how Foster and Jill came to be—Claire was feeling fresh pangs of anger. She'd kept her annoyance at bay during dinner, but she didn't trust herself to keep it quiet at this late hour.

When they passed In the Curl, it was Luke who saw the telltale glow in the upstairs windows.

"Hey, Grams is home!" he cried. "Let's stop."

Claire glanced in her rearview mirror, a rush of excitement flooding her.

But it was so late. "I don't know, Luke. I can't just show up . . ."

"Of course you can."

"What if she's asleep?"

"Before midnight? Are you kidding?"

At the next intersection, Claire turned them around and steered into the shop's parking lot. Luke was out of the car and up the steps before Claire could stop him. His advance did the trick; Ivy appeared and hurried down the store's front steps, arms out, before Claire had even exited the driver's seat.

"Pepper." Ivy pressed her palms to her own cheeks. "Oh, honey."

Claire never would have imagined she could sink into another person the way she melted into Foster's mother's arms. Whatever return she thought she'd made to Folly in the days since her arrival had only been a rehearsal.

Until this moment, this embrace, she wasn't yet back.

*S*he and Ivy never had a proper good-bye. Her departure had happened so fast—after learning that Foster and Jill were in love and preparing for a baby, Claire had packed up that same day.

Months after leaving Folly, when she'd moved into a new life in Florida, Claire had sent Ivy a long letter, an apology, for what she wasn't even sure, but it had been important to her, Claire, that Foster's mother know how much she had meant to her. Unlike Claire's own mother, Ivy had been a source of strength and comfort. The pain of Foster and Jill's betrayal was doubled. Jill didn't understand. She hadn't just taken Foster; she'd taken Ivy too.

Now, seventeen years later, Claire sat at the same breakfast table where she and Ivy had shared a final pot of tea the night before the Folly Classic, the night before everything had changed. She watched Ivy maneuver her way through the apartment's tiny kitchen, the rich scents of coconut oil and spiced tea the same as Claire remembered.

Ivy set down a pair of mugs, the scent of clove rising with the tea's steam.

Her eyes twinkled with excitement. "So, tell me everything! Did ESPN wear you out with all their questions?"

Claire sighed, wishing she didn't have to dampen Ivy's enthusiasm with the truth. "There's not much to tell, I'm afraid," she said, taking up a mug. "The director had a vision for me that was less than flattering."

Ivy stared at her quizzically.

Claire smiled. "Let's just say if I wanted to feel old I could have turned on MTV and saved myself the air miles."

"Punks," Ivy spat. "I suppose Luke told you they didn't even have the courtesy to come to the shop?"

Claire nodded. "I tried my best to get them here. But you can guess how much influence I had."

The pleated laugh lines around Ivy's eyes softened. "It can't be easy for you, honey. Being here. After all this time."

"I was just thinking the same about you."

Ivy shrugged and looked around the kitchen. "Ghosts aren't always bad, you know. I've come to love them, honestly. It's when they go away that I get scared. Besides . . ." She looked at Claire with glistening eyes. "I could never leave my grandson. My baby's baby. That boy's my whole world. He's my hope. My memories. My heart. I could no sooner leave him than leave my own damn body. Not that I haven't wanted to do that some days."

Claire reached out and laid her hand over Ivy's, startled at the unfamiliar feeling of loose skin and bones so close to the surface. What had it been like for Ivy after Foster died, to stay in the same place where you'd raised your child and then buried him? Claire had left Folly over a betrayal, fled after a single night. What sort of cowardice was that?

Tears soaked her eyes. Claire lowered her face, shame and regret colliding with a force ten times harder than any wave that had smashed her body earlier in the night.

Claire whispered, "I'm so sorry I wasn't here for the service. For you. I wanted to be. Please know that—"

"Shh . . ." Ivy pressed her palm over Claire's hand. "You *were* there. In my heart, you've never left, Pepper."

Claire shook her head, undeserving of absolution. "The way I took off that night . . . that I never came to see you, to say good-bye in person. To *explain*."

"What was to explain?" Ivy asked, drawing closer to sweep back a loose strand of salt-thickened hair from Claire's lowered face. "Your whole life was torn into pieces. You were in agony."

"It doesn't compare to what you lost."

"It doesn't have to. Your anguish was everything to you. The worst pain you could imagine. Everyone's pain is their own, honey."

Claire searched Ivy's wide-open face, her features weathered by sun and time, heartache and disappointment. If anyone deserved to judge, it was Ivy.

"After you left, I kept my ears open, hoping I'd hear something," Ivy said. "I was sure the next time I saw you it would be on the cover of *Sports Illustrated.*"

Claire sighed. "Me too."

"So, what happened?"

"I don't know, really. I went down to Florida for a few months, but I couldn't seem to get my groove right on their barrels. I entered a few heats and didn't even place." Claire shrugged. "A few of the waitresses at the restaurant I worked at were moving out to Denver for the winter, so I thought, why not?"

Ivy smiled knowingly. "Not many waves in Colorado."

Claire sipped her tea, unable to meet Ivy's gaze.

Ivy patted her hand. "You remember that heat in 'ninety?"

"You mean when I had strep?"

"Not just *any* case of strep," Ivy corrected. "I believe the doctor at the clinic said it was the worst case he'd seen in thirty years of practicing medicine." Ivy shook her head and laughed. "Boy, honey—when you did something, you did it all the way."

Claire laughed too. "Foster begged me not to ride that day."

"That was your first win," Ivy said, gesturing to the busy wall beside them. "The first of many."

Claire looked up at the spread of framed pictures, so many of her and Foster, of the old days. Her gaze slowed on one of her sandwiched between Foster and Shep after the '91 Classic. Later that night, Foster had surprised her with champagne on the beach and a tub of mint chocolate chip. They'd grown so drunk they ended up falling asleep on the sand and were woken by a pair of damp golden retrievers on their morning walk.

Claire smiled helplessly, swept up in the memory.

"Those were great times," she said softly, her eyes still fixed on the photograph, the firmness of Foster's hand around her waist. He'd been so proud of her that day. He'd practically teared up when she'd come out of the water. "Is it true he'd stopped surfing?"

Ivy nodded. "He wouldn't admit it, but I know it was because of Jill. You saw her all those years. She never liked our way of life. You could count on one hand the times she came into the store when y'all lived here. I know she didn't want him being part of all this. He says it wasn't her idea to get him into real estate, but I never believed him."

"But Luke surfs."

"She tolerates that—what can she do? But I think that's only because she knows he's leaving for school—and that the shop's for sale."

Claire frowned, reminded of the unfortunate fact. "Luke doesn't want you to sell it."

"Most days I don't think that boy knows what he wants. But what boy does at his age?"

Foster, Claire thought reflexively. Foster had wanted her at that age. Wanted her completely and with a confidence that could have parted waters.

She slid her fingers around her mug and lifted her tea to her lips. "Luke and Shep seem to get along well." She took a careful sip. "It's strange, though. Seeing Jill and Shep together again."

"I wasn't surprised he took her back," said Ivy, lowering her chin to her upturned palm. "Shep had never moved on from Jill. Some people don't move on. But you did . . ." Ivy gave Claire's hand a questioning squeeze. "Didn't you?"

Had she? Claire dragged her eyes to the window, not sure what she hoped to see in the black glass.

"I think it hurt Foss terribly to see Shep alone all those years afterwards," Ivy said. "He loved Shep. He wanted him to be happy. We all did."

Just not like this, Claire thought, knowing Ivy was thinking the same. *Not this way.*

She set down her mug and looked at Ivy. "Are you really okay with selling this place?"

Ivy shrugged, sighed. "If there's one thing I've learned, it's that you're never ready to say good-bye."

"So don't sell it. Luke said Jill and Shep are the ones pushing you to do it. If you're not ready, then tell them to back off."

"Oh, that boy . . ." Ivy smiled fondly at the door to the shop where Luke had disappeared. "He means well, but he can't know all the layers. I wouldn't want him to."

"He told me Jill lied to him about me leaving Foster."

"She did."

"And you went along with it," Claire said, careful to keep the comment from sounding like an accusation.

Ivy didn't appear to take it that way. "Lies are such damnable things, Pepper. They start small, but the longer they live, the bigger and the heavier they grow. After a while the truth would have made us all look like fools. And you weren't here, honey. What was the harm in it?"

Luke's footsteps thundered up the stairs; Claire glanced at the clock above the sink. "I should go."

"Don't be silly," said Ivy. "You'll stay here tonight."

"I can't. I have an early flight. I have to get back to the hotel and finish packing."

"Then you'll change your flight and stay on a few more days. You'll take my room."

"And where exactly will *you* sleep?"

"There's still a foldout in the office. I mean it. You could come and go as you please for as long as you like."

Luke came into the kitchen and crossed to the fridge. His arrival brought with it the reminder of Lizzie, the terrible terms of their parting. Claire wished she were here now, wished she could hug her. The longing was agony.

"I wish you could have met my daughter," Claire whispered. "I wish she could have met you. I wish she could have seen us together."

Ivy took her hands. "There'll be another time."

Claire glanced around the kitchen, reminded of all the things she'd hoped to squeeze into this visit, the years of heartache and joy that she'd foolishly thought she could share with Lizzie; that it might have been as simple as flipping the pages of a photo album. *Here's where I won my first surfing competition. Here's where I fell in love with Foster. Here's where I was happy. Here's where I belonged.* Suddenly the life that she'd left behind seemed so much more important than she'd remembered. And Lizzie had come and gone, and understood none of it. Claire had failed them both.

"I just wanted her to see this piece of me. How complete I was here. I don't think I realized how much I wanted it until we got here, and then before I knew it, before I could help her to see, she was gone."

Ivy leaned closer. "Did you never tell her about your life here?"

Claire shook her head. "I meant to. I kept waiting for the right time, I guess. When she was older, when it might mean more to her. When she could be proud of me. I had all these reasons. It never occurred to me not to wait."

"I know." Ivy smiled, but Claire could see tears shine at the edges of her eyes. "We think we have all the time in the world," she said, "but we don't."

18

The night before Foster left her for Jill, Claire and he took a long shower together: something they rarely did. When you were in the water as much as they were, showering was utilitarian, equipment maintenance the same as any in surfing, no more erotic than hanging up your wet suit or storing your wax.

But that night, without warning, Foster had eased off his suit and stepped into the steam that Claire had built up as she scrubbed the salt and sand from her hair. When she opened her eyes, there he was, smiling down at her through the pelting mist. She turned and let him rake his long fingers through her soapy hair until the water had run clear around their feet. Then she watched him whittle down the silver of soap to a remarkable froth in his hands. The smell of grapefruit rose around them, ripe and sweet. When he laid his palms on her and began to work the lather down her body, she closed her eyes again.

They'd been on the water for most of the afternoon—a luxury they hadn't known in years. Now with them all in their midtwenties, work schedules and responsibilities didn't allow them the languishing surfing days they'd enjoyed in their teens. But that day, Shep, Foster and Claire had shared a mutual day off and spent it on their boards. Jill had come later, arriving with crab salad sandwiches and watermelon slices. Afterward, stretched out on the sand, nicely buzzed from beer and sun, Claire had stolen a quiet moment to drink them all in, and the significance of the day. She'd surfed well, nailing roundhouses and floaters with the same reckless passion she'd impressed Foster with years earlier.

The shower's stream felt heavenly: just enough pressure and heat. She slid against Foster, his body slick and warm.

"I can't believe I'm saying this, but I'm actually nervous about tomorrow," she admitted.

He snorted. "Hot Pepper Patton, nervous? You won it last year. *And* the year before that."

She had; the proof still hung from the cluttered front of their fridge, a half page of newsprint faded from too many mornings in full Folly sun. Claire Patton, winner of the Folly Classic, second year in a row. Surely she'd go pro and join the circuit at last?

"Pretty soon I'll be Hot Pepper *King*," she reminded him. He nodded; she lathered the pale tuft of hair above his belly button and asked, "Aren't *you* nervous? Even a little bit?"

"Actually . . . I was thinking I might pass this year."

"Pass?" She laughed, the idea absurd. "What are you talking about?"

Foster shrugged. "I've competed almost as long as I've been eating solid foods, Pep. I just think it's time for a break, that's all."

Was that all? Claire stared up at him through the thinning steam. He looked tired, worried.

"Then I'll pass this year too," she declared.

"No." His voice was firm enough to startle her. "You can't miss one."

"You said it yourself; it's time for a break."

"For me," he said. "Not you. This is who you are, babe. This is who you're meant to be."

"I'm meant to be your wife, Foss. That's who I'm meant to be."

Foster nodded, but his smile waned. "Promise me you'll ride tomorrow," he said, then again, harder, "Promise me."

"I promise," she agreed, only because something in his eyes alarmed her too much not to. Then he grabbed her face between his soapy hands and kissed her, deeper and fiercer than he had in a long time, as if he were trying to bury something inside her mouth.

Looking back, when she finally could, Claire saw what he was doing, masked by all that steam and heat. The words of encouragement were a plea, loud and desperate, a warning that sooner than she could imagine it would all be gone, and this was her chance to hold on to one piece of herself.

But their love, their life, it was all one great big world,

every part linked to every other part. There could be no separating her pieces from his.

Surely Foster had known that when he set her adrift?

Now as she sat in Charleston International at nine ten and stared out at the runway, Claire wished she'd been smarter that day, any of the days. Even one day of good sense might have helped.

Driving to the airport, passing Charleston, Claire had slunk down in her seat like a twelve-year-old afraid to be caught with her first cigarette. It would have been the crowning shot of this entire trip to be spotted by her mother on her way to the airport.

Why had Claire not told her mother she was in town? There had been reasonable excuses at the beginning of the trip, reasons that now didn't hold up.

She shifted carefully in the upholstered seat, the slightest movement causing the muscles across her back to cry out. The effect of the two ibuprofens she'd taken earlier was fading. She'd meant to take some before bed in the hope of staving off the inevitable pain she'd wake with, having stretched her poor body far beyond its reach the night before. It served her right, she thought, as she rubbed her neck.

You'll change your flight and stay on a few more days. There's still a foldout in the office. . . .

Stay on. The possibility wasn't so outrageous, was it?

She thought about her talk with Luke, the truth that it was Jill and Shep who'd forced Ivy to close the shop; then she thought of Ivy in her kitchen the night before. Her thin fingers shaking as she'd set down their tea. The woman had lost everything. Her only child, and now her thriving business—her *home*. Rage flushed anew. Claire had been pushed out of Folly once before, been made to leave before she was ready. She'd abandoned Ivy then, but she wouldn't this time. Claire could help, could be useful. Here, she could have a purpose. She could be wanted. *Needed.*

Lizzie's accusation swam back, that Claire leaned on her too much, that she didn't have a life of her own. It wasn't true. And maybe staying on in Folly would be the best way of proving it.

Last night, sitting with Ivy, revisiting all the memories, Claire had forgotten how content she'd been here, how hopeful, how free.

If she stayed, she could make time to visit her mother.

She could tell Luke more about his father.

She could even get back on that board and show Gus Gallagher she could still carve harder than any girl he'd ever seen.

Consternation rose through her aching limbs. Claire rose with it.

The line at the ticket counter was a dozen passengers deep; she didn't feel like waiting. Instead she wheeled her luggage out into the corridor and looked down the crowded carpet for the exit signs.

You think you have all the time in the world.

But you don't.

19

*A*nd so, barely three hours after she'd left, Claire was back in Folly again. The taxi took her over the bridge, just as she'd steered herself and Lizzie along the same road a few days earlier; only this time her arrival was without fear or doubt. She glanced down at her phone in her hand. She'd left two messages with Lizzie to let her know she'd changed her plans. Nick needed to know too. He'd sent her a terse text the night before to assure her that Lizzie had arrived safely; Claire had texted him back immediately with more questions. He'd never replied.

Defiance coursed through her; no more texts, no more blow-offs. It was time for a call.

After five rings, Nick picked up. "Claire, she's fine."

"Then why won't she call me, Nick? You need to tell her to call me. This is ridiculous."

"I will ask her to call you."

"Don't ask her, Nick. *Tell* her." She worried her thumb-nail. "How is she *really*?"

"She's a little mopey but she'll get over it. I was think-ing it might help if we took her over to Breckenridge for a few days," Nick said. "Stay in the village. Do it up."

Claire swallowed a mouthful of jealousy, determined not to go down that sour road again. She would fix this with Lizzie, she would prove to her daughter she was wrong about her mother; it wasn't too late. Then she and Lizzie would get to have trips like that too. The mother-daughter trips Claire had always imagined.

Trips like what *this* one was supposed to be.

"When are you getting in today?" Nick asked.

"Actually, I've changed my plans." Swaths of marsh-grass came back into view. "I'm staying on in Folly for a few more weeks. I have an old friend here whose surf shop needs a lot of work and I want to help her."

"Wait, I thought this trip was for the interview."

They thumped over the bridge and passed the marina; Claire smiled wistfully. "It was."

"So, how many weeks?"

"I don't know yet. As long as I want. As long as it takes."

"Claire, is everything okay with you?"

You mean, besides the fact that my daughter blames me for something I didn't do, and her father whisks her away on a plane without even asking me?

"It's fine," she said. "Why wouldn't it be?"

"This just seems a little manic, that's all. One minute you won't talk about a whole chunk of your life, and the next you're back in it trying to relive some kind of, I don't know, teenage fantasy."

Claire closed her eyes. How could she expect him to understand?

"Tell Lizzie to call me, okay? Tell her that I love her and that I miss her and to call me."

Claire hung up and sat back, taking several deep breaths. She asked the driver to take her straight to In the Curl, but when he delivered her to the parking lot and twisted in his seat, hand out for the fare, Claire felt the first prickle of apprehension. Had Ivy really been serious about her offer? In her impulsive fever, Claire hadn't even called Ivy to make sure.

"Ma'am?" The cabdriver shoved his opened palm at her.

"Right. Sorry." Claire rummaged through her purse and found her wallet buried at the bottom. "Keep the change," she said, handing him a pair of twenties.

She slid out with her luggage and waited while the taxi swerved back into the street.

The breeze picked up, ruffling the loose tendrils she'd been unable to stuff into a ponytail. Claire closed her eyes and filled her lungs with sea air, just the way she'd done at eighteen, when Foster had hurried her up the steps in his excitement to start their lives in earnest, working side by side in the shop that was to be his legacy, a legacy he intended to share with her.

So it was only fitting that his son should be there when she stepped inside.

Luke stood in the back of the store. An older man with

a mop of white hair stood beside him and ran his hand reverentially along the edge of a long board. At the tinny sound of the bell, Luke looked over.

"Miss Claire?" He blinked at her. "I thought you left."

Claire smiled. "Me too."

*E*ven though Foster had assured her she had nothing to worry about when he pulled the truck into the parking lot for her first official day of work at In the Curl, Claire was certain every one of her limbs trembled. Not even nine and already the parking lot and grass around the store were teeming. Young people, their age or just slightly older, milled about in shorts, barefooted or flip-flopped, their voices loud, their laughs louder. Reggae music swelled from the stereo of a roofless Jeep. A few young women in cutoff jeans and bikini tops wandered around, holding fountain drinks. A pair of dogs chased a ragged tennis ball along the rise.

Claire stared at it all like a child at a carnival, not sure where to look first or longest. Her heart raced.

Foster killed the engine and reached across the seat for her closer hand, gently loosening the fingers she'd kept fisted in her lap.

"You're not still nervous, are you?" he asked.

"Maybe a little," she admitted.

"You could ride circles around any one of these guys. In an hour, they'll be coming to you for pointers. You wait."

"It's not just that," she said. "I'm not one of them. I'm not from here and everyone knows it."

"You may not be from here, but you're here with *me*."

Claire turned her gaze from all the activity to meet his smile, his periwinkle eyes, calmed at once by the confidence she saw within them.

But what Foster couldn't understand—what he never could, Claire would eventually decide—was that her nerves weren't over the job. After all, she had yet to see how selling boards and teaching people how to surf could be considered "work." Her worries ran deeper. What terrified her, what had kept her up the night before and might very well keep her up many more, was the knowledge that this plan simply couldn't fail. Everything she wanted, everything she hoped to be, now rested on this life with him, and no one part alone could succeed without the success of the other parts.

"Ready?" he asked.

She wasn't, but somehow she managed a nod and to steady her legs enough to slide out of the passenger seat.

Foster raced to her side and scooped up her hand in his. "Here we go," he said.

But she remained still. "Wait," she said. "I just want a minute."

"A minute for what?"

"To savor this moment." She scanned the property. "To remember this."

"Are you kidding? You'll be here every day. Most nights too. And then, when my mom wants to retire, it'll be our store. Yours and mine." He took her hand and pulled her close enough to land a kiss on her mouth, the promise sealed. "Heck, you'll be so sick of this place you'll only *wish* you could forget it."

She shook her head, her thoughts spinning. Never.

And as he tugged her forward, Claire closed her eyes and inhaled extra deep. As much as he wanted to understand, Foster King couldn't know that freedom had a scent, and dreams a taste. Those were flavors she'd waited a long time to enjoy. She wouldn't rush them from her senses.

*C*laire came right out with it: "Ivy, I don't think you should sell the shop."

Ivy stared at her, the smile of surprised joy still pulling up the ends of her lips. "What?"

"I'm serious," said Claire. "It came to me this morning and I haven't stopped thinking about it since. It's obvious you're not ready to let it go, it's obvious Luke isn't either, and if you can swing the taxes, why not just keep it open?"

"Oh, honey . . ." Ivy gave her a weary look. "Sugar, it's not just that."

"I know, I know; the repairs. Which is why I've decided to stay on a few more weeks and help you get it back into shape."

"We're not just talking a coat of paint, Pepper."

"So we'll get quotes. People do it all the time."

"Pepper, honey, you know I love you, but you can't just pull out of your life—"

"Who said anything about pulling out of my life? My

daughter's with her father for the next four weeks. I don't have any reason to hurry home. If that offer's still good for the pullout couch, I can stay on here and help you." Claire smiled. "I may not be much on a surfboard anymore, but I know my way around the shop and I know the equipment. If we work fast, we could even have a grand reopening before summer's out. Show those punks at the network what they missed."

Ivy came toward Claire with a loving smile, wagging her finger. "You sound exactly like that good-looking guy from Fins. I take it you've already been in his store?"

"Excuse me?" Claire set her hands on her hips. "What kind of traitor do you think I am?"

Ivy laughed. "He's not as bad as all that, you know. He actually offered to help me boost traffic to the store last year. Told me he wanted to see In the Curl busy as a surfing school again, wanted to bring in some West Coast guys he'd surfed with, said our stores could partner up. He was a real peach about it, but I just couldn't see it working out."

"All I'm saying is, why not give it one more try?" Claire pressed, glancing at Luke and seeing the look of pure longing on his face.

"Come on, Grams. It's not too late."

Ivy walked to the counter, her expression shifting as she deliberated. A myriad of emotions passed over her deeply wrinkled face—elation, concern, hope. Claire studied them like a gambler waiting for the reels of a slot machine to settle—which expression would win?

Impatient, Luke followed. "Say yes. You know you want to."

"It's not about what I want."

"Since when?" Luke demanded. "Don't you at least think it's worth a shot?"

"Just give it a few weeks," said Claire, meeting them at the counter. "If it seems too much, I'll step back gracefully and get out of everyone's hair for good."

Ivy reached out and cupped Claire's face, holding it firmly in her hands. Her eyes welled. "You rush off on me again, and this time I won't forgive you."

20

*I*t was bound to happen. Claire knew one day that first summer in Folly her parents would arrive unexpectedly and learn of her love for Foster without her having time to prepare them. There had been opportunities, of course, phone calls with pregnant pauses ideal for confessions, but Claire had denied them. So when a taupe Mercedes pulled into the Glasshouse's driveway on a bright August morning while she was watering the porch plants, Claire didn't recognize the car, but she definitely knew the chauffeur, a long-faced man named Harvey who had worked for their family for years.

Harvey swung open the door to the backseat and Maura Patton stepped out in a linen suit, blinking up at Claire.

"Mom?" Claire lowered the watering can so fast it sloshed over the side and soaked her bare feet. "I—I wasn't expecting you."

Maura smiled thinly. "Clearly."

"How did you find me here?"

"I went to your address, but no one was home, so I asked your neighbor where I could find the closest surf shop and he directed me to In the Curl. That is the name, isn't it?"

Claire reached for the railing to steady herself, dizzy suddenly.

She swallowed. "You went to the shop?"

"That Ivy woman seems to think the sun rises and sets on you. Interesting woman. Very *colorful*." Her mother glanced at the railing, the row of pots still dripping from their recent drinks.

"This is just a friend's house," Claire said. "I come over and water their plants when they go out of town."

"How thoughtful of you."

Claire looked around the porch, the driveway. What to do now? For any other visitor, she would have welcomed her inside, thinking nothing of it. But letting her mother into the Glasshouse was dangerous. Claire had left pieces of herself all over the living room, the kitchen.

In the awful silence, she madly cataloged the possible land mines of evidence behind the front door.

Her hesitation was her undoing.

Her mother stepped forward. "Would your *friends* mind terribly if I came inside for a drink of water? That is, if they leave you a key."

Claire's stomach knotted. *Crap.*

"Of course," she said pleasantly, calmly, for what else

could she do? But only after she'd turned the knob and pushed the door ajar did Claire realize she'd revealed the house to be unlocked. Too late now, she thought as she led her mother through the front room, seeing the mess of the men's interior freshly, clutter she'd never minded before. Now every pile of towels, every discarded shirt or shoe, every forgotten coffee mug, screamed at her as she walked by. Claire scanned the chaos, panicked. What items would signal alarm, suspicion? A fashion magazine on the couch, a purple cardigan of Claire's slung over the arm of a chair. Would her mother recognize it as the one she'd received last Christmas—or was her mother too horrified by the volume of litter to notice?

When they reached the kitchen, Claire took a glass from the cabinet. "We have filtered if you'd rather."

We. Shit.

"They," Claire corrected. "I mean, *they* have filtered water. My friends."

"Tap water's fine," her mother said, surveying the kitchen with bald disdain. Dirty dishes stacked in the sink, bowls of uneaten cereal left on the table.

Claire shoved a glass under the faucet and willed the water pressure to speed up its trickle. With it three-quarters full, she handed the glass to her mother.

Her mother took a tentative, decidedly unthirsty sip, her eyes continuing to dance around the kitchen, two birds that couldn't decide where to perch.

At last, they settled on a spot behind Claire. She turned to see what had caught her mother's interest, and her skin burned.

A tilted strip of pictures from a photo booth; four damning black-and-white squares of her and Foster kissing. Deeply.

Claire stiffened, her secret out.

She fell against the sink. "His name is Foster and he's wonderful."

"They always are," her mother said dryly.

"You can meet him and see for yourself."

"I already did. He was at the store."

Claire blinked, feeling cornered, duped. "Then you knew," she said. "When you pulled in here, you already knew why I was here. Why didn't you just say so?"

"Don't get indignant with me, Claire Louise. You're hardly one to point fingers just now."

"Are you going to tell Dad?"

"And what exactly would you recommend I tell him? That his daughter has done exactly what he feared—what she promised she wouldn't do—and lost her heart, not to mention her mind, to a surf bum?"

"He's not a bum," said Claire. "And I haven't lost anything."

Her mother opened her purse, pulled out a fat envelope with the College of Charleston seal on the top, and thrust it at Claire. "I thought you'd want to look over your final schedule for next semester. It seems a little thin to your father and me. He thinks you need at least one more class."

"I'm not going back," Claire said evenly. "I've already withdrawn."

"Yes, yes, we know about all that. You made some

absurd phone call to the registrar, and thankfully, she had the good sense to contact Neil, who promptly contacted us and we assured him you'd been under a great deal of stress, which he completely understood, so it's fine—"

"I'm not going back to school, Mom," Claire said again, firmer this time. "I'm not leaving Folly. I love it here. I love Foster and we're going to get married and run his family's surf shop together."

Her mother set the letter on the counter. "Are you angry with your father? Is that what all this is about?"

Claire stared at her, incredulous. "Do you really think that's why I'm here?"

"I don't know what to think. How could I? You won't return our calls. You won't return to your home."

"Folly *is* my home now."

Her mother snapped her purse closed and shook her head. "I can't speak to you when you're like this. I just can't. But you are to call the school and confirm your schedule by Friday or you risk losing your first-choice classes."

"Mom, wait." Claire reached out to touch her mother's hand where it remained on her purse. "I don't want to fight, okay? I just want you and Daddy to be happy for me."

Her mother slid the strap of her purse over her shoulder and held it there. "Then you've no idea what it means to be a parent. But of course, you wouldn't."

The refrigerator shuddered as the ice maker spilled fresh cubes into the freezer, startling them both.

Claire smiled weakly. "We could walk the beach awhile."

"Oh, Claire, really. I'm not dressed for the beach."

"Then go barefoot."

Her mother tilted her head, exasperated. "You can walk me out."

At the door, Claire asked, "Why aren't *you* angry with him?"

Her mother stopped. "What?"

"You asked me if I'm living here because I'm angry at Daddy. But if anyone should be angry with him, it should be you."

Her mother squinted out at the driveway. "I shouldn't keep Harvey waiting."

But this time, Claire wouldn't be put off. "Not even a little bit?" she asked.

"Every marriage has its challenges, Claire. Mine are no worse or better than anyone else's." Her mother smiled. "You'll see for yourself someday. And then we'll talk."

*F*ins was everything Claire had expected. Loud music, crowded with customers, and wall-to-wall merchandise. Gus Gallagher saw her before Claire saw him. When she rounded the display of rash guards and found him behind the register talking with a customer, his eyes—and smile—were already fixed on her. Three days ago she had refused to stand within ten feet of his store. Now she was inside and walking toward him, not sure if the hastening of her pulse was from the ride over on Ivy's borrowed bicycle or from seeing him again.

He excused himself from his exchange and came to the

end of the counter to meet her, his eyes narrowing quizzically as she approached. "I thought you were supposed to be on a plane today."

"I was." She smiled at him. "Then it occurred to me I couldn't leave Folly without visiting everyone's favorite surf shop."

"Ah. So that chill I felt this morning *was* actually hell freezing over."

"I'll have you know I got approval from the top to be here. "I wouldn't have come otherwise."

"That's because Ivy likes me."

"So you said. I'm starting to wonder if there isn't a woman in Folly who doesn't."

"I don't know. . . ." Gus rested his elbows on the counter and leaned forward. "I think there's one left who's still undecided."

Claire met his teasing eyes. "Why didn't you tell me you offered to help her get In the Curl back on its feet?"

"She turned me down flat. Broke my heart."

"I'm sure you healed quickly."

"Does this mean I can take you out to dinner?"

"That depends," Claire said. "Does it involve putting on a pair of board shorts?"

"Absolutely not." He grinned. "Clothing is entirely optional."

"Good, because I'm so sore from yesterday I could barely bend over to get on my shoes."

"I could help you with that."

"My shoes?"

"Your sore muscles."

Claire would bet he could. She searched his face, his eyes. It had been a long time since she'd felt the flutter of attraction, the deep heat of flirtation. She'd forgotten how delicious it was.

"So." Gus leaned closer. "Is that a yes?"

She had to be out of her mind, really. She had no business feeling so carefree, so reckless. But all she wanted was to have Gus Gallagher pour her a huge glass of wine and to sink into those gray eyes of his while she drained it.

Remember, Pepper: The curl doesn't care.

"Yes." Claire wasn't sure if she said it or sighed it, so she answered again to be sure. "This is a yes."

21

*S*he needed a new dress.

Something summery, breezy. Undeniably sensual. Gus Gallagher had only seen her in various stages of disarray—sweaty, salty, frumpy—so let him see her sexy. All around her on Center Street, women strolled in filmy sundresses and rhinestone-dotted sandals. Racks of the same strappy dresses lined storefronts, swinging in the breeze like curtains. All Claire had to do was pick a print.

Sailing down Ashley an hour later, the colorful nest of batiked silk shuddering gently in the bike's wicker basket, Claire couldn't remember the last time she'd been this excited over a new dress, the chance to style her hair into something other than a utilitarian knot, to smooth gloss over her lips, to dab fragrance on her skin.

A real-live, honest-to-God *date*.

. . .

*I*t was Jill who pointed out the simple fact: For as long as Foster and Claire had been living in Folly that first summer, which by that point was two months, Foster had never taken Claire out on a proper date.

The revelation had come when they were all sharing a bucket of crab legs on the Glasshouse deck, their fingers and lips sticky with butter.

Claire had waved the point off and taken a swig from Foster's beer. "It's okay," she said. "Really."

"No, it's not," Jill insisted, pointing a corncob for emphasis. "Foster King, you need to take Claire out on a real date."

Foster had agreed.

A few days later, INXS on the stereo and a moist breeze sailing through the screens, Jill was in Claire's room helping her get ready for dinner at Folly's fanciest restaurant, Pearl's.

"Now," said Jill, "since it's an official date, you need to wear a real dress and makeup."

A real dress? Claire hardly knew what that meant anymore. When she wasn't in her red swimsuit, she was in shorts or one of Foster's oversized T-shirts *waiting* to get into her suit, so her wardrobe didn't offer much in the way of dresses, real or otherwise. Jill happily let Claire pick from her closet: a too-short spandex dress that crept up every time she breathed. She tugged at the hem incessantly, sure she revealed less skin in her swimsuit.

Hair and makeup was next. The two friends went into the bathroom. Jill searched the crowded vanity surface. "Where do you keep your makeup?"

Claire shrugged. "I don't."

Jill stared at her. "You don't have *any*? Not even lip gloss?"

"You make it sound like I don't have a toothbrush, for God's sake."

"Well, it's kind of close! Never mind. You can borrow some of mine."

Claire sat down on the toilet and watched as Jill tested shadow colors on the back of her hand. "Don't go crazy now," Claire said. "I don't even know if Foster likes makeup."

"Trust me, *every* guy likes makeup," Jill said, deciding on a soft plum. "And every guy definitely loves lipstick. It's like a big shiny you-know-what on your face."

Claire couldn't resist. "A big shiny *what*?"

"You know what," said Jill, blushing now. "Close your eyes."

"Hmm. I'm not sure I do," Claire teased. "Maybe if you used the real word . . ."

Jill made a face at her. "I am *not* saying that word!"

Claire tried to stifle a laugh.

"Sit still," Jill fussed. "You'll make me smudge."

A few minutes later, Claire turned to face her reflection while Jill made a soft twist with Claire's hair and pinned it high, loosening a few tendrils to soften the look.

"You were right," said Claire. "This feels different."

"It should," said Jill.

"I think the only time Foss has ever seen me in a dress was when we met."

"Then this will knock his socks off."

Claire smiled at Jill's reflection. "When I first got here I worried you'd hate me."

At the confession, Jill's head snapped up. She stared at Claire in the mirror.

"Okay, maybe *hate*'s a strong word," Claire corrected, seeing Jill's reaction. "Maybe more like mistrust. That you'd think I was spoiled or a know-it-all just because I wasn't from here."

Jill teased, "Oh, but you *are* a know-it-all."

Claire snatched a bottle of hair spray off the sink and reached back, pretending to spray it. Jill laughed.

"A lot of girls would, you know," said Claire, setting the bottle back down.

"Then we're even," said Jill. "Because I worried that you would think you were too good and too smart to live with a girl from the beach. So there."

Claire smiled. Even. So they were.

"Ta-da!" Done, Jill stepped back and admired Claire's reflection. "What do you think?"

"I look fake."

"You look beautiful."

Not convinced, Claire turned her head from side to side, studying herself. Maybe she did like the way her eyes popped, the way the lipstick made her bottom lip look especially full.

"You really think so?"

"Believe me." Jill grinned. "Foster's gonna flip."

*I*t was only when Claire climbed the steps to the shop and saw Ivy's cloud of gray hair through the window that she realized she would have to tell Foster's mother she had a date. With Gus Gallagher. Not that she had to tell Ivy right away, or make a big deal out of it. After all, it *was* just a date. Just dinner. Maybe in a few hours, Claire could mention it casually, soften the blow over a cup of tea or a walk on the beach.

Claire needn't have worried. As soon as Ivy saw the dress in her hands, a knowing smile spread across her lined face. She looked at Claire and said, "You've got a date."

"Because I bought a new dress?"

"Because you're glowing like a giddy teenager," Ivy said. "So who's the lucky guy?"

Claire smiled. "Gus Gallagher."

"Good for you. Good for *him*."

"I don't know about that." Claire came beside Ivy and set down her dress, spreading out the fabric thoughtfully on the counter, her fingers grazing the remnants of stickers that had decorated the surface over the years, now faded and peeling away. "It's been a long time since I've been out on a date. God only knows how everything works nowadays."

"I'm guessing the same way everything worked back then," Ivy teased.

Claire laughed. "You know what I mean. The *rules*."

"Well, if you're looking for advice, don't ask me," said Ivy. "I never could keep all that crap straight. To kiss him or not kiss him, to let him take you to bed or pretend you hate his guts. It wore me out, all those damn do's and don'ts. I always said: you like him, then like him. The heck with rules."

Claire searched Ivy's warm eyes, the impossibility of the situation hard to ignore. "This is strange, isn't it?" she asked. "Me being here. Going out on a date."

Ivy scoffed. "What's strange to me is that you've gone *without* one so damn long."

For the rest of the afternoon they remained in the shop, reminiscing and planning as they wandered the aisles, then later as they wandered the beach, following the surf as far as they could.

When they returned to the shop, Gus was waiting for them on the porch in a fitted gray T-shirt and khakis. Claire waved, longing rushing to the surface of her skin.

God, she was in such trouble.

"Hi." He smiled down at them as they approached. "I'm a little early."

Claire glanced over at Ivy, seeing the warm glow of approval in Foster's mother's eyes.

"Give me fifteen minutes," Claire told him.

She was done in ten. Wearing her new dress, her wet hair swept up in a messy twist, peach oil dabbed on her throat and wrists, Claire hugged Ivy good night, grabbed her purse, and followed Gus Galla-gher out to his truck.

Inside, she turned to watch him start the engine, allow-ing the flutters of excitement to rise in her again to be near him, alone with him.

He yanked on the gearshift and looked over at her. "You smell great."

She watched him as he steered them out onto the road, thinking as he picked up speed and the air blew harder through the cab that the last time he'd had her in that seat, she told him she wouldn't sleep with him.

Had he known even then she couldn't be held to that vow?

He must have, she decided. Because he was driving them away from town, not toward it.

"I thought we were going out for dinner?" she asked.

"We are. It's this little place up the road," he said with a grin. "The views are out of this world."

She smiled knowingly. "I'll bet."

*M*argot was waiting for them in the entry, the black Lab's tail furiously sweeping the floor as Gus led them inside. He'd cleaned up, Claire noticed as he steered her through the kitchen to the deck door and slid open the glass. An unobstructed view of the shore greeted her. The deck was as cluttered as the home's interior, but with the sea as its backdrop, the mess was downright charm-ing. A tiki bar had been built at one end, the bamboo posts rough and weathered, the frond roof equally sunbaked.

Three bar stools hugged a crescent-shaped counter; Claire took one at Gus's urging and settled in to watch him work.

"What's your poison?"

She leaned her chin on her palm. "What do you recommend?"

"The house margarita. No contest."

Claire eyed the bottle of tequila already in his hand, reminded of all the times she and Jill had concocted their version of the sweet-and-sour drink at their apartment. It had been a Friday night ritual, a shared drink to purge the week's highs and lows before meeting up with their boyfriends. Jill had never liked hers with salt; Claire always had. Now she could almost taste the prickly crystals sticking to her bottom lip.

"Maybe just one," she said.

Gus reached down for a pair of tumblers and wiped the rims with a lime wedge. He upended the glasses into a saucer of salt and gave each one a hard twist. "This recipe comes from a guy I surfed with in Puerto Rico. Johnnie Randolph, but everyone called him Curly. Big wave rider. Craziest guy you ever met . . ."

He talked easily while he made their drinks, his movements automatic, never slowing, mixing and conversing in one seamless motion.

Claire smiled. "You were a bartender, weren't you?"

"I don't think there's a surfer who hasn't either waited tables or tended bar," he said, capping the cocktail shaker and giving the stainless steel cylinder several hard shakes. "I take it you didn't pursue a career in the food industry?"

She laughed. "No," she said. "I'm a high school teacher now."

"That's a far cry from wave riding."

"It was my ex-husband's idea. He was a professor—*is* a professor—and he thought it would be a good thing. I suppose it made as much sense as anything. I'd taught surfing for years and loved it."

Gus emptied the shaker into their glasses and set one in front of her. "Your ex must have been pretty impressed when he found out what a superstar surfer you were."

"The only things that impress my ex-husband are good core samples and overly endowed graduate students." She looked up at Gus. "That wasn't very nice of me, was it?"

He offered her an absolving smile. "No one's nice all the time."

"It's just that I hate being that wife," she admitted. "The one that got dumped for the younger woman. I hate being a cliché."

"So don't be one," he said matter-of-factly.

His eyes held hers as he took a quick swig of his drink.

Claire felt weightless, soft; desirable for the first time in so long.

"I never expected this, you know," she whispered.

Gus leaned in. "Now, see, that's what I love about living here. Some months, you think you won't have a single good wave. Then out of nowhere you get this surprise swell and suddenly you're riding big breaks you never saw coming." He raised his glass to hers. "To surprise swells."

"To surprise swells," she repeated, meeting his toast.

He grinned. "And to carving the hell out of 'em."

*G*us banished Claire to the deck while he cooked dinner. As she sat, the air warm and feathering, the beach seemed both near and far, the deck separated from the sand by a rolling stretch of dune grass. Claire could pick out faint voices of swimmers and combers on the wind, the gentle sweep and roar of the Washout's surf farther down the sand. She had always loved the way the beach quieted at the end of the day. Everything slowed, like the steady rhythm of a body sliding into sleep. Even the waves seemed to yawn.

"Okay, hot stuff," Gus ordered from the doorway. "Close 'em."

She sat straighter and obliged, catching the faint scent of toasted bread just before he gave her approval to open her eyes.

When she did, she blinked down at a sad pair of triangles swimming in a wreath of potato chips. "Grilled cheese?"

"With tomato," he said proudly, taking his seat. "The tomato really makes the sandwich. Gives it that extra something."

"You promised me dinner out, Gallagher."

He gestured to the deck. "We *are* out."

Clever. She gave him a playful scowl. "God, you're such a liar."

"I thought I was being creative."

"I was thinking more like *cheap*."

He chuckled. "I didn't lie about the view, though."

"No, you didn't." Claire looked at him across the table, appreciation flooding her. "Thank you," she said.

He nodded to her plate. "You might want to try it first."

"No, I mean for everything," she said. "For tonight. For getting me back here. Even if I had no business being on that beach yesterday."

"Hey." Gus leveled a stern look at her. "You had every right being on that beach. Anyone worth their chops knows that."

"Maybe." Claire tore off a piece of her sandwich and watched the threads of melted cheese thin. "My ex-husband thinks I'm having a midlife crisis."

"This coming from a man who left his wife for one of his students."

She smiled gratefully at him. "Maybe he's right."

"What if he is?" said Gus. "What's so wrong with mixing things up?"

"Because I'm not that kind of person anymore."

"And what kind of person is that?"

The kind that agrees to a date with a man she barely knows, Claire thought as she stared back into his unrelenting gray eyes. *The kind who, just an hour earlier, sprinkled scented powder all over her skin like fairy dust because she hopes this man she barely knows will make love to her before the night is out.* She bit deeply into the fattest part of her sandwich, the bread soaked with butter, the cheddar still soft and warm, the sliced tomato slightly crisp.

A simple grilled cheese sandwich.

She couldn't remember anything ever tasting so good in her whole life.

Gus studied her. "The woman I saw that day on her board was fearless."

Claire lifted her glass, considering the sprinkling of salt along the rim. "The woman you saw that day was a girl who didn't know better."

"I know what I saw," he said. "And I know what it takes to ride like that. That kind of nerve isn't something you lose. You can bury it but it's still there."

"I was fearless then because I had no reason to fear anything. It never occurred to me to be afraid that something might not work out."

"And now?"

Claire took a sip and shrugged. "Now I know how fragile everything is. How quickly it can all be taken away."

"You asked me why I left the West Coast. . . ." Gus reached for his drink. "It wasn't just wanting out of the surfing scene. It was more like resigning before they could fire me."

Claire considered him over the top of her margarita, wondering if it was the cast of the sun or the shift in topics that tightened his features, the easy rise of his smile nearly gone.

He took a sip and swallowed hard. "I was a kid when I got on the circuit, and I got big fast. Sponsors wooing me,

money all over the place. I wasn't exactly well-behaved."
He looked at her. "Stop me if you've heard this one before."

"Everyone's story is different."

"I don't know about that," he said. "I came here to hide
out, just like everybody else who burns their bridges and
wants to pretend they don't need them to get back."

"Did you?"

"Absolutely," he said. "It took a while, but I built them
up again. Now you know." He shook the ice around in his
glass and took another swig.

She searched his face as he drank, moved by his confession, his honesty. It comforted her to know she wasn't
the only one who'd seen dark days. Not that she imagined
she was.

"Did you ever compete again?"

"A little," he said. "Charity rides, mostly. Good causes,
good people. Honestly, I was glad to quit the circuit. Now
I'm the sponsor who has to put up with the punk kid I *used*
to be."

"Ah." She smiled. "Karma."

"So what brought *you* here?"

"You did, apparently."

"No, I mean, what is it you wanted to do here?"

Claire shrugged. "At first, I just wanted to get away
with my daughter for a few days, to get her away from her
boyfriend. But now . . ." She looked at him. "Now there are
other reasons. Other people."

Gus nodded. "Ivy."

"I want to help her keep her shop. It's everything to her."

"Maybe it's still something to you too."

His eyes searched hers; Claire felt certain he could see a part of her she'd lost. That girl who knew that timing was what you made it, that opportunity was something to be seized. The one who took on Harp Patton and didn't surrender. The one who cut her own path and carved her own wave. The one any daughter would be proud to have as a mother.

Claire wanted that woman back. She had left her here, on this beach. She could retrieve her. It wasn't too late.

She shifted her eyes to the water. Out there, her world had been exactly what she'd wanted it to be.

Out there, everything had been perfect and possible.

To know that kind of bliss once more, even for a second.

She clapped her hands clean of crumbs and grease and rose.

"I want to ride," she announced.

Gus blinked at her. "You sure you're not too sore?"

She was, of course. Just standing up had brought with it reminding bolts of pain.

So what?

Claire reached for her margarita and drained it. "I'm sure."

This time, she didn't stop to survey her hips or her belly or the cut of her rash vest or the rise of her board shorts. She slid out of her clothes and into her uniform with the speed she had possessed twenty years earlier. When Gus handed her a long board, she tucked it under her arm and carried it down to the beach, walking beside him toward the Washout. If he was right—that nerve was something you buried—then all she had to do was paddle out to uncover it. She squinted into the sky, the sun hanging in that sweet spot of dusk, its harshness faded. You could almost stare at it, its glow as soft as that of a flickering porch bulb.

She was determined not to exhaust herself getting through the surf, so she paddled around the waves she couldn't duck-dive or turtle-roll. Finally outside, she joined Gus in the stillness where he sat on his board, bobbing easily on the calm water. Nothing could touch her now.

When the first break neared, she dropped down beside Gus, turned to face the beach, and paddled hard.

This time, her body moved without a thought. In one smooth motion, she threw her feet under her chest with the speed she'd feared she'd lost. The day before, her pop-ups had been choppy, clunky, too slow. Once she was up, everything came back—and everything fell away. Fear, doubt, regret, longing—all of it blending into one big soup that washed into the break. Arms and feet moved in unison. All the moments she'd treasured returned: the sunlight through the wave, seeing the white water come down her back.

For nearly an hour, even as her muscles cried for her to stop, Claire kept pace with Gus until the fortunate breaks waned. Gus waved her to shore; she followed him in.

Out of the water, they climbed the beach to where the sand was dry, abandoned their boards, ripped off their leash straps, and collapsed side by side. For several moments, they didn't speak, only lay there, winded, blinking up at the sky and letting their breathing slow.

Gus rose on his elbows and looked over at her. "How do you feel?"

"Incredible." Claire turned her head to his. "How did I look?"

He rolled toward her. "Fierce."

"Liar."

This close, she could feel the cool water on his skin, his breath. Droplets glistened on his beard, the curves of his hair.

"I told you I won't sleep with you," she said.

He leaned closer and whispered huskily, "So we won't sleep."

*I*t was almost fully dark by the time they returned to the cottage. Gus laid their boards against the railing and led Claire up the steps to the deck. Margot waited by the slider and stepped back when they came inside.

"She seems nervous," said Claire.

Gus pushed wet ropes of hair off her face. "So do you."

"I'm not nervous."

"Your teeth are chattering."

"I'm cold."

"You're soaked," he said, cupping her cheek. "You need warming up."

Claire stared at him as he traced her bottom lip with

his thumb, her stomach as tight as her hands at her side. Why hadn't he kissed her yet? Didn't he want to? She felt young and foolish and unsure and a thousand other things that were pulling her farther and farther from the delirium she'd felt on the water and then the beach.

"Maybe I *am* a little nervous," she confessed. "It's been a long time for me . . ." She looked up at him expectantly. "And this is the part where you say, 'Don't worry, Claire. It's been a long time for me too.'"

Gus shrugged. "It's been two weeks."

Two weeks? Color flooded her cheeks. "You really know how to make a girl feel special." Embarrassed, Claire tried to wriggle free; Gus held her fast.

"Hey," he said, his voice deep but tender. "Give me a break, okay? I didn't know you two weeks ago."

She stilled, relenting. He searched her face and she let him, feeling her comfort return, her desire, her longing.

"I don't want to be alone," she whispered.

He lowered his mouth over hers. "Then don't be."

*T*hey made love twice before they finally gave in to sleep, collapsing, deliriously spent, as they had done on the beach hours earlier. In the shower, he'd pulled seaweed off her skin where it had snuck under her rash guard, pressed into her rear, the backs of her thighs; he'd peeled off shell chips from the fullest part of her breasts and just below her belly button; he'd combed sand and salt from her hair with his fingers, turned her around, and scrubbed her scalp hard enough to make her moan. By the time they turned off the water and climbed into his bed, her body was a freshly lit match, every inch of her skin inflamed, and he knew what he'd done to her. He grinned as he did even more, licking off whatever salt remained, hard-to-reach places, and places all too easy to find.

Drifting off, she listened to the lullaby of sounds, the lazy crash of surf, the faint tapping of dog nails across the bedroom floor, the even breathing of the man lying beside her whose callused fingers remained curved over her bare hip. She felt a fleeting pinch of guilt for all she'd put aside to have this moment to herself, for herself, this night, fears that she was selfish and a bad mother, but then sleep rescued her, forgiving her so she didn't have to forgive herself.

22

*I*vy woke to the sound of a lawn mower starting, a sluggish groan that could have belonged to a snoring lover or a hungry mosquito. She rose and dragged her hair behind her ears, slowing at the window to test the breeze that blew in. At eight thirty, the sun was already strong and the air thick with its heat. On her way to the kitchen, she stepped downstairs into the guest suite and smiled to see Claire's bed was still made.

Women could predict things about each other. Tiny signals, missed so often by men, even those men who imagined themselves psychic when it came to a woman's moods and needs; a look cut short; a laugh that started small and turned loud in an instant. To those who witnessed impending lovers, attraction was as apparent as a smell. The moment Gus Gallagher arrived, the breeze had hastened with electricity, like the thick air in those moments before an afternoon thunderstorm, when the light turns a silvery pink and nothing moves.

Ivy had felt that way about Foster's father, sure everyone within twenty miles of them had sensed their passion. She'd been chased by boys her whole life and grown accustomed to their clumsy urgency, boys who kissed as if they were trying to squish a bug on her lips, boys who touched her as if the end-of-the-quarter horn would blow at any second, which, at their undisciplined age, was an accurate comparison.

But Ladd King was a man. He was only twenty-six days older than she was, but he had already lived all over the world. He'd surfed Pipeline and Mavericks. He'd made love to women twice his age and claimed, when Ivy had finally dared to press, they had enlightened him on the beauty of leisure in bed. He'd told Ivy that making love wasn't so different from surfing, that he understood waves as he understood women, both unpredictable, needing total attention and focus, and that no two were ever alike.

Ivy had been seeing two boys when Ladd King rode into town the summer of her nineteenth year. By the end of his first week in Folly, she belonged to him as firmly as a star belongs to the sky. She hadn't known then that stars were nothing more than explosions of gas.

The first time Ivy met Claire Patton, it was like looking into a mirror. Claire was fearless, feisty, and unabashedly enamored of her son. Ivy had adored the girl at once. When it was clear that Foster did too, Ivy mothered their affection as if it were a rescued baby bird with slim chance for survival. Ivy knew how distance could cool the fires of young love, but with every letter that arrived, every phone call, Ivy watched her son's eyes ignite all over again. When Claire moved to Folly the following summer, Ivy was relieved but she wanted to be certain.

"You love her, don't you?" she had asked.

Foster had hesitated in answering; Ivy was sure she knew why. He worried that she, his mother, would feel unneeded, cast aside, that there would be a question of having to choose.

"I think you do," she said, wanting to put his fears to rest. "She's one of us, Fossie. And she's so good for you. Anyone can see that."

Still, he'd looked unsure.

"There are all kinds of love, baby," she said, taking his hands. "One doesn't have to replace the other. They can all live in the same heart. You don't have to worry about that."

Breaking someone's heart is a certain kind of pain—for both lovers. Ivy had grieved as much for her son having to hurt Claire as she had for Claire being hurt. It shredded her soul. And then, without a good-bye, Claire left.

Now she was back. And she'd returned with a dose of inspiration that Ivy had been missing. She, Ivy, had woken this morning with the same excitement she'd gone to sleep with the night before; the shop would remain hers, and they'd reopen it for business. She would have to tell Shep and Jill her decision, of course. She'd already spoken with Lee Reynolds, the Realtor, instructing him to remove the listing, so it was only a matter of time before the news made its way around. Shep and Jill would be contentious, maybe even outraged. Let them be, Ivy thought as she nursed a mug of green tea at the sink and stared out at the view of the beach. This was still her property, still her decision to make. Still her life.

Coming downstairs into the shop a few minutes later, she smiled to find Claire kneeling in front of a display of fins, carefully working a sponge over each one, a bucket of soapy water beside her.

"Good morning."

Claire spun around. "I hope I didn't wake you."

"How long have you been down here?"

"I don't know."

"Well, judging by the fact that the lights are on and it's bright sun, I'll guess you got here when it was still dark, you crazy girl."

"What can I say?" Claire shrugged. "I was excited to get started. It's been a while. I needed to reacquaint myself with the inventory."

"I think the better question is why are you here wiping down fins when you could be eating scrambled eggs in bed with that yummy man?"

"I left him a note."

Ivy sighed. "Oh, honey. You don't leave a man like that a note."

Claire returned the fin to its slot and looked at Ivy. "I can't believe I'm here with you. I can't believe I'm here at all."

She dropped the sponge into the bucket and wiped her hands on her rear. When she looked up, her eyes pooled with tears. "I'm sorry." Claire swallowed, sniffed. "It just hits me every now and then, you know?" She swiped at her wet cheeks. "It's not that he's not here with me. . . . It's that he's not here *at all*."

"But he is, sweetie." Ivy came down beside Claire and wiped at the tear she'd missed. "He's all over this place," she said, gesturing to the displays. "He's everywhere I look. Everything I touch. Why do you think I never changed a damn thing in all these years? This is my memorial. This is where I come to be with my son. Don't make me go to some hole in the ground."

Claire's body shook with sobs, an unstoppable rush of sorrow that Ivy suspected she had been swallowing since she arrived. Ivy turned, arms out, and Claire fell against her.

Ivy stroked her hair. "Speaking of mothers . . . have you seen yours yet?"

Claire leaned back to meet Ivy's eyes. "Not yet," she admitted. "I should. I *will*." She looked away. "I didn't tell her I was coming."

The complicated stitches of children and parents, Ivy thought: a sweater never quite finished.

Claire looked past Ivy to the wall, her gaze drifting over the photos of her and Foster surfing. "I think he just loved me because you approved of me. Because he wanted to please *you*."

"No. His love was his own."

"But it wasn't enough."

"What's enough?" asked Ivy. "We love as deeply as we

can. For as long as we can. Sometimes that measure isn't the same for two people. But it doesn't mean it isn't real."

Ivy reached out and smoothed a loose lock of hair behind Claire's ear. The soft crunch of bicycle tires sailed through the open window. In the next minute, Luke appeared at the door, wearing a proud smile and holding up a pair of white take-out bags.

"Breakfast is served. Anyone hungry?"

At the counter, they unpacked egg sandwiches, bowls of cheese grits, and dug in. Between bites, they scanned the shop, but Ivy's eyes kept returning to one area of the store in particular, one door, to a room she hadn't ventured into for too long.

To Claire and Luke, she said, "If we're serious about getting this place back into shape, then we need to clean out more than just dust."

Still chewing a chunk of his sandwich, Luke looked at her, his eyes shining with understanding.

Ivy reached out and stroked his cheek. "You up for it, honey? That room's a biggie."

He smiled, tears rising. Ivy watched him swallow and take in a long breath, a swimmer preparing for a deep dive.

"I am if you are, Grams."

23

*J*ill shifted in her chair to loosen the denim seat of her skirt and watched Shep wander the perimeter of Lee Reynolds's small office in the back of Folly Realty, searching the listings on the papered walls.

The heavy smell of licorice hung in the air, a mix of cologne and stale cigarette smoke. Lee had quit for years. It seemed he'd taken it up again.

"I'm sure Lee would have called if there was any news," said Jill.

Shep shrugged. "Never hurts to ask."

Jill rubbed her arms, chilled, the room's familiar smell drawing her into memory.

Sixteen years earlier, she and Foster had sat in this same office, excited and terrified to sign off on their new home, a simple cottage Lee had found them several streets up from the water. The cottage where Foster had bought

Luke his first bike and taught him to ride. The cottage she and Luke had come home alone to after Foster's funeral. The cottage she had sold to move in with Shep to the Glasshouse. The Glasshouse where Shep and Foster had lived when Claire had loved Foster and she had loved Shep.

Time seemed to race backward; she'd imagined every piece separate when it was all really one chain, each event linked to another.

The last time she'd sat in this office, it was spitting a warm rain after three weeks without a drop.

The last time she'd sat in this office, her hair fell to the middle of her back.

The last time she'd sat in this office, she was Foster's wife.

*C*ontrary to Ivy's long-held belief, it was Lee Reynolds—and not Jill—who first suggested Foster become a Realtor. Three months after they'd bought their house, Jill had run into Lee in the Piggly Wiggly parking lot, loading bags of ice into his trunk. "He'd be a natural, you know," Lee had said. "Your husband could sell a turtle the shell off its own back. Everyone loves him."

It was true, and yet Jill had resisted sharing her conversation with Foster, knowing how devoted he was to his coworkers at the marina, knowing how much Ivy depended on him at the shop. Until two weeks later when Foster came home late from work, breathless with excitement, just as she was fixing Luke's dinner and theirs.

His eyes were huge, his skin flushed. "Babe, you'll never guess who I just had a drink with."

Jill drained a can of peas. "Who?"

"Lee Reynolds. He wants to bring me on board at the agency. He said he'd mentioned it to you a while back."

She pressed the soft peas into mush. "I didn't think you'd have any interest."

"Are you kidding? I'd love to get into real estate." Foster reached into the fridge for a beer, twisting off the top with his shirt. She waited while he swigged. From his high chair, Luke watched his father, tiny fingers reaching. Foster came around and planted a loud kiss on his son's curly head. "I'd be great at it. You know I would."

"It's not that easy, Foss," she said gently, handing him Luke's mashed peas and a baby spoon so she could finish fixing dinner. "There are exams, licenses—"

"Lee said he can fast-track all that. I'd work with him for a while, get a few sales under my belt, and then he'd make me an agent." Foster pulled up a seat beside Luke's high chair, spooning a generous bite. Luke gummed the green puree, blowing emerald bubbles. "Come on, babe. What do you say?"

What *could* she say? Certainly not the truth: that the idea of him moving into a new career, one that would draw him away from the surf shop, one that would find him spending less time surrounded by all those memories of Claire and the world they'd blown apart with their love, thrilled her to bits? But it did. God forgive her, it did.

"Jill, I grew up not knowing my dad. And what I did

know, I didn't like." Foster paused to refill Luke's plastic spoon with peas. "I don't want Luke to think of me that way. To think I didn't care enough to do the right thing by him. That I didn't want to get serious about my life."

"It's not the same," she said. "Your father was gone. You're here."

"I know, but I want to be more than just here." Foster rose and came beside her at the stove, lowering his hands to her shoulders. Jill turned and fell against him.

"It's time, baby," he whispered into her hair. "Time to let that life go. I don't want to be that guy who used to show up at the surf shop at four in the morning on a Sunday because he didn't know what else to do with himself. I want Luke to grow up eating dinner at a table, not on a beach, or on the bed of some dude's truck."

Not yet convinced, she leaned back and looked up at him, searching his face. "But the shop . . ."

"It's not my dream anymore. I don't know if it ever really was."

But all Jill could think about was Ivy, her reaction, her outrage. "Your mother will be devastated."

"She'll be disappointed, sure, but she'll understand."

Jill lowered her eyes, her heart racing with another fear, her *real* fear. "She'll think it was my idea. She'll blame me. Foss, she'll hate me."

"She won't. She'll see it's what's best for Luke. For our family."

Our family. Tears pooled, blinding Jill as she stirred their soup and Foster returned to the table to be with Luke.

Her relief was so overwhelming she could barely breathe.

And that quickly, Foster shifted into a new role. The same wonderful man with a new focus. His trips to the shop grew less frequent, and shorter; his wet suit rarely dried on the railings, his board rarely stuck out of the back of their station wagon. And every night, heads on their pillows, before he clicked off the light and she had one last chance to look at the day's wear on his kind face, Jill searched his sky blue eyes for proof that he regretted his choice. Not just the new job, but her, Luke, all of it. And every night she would see only the calm of conviction, and every night she would sleep well and deeply. Grateful.

*S*orry to keep y'all waiting."

Lee Reynolds greeted Shep with a handshake and Jill with a kiss on the cheek, then took a seat at his desk. "Did Gwen offer you some coffee or iced tea?"

"We're good," said Shep. "We were in town, so we thought we'd swing by and check in, see how it's going."

"I appreciate that, but I think we're all set. I'll keep the listing on file, and when Ivy wants to put it back on the market, we'll just pick up where we left off."

Jill blinked at Shep.

Shep darted forward. "I'm sorry, Lee—did we miss something?"

Lee looked between them, confusion pleating the edges

of his eyes. "I assumed Ivy told y'all before she called me," he said. "She's changed her mind. She wants to take the property off the market. She didn't tell you?"

"What?" Jill reached for the edge of the desk. "When?"

"Last night," said Lee. "She said she's not ready. She thought she was, but she's not. Heck, I just figured she'd gone over it all with you first."

Jill watched Shep suck in a long, hard breath, the kind he used to take in just before walking out into the water to surf on a blustery day.

*I*t was Claire's idea; I guarantee it," Shep said tightly as they marched out of the agency and down to the sidewalk. The morning clouds had finally thinned and now the sun burned hot. Jill squinted against it as she pulled open the passenger door to the van and climbed inside.

"We don't know that," she said, but it was a hollow tempering. Shep was likely right, and even though she was determined not to let her emotions flare before knowing the whole story, Jill felt the swells of irritation bloom.

Shep pulled them into traffic. "You heard Claire at dinner. You were the one who pointed it out to *me*. She was obviously put out that we'd convinced Ivy to sell."

Jill frowned out the window, trying to understand. "But Ivy's only just gotten back and Claire already left. When could they have talked about this? When could they have made this plan without us knowing?"

"Claire and Ivy probably got talking about the old days and Claire lit a fire under Ivy not to sell yet. I'd put money on it."

She sighed. "We have to talk to Ivy."

Shep had already steered them onto Ashley. He flashed her a knowing look. "Way ahead of you."

They'd gone through it all. Every box, every notebook, every album. They'd sorted through trophies and filed through newspaper clippings. They passed around photograph after photograph. Nearly two hours of tears, laughter, quiet wonder, loud cries of recollection. If there had been any doubt in Claire's mind that Ivy had it in her to keep In the Curl alive, there was no longer. Now, with the room's treasured memories consolidated into a half dozen boxes, the need to preserve the shop's history and worth was stronger than ever.

Claire pulled her phone from her pocket, startled to see the time. Was it really almost one? She plucked a Kleenex from the box Ivy had brought in for them earlier in the excavation and blew her pinked nose. She hadn't expected to cry so much. And she wasn't even sure all the tears had been for Foster. Many had been for Lizzie, and for all the ways Claire longed to make things good again. Now Claire wanted desperately to call her daughter and tell her that she wished Lizzie might have been in that room of boxes and ghosts and hope with all of them just now, that she could have seen the evidence of the fearless, independent woman her mother once was.

Claire texted a short message instead: *Thinking about you, Zee. Love you. Miss you. Mom.*

An engine rumbled into the lot. Luke craned his neck to reach the window and announced, "It's Mom and Shep."

Claire stood and wiped quickly at her eyes, her nose, panicked at the news. In all her impulsive excitement, she hadn't considered the possibility of seeing Shep and Jill again after their strained meal. They believed she was back in Colorado. Finding her here, learning that she planned to stay on, that she'd encouraged Ivy to keep the shop—what would they say?

"Ivy, maybe I should go," she said. "Walk the beach, or something."

"What for? You stay put. You're not some stranger. This was your home too, you know."

Claire smiled, fortified, reaffirmed. Ivy and she had always spoken the same language. She glanced at Luke while they waited for Shep and Jill to climb the steps, curious how he would receive his mother and Shep after emptying the storage room, after their emotional purging.

Shep came inside first. "Claire?" He stared at her. "We thought you were leaving after the interview."

"I was," she said, meeting Jill's startled gaze behind his. "I changed my flight."

"Oh."

Claire watched Jill quickly turn her shock into a polite smile.

"Where's Lizzie?" Jill asked.

"She went home early," Claire said. "She'll be with her dad for the next few weeks."

Jill and Shep shared a quick look—a nervous look, Claire thought.

Shep's gaze drifted past them to the opened door of the storage room. "I see y'all've been busy."

"It's Dad's stuff," said Luke. "We finally went through it. And guess what? Grams decided not to sell the shop!"

Claire swore the air in the room cooled ten degrees.

"We know," Shep said evenly. "We stopped by Lee's office."

Claire looked at Ivy, feeling a prickle of guilt; Ivy hadn't told them yet?

"Miss Claire said she'd stay on longer and help us fix it up too," Luke continued. "Isn't that awesome?"

Shep turned to Ivy. "Can we talk to you outside for a second?"

"We can talk right here," said Ivy. "It's hot as hell outside."

"We really wish you came to us first before going to Lee," Jill said. "He's put a great deal of his time into this listing, Ivy."

"I thought we agreed not to revisit this discussion," Shep said.

"We're not revisiting it," Ivy said firmly, stepping behind the counter and facing them, palms flattened challengingly on the divider's surface. "I've made my decision and we'll reopen as soon as possible."

"You know what the building inspector said: You can't

do that until you make the necessary updates," Jill reminded her.

"That's what the three of us plan to do," said Luke, joining Ivy on the other side of the counter and smiling at Claire. "Isn't that right, Miss Claire?"

Shep rubbed his temple. "Claire, I don't know if Ivy's explained to you the scope of what's required. It's not something y'all can fix in a couple of days. We're talking wiring. Roof repair. Fire safety systems. We're talking big stuff here."

Claire shrugged, undaunted. "I'm sure between the three of us we can track down someone fair and competent to do the work."

Jill spoke softly, but her strain slipped through. "Luke, baby, why don't you wait for us in the van? We'll be down in a second."

"But I'm not ready to go."

"Yeah, you are," Shep said, his voice harsh. "Get in the van."

Claire looked at Jill, sure she wouldn't let Shep tell her son what to do, but Jill made no motion to reverse his order and the look of betrayal on Luke's face broke Claire's heart.

Shep was angry; Claire could see it. Many times she'd watched him boil over at the Trap's bar after too many beers on a Friday night, red-faced and ready to pounce, until Foster would steer him outside and cool him down. The years might have drawn out the length of his fuse, but Claire suspected it was still every bit as quick to light.

"The boy wants to stay, let him stay," Ivy said, moving her hands to her hips.

"Ivy, please," said Jill. "Luke, sweetie, just do this for me."

Shep said, "Claire, would you mind giving us some privacy?"

"She's not going anywhere," Ivy said. "Pepper has as much right being here as anyone, and I want her here. Which is more than I can say for the two of you right now. Excuse me."

Then Ivy walked through their tense semicircle to the upstairs door, threw it open, and slammed it behind her, the sound of her bare feet smacking the treads to the apartment.

Shep closed his eyes and pinched the bridge of his nose.

Luke stormed out from behind the counter. "I'm outta here."

"Baby, we'll be right down," said Jill.

"Don't bother, I'll walk home," he muttered, reaching the door and giving it a hard shove. "See ya, Miss Claire."

Jill moved to follow him, but Shep touched her arm to stop her. "Let him cool off." He turned to Claire and said low, "Claire, look; we appreciate what you think you're doing here, but Ivy has no business keeping this shop one more day."

"It's what she wants," Claire said.

Shep looked at Jill. "That's news to us."

"Well, she didn't hesitate when I suggested it."

"So it *was* your idea," Shep said.

Jill turned for the door, her features strained with

worry. "I'm going to catch up with Luke. I don't want him going off angry about this."

Claire watched Jill rush out, reminded of her own recent attempt to stop her child from leaving in a rage, the helplessness she'd felt, the regret. She followed, sure she would see Jill endure the same. But from the height of the porch, Claire could see Jill reach Luke at the end of the street. He stopped, appearing to listen. Envy swelled, shifting quickly to bitterness. It was hard not to resent the simple fact that Jill *had* lied to her child, whereas she, Claire, had been accused of it and was suffering her child's anger unfairly.

Shep came out too, yanking the door shut behind him. "Is this because you're still mad at Jill?" he demanded. "Is that why you're doing this?"

Claire turned to face him. "This has nothing to do with Jill. This is about Ivy. This is about taking care of her."

"Christ, Claire—what do you think we've been doing for the last ten years?"

"I think she's not ready to let this place go."

"How would you know? You've been back in her life for all of forty-eight hours."

"That's not fair." Claire could feel the bubble of tears climbing her throat. "I know her, Shep. I know her just as well as you do."

He rubbed his face with his palms, as if to wipe away his frustration, but when he looked back at her, the flush of exasperation remained. "I thought we made it clear at dinner

that this decision was something Jill and I had been working toward for a long time, that it was best for everyone."

"Including Ivy?"

He squinted, as if it hurt to look at her. "Do you have
any idea how hard this has been for us?" he demanded.
"How good it felt to know we could finally move on from
this place? Then you show up, out of the blue, and stir all
this up again. Did it ever occur to you that this isn't just
about what's best for Ivy?"

"Then what about Luke?" Claire said.

"Don't bring Luke into this."

"Why not?" said Claire. "Doesn't he have a say?"

"I just can't believe that you'd come back here and
make this kind of trouble for us."

Claire's heart raced so fast that she nearly stumbled
over her words. "And I can't believe after everything Jill
did, you—"

She stopped herself, trapping the rest of the accusation
safely behind her teeth, but Shep wouldn't let her off the
hook. He stared at her, waiting.

"Go on and say it," he ordered, low. "You can't believe I
took her back. That's what you wanted to say, isn't it?"

Claire straightened, too angry now to pretend otherwise. "You just scooped everything back up like nothing
had changed. You're living in the Glasshouse, for God's
sake! After the way she treated you, the way she lied to *both*
of us, you just take her back like it's no big deal, like none
of it mattered."

"I don't have to justify my decision to you, Claire. I

made the choice I made. You made yours just the same. And I think if you'd had the chance, if Foster had begged you to come back, you'd have done the same damn thing I did and you know it. And I'm sorry if you're angry about that, or jealous, or what—but it doesn't give you the right to come back here and upend all of our lives."

Shoving his hands deep into his pockets, Shep turned for the steps and took them to the gravel, headed for the van.

Claire followed him down. "This has nothing to do with me, Shep. I'm here to do what's best for Ivy."

Shep didn't respond, just gave her a cool look as he yanked open the driver's door and climbed inside.

When he'd sent the van lurching into the road, Claire stood frozen, too numb with hurt to move.

She looked around, feeling small and out of place. Lost.

She needed a compass.

24

Claire wasn't sure Gus would be home. She wasn't sure he'd be happy to see her; she wasn't sure of *anything*, but still she steered her bike up his driveway without slowing, deciding she'd take her chances. If he wasn't alone, she'd flee, unnoticed. But, God, she hoped he was.

She heard the wail of blues guitar coming from the back of the house. When she rounded the deck and saw him leaned over a flipped board, she stopped before he spotted her and watched him for a moment as he waxed, relishing too much the sight of him stroking the rails to disturb him, the peaceful set of his mouth, the intense focus in his eyes.

She wished she could trade places with that board.

"Going for a ride?"

Gus looked up, startled for a moment until he located her.

Please don't make me go, Claire thought, a girlish panic

and need sloshing around in her stomach, making her dizzy. She couldn't take another rejection today.

He set down his wax and reached over to turn down the music.

She made her way to him.

He wiped his palms on his thighs. "She lives."

"Barely," Claire admitted with a weak smile.

When she reached him where he waited at the edge of the deck, his gaze was searching, wary. "For future reference, I hate notes. You want to sneak out in the middle of the night, wake me up and tell me, okay?"

She nodded. "Duly noted."

He touched the swollen skin above her eyes. "I don't think you got enough sleep."

She smiled wearily. "But I'm not tired."

He dragged his thumb down her cheek and smiled back. "Yeah. Me neither."

She'd forgotten what it was to make love in daylight. The decadence, the feeling of doing something forbidden, like skipping class or getting drunk at lunch. She rolled drowsily onto her stomach and surveyed Gus Gallagher's cluttered bedroom in the watery glow of late afternoon. Beyond the door, out of sight, she could hear him in the kitchen, whistling as he cooked, dishes clinking, water flowing.

She'd craved pasta; he'd obliged with boxed mac and cheese.

Exhaustion tugged at her, the smoothness of his sheets tempting her to slide deeper into his bed and drift off to sleep. She closed her eyes, the cotton cool and smelling faintly of salt and damp skin. She'd arrived as tight as a knot; now she felt like a piece of taffy that had been warmed and pulled. How quickly the mind could shift from despair to pleasure. Just a few hours earlier, she'd been swamped with such sadness, such regret.

It wasn't that she hadn't cried for Foster before that morning in the storage room. Learning of his death ten years earlier, Claire had wilted against her kitchen counter in Colorado and wept a different kind of tears. Two thousand miles away from Folly, the words on the paper had belonged to someone else, a life too distant to hurt the way loss should hurt. But there in the shop, the anguish had arrived at last, in whole, the intersection of grief and reality, and she'd stood in the center of it and let it pummel her. Until she'd come back to Folly, until she'd stood inside the shop without him, Foster could never really be gone.

But he was.

Gus returned, lay down next to her, and slid the bowl of mac and cheese between them.

She smiled sleepily. "Why do I feel like I just called in sick to work and any minute now my boss is going to find out that I lied?"

"Because great sex always makes people feel guilty." He speared a stack of macaroni and fed them to her.

She grinned as she chewed. "You too?"

He snorted. "Hell, no. I need all my guilt for those

mornings I leave without remembering to refill Margot's water bowl, or when I forget her heartworm pill. I can't be wasting prime guilt like that on great sex."

Claire laughed. "I'm sure Margot appreciates that."

"Yeah, well. She'd appreciate fresh water more."

They shared the rest of the mac and cheese, shiny and gooey and electric orange, until the bowl was emptied and Gus lowered it to the floor. Margot trotted over and lapped it clean.

Claire dropped her cheek onto her folded arms. "You must need to get to the store," she whispered.

"Later." He rolled her onto her back, lifted her hands above her head, and came over her.

She searched his eyes. "They don't want me here."

He frowned down at her. "Who?"

"Ivy's family. My old friends. They're angry that I encouraged Ivy not to sell the shop. They think I'm interfering." She reached up and wove her fingers through his hair. "I'm not."

"Then what does it matter what they think?" He drew down the sheet, baring her breasts to the breeze, and dropped a kiss on each one. She closed her eyes, trying to lose herself and all worry in the sensation of his mouth on her body, the roughness of his beard as it swept a circle over each tip.

He was right. This time, it didn't matter. It couldn't, she thought.

Then she stopped thinking entirely and sank like a stone.

25

*B*efore the affair, Jill had been a terrible liar. Sure, she'd dabbled in the age-old tradition of the kind white lie, the ability to reshape hard fact into something soft and pleasant, but pure deceit, the kind that broke friendships or crushed hearts, was something else entirely, something deplorable, something ugly.

Until she and Foster had made love for the first time, and a talent for falseness had arrived overnight. Lies over the smallest things—lost keys, leftover coffee—had danced out of her mouth with the grace of a heron in flight.

Then came the day she and Foster agreed to tell Shep and Claire the truth of their love. And suddenly honesty terrified her. Worse, she wasn't even sure she knew how to tell the truth anymore. When they'd stepped into the kitchen where Claire and Shep were setting out the pizzas they'd picked up for dinner, Foster asked Claire to walk the beach with him. Just a quick walk before they ate, he promised. They'd put the pizzas in the oven so they wouldn't get cold. The look of excitement, of unquestioned anticipation, in Claire's eyes had squeezed Jill's heart so hard she struggled to breathe.

When they'd gone and Jill turned to Shep, his eyes darkened with dread. She'd had everything planned, imagined she knew him well enough to know exactly what he would say. But his expression undid her. The words she'd practiced, the gentle phrasing she'd composed, abandoned her. She blurted everything out in one frantic breath, dropped her head into her hands, and began to weep.

She was the girl who spared spiders in the bathroom, the girl who set out water bowls in the heat of summer for neighborhood dogs. She was the girl who gave up her place in line, who donated canned goods and blankets, who potted marigolds and asters for monarch butterflies. She wasn't supposed to hurt someone this way.

She wasn't that girl.

And then she was.

Shep sat stiff and straight, rubbing his palms up and down the tops of his thighs. "He's telling Claire now, isn't he?"

She lowered her hands. "Yes."

Shep kept his gaze fixed on the table, his brown eyes always liquid soft, like melting chocolate, burned hot on a pile of junk mail that had been forwarded from her old apartment. It struck Jill sharply—she and Shep had only just moved into this house together. They had barely had time to start receiving mail.

"How long has this been going on?" he demanded.

"It doesn't matter," she whispered.

"It matters to me." The anger in his voice seemed to shake the legs of her chair. She looked up. "How long?" he asked again.

How did she answer that? Did she say that night she and Foster shared the dinner she'd cooked for him, Shep, or did she say the first time she and Foster lay in the bed he had shared with Claire for nearly six years? Either answer would have been true.

"I'm pregnant."

Whatever air remained in the room vanished. She watched Shep take in the impossible news, waiting for the blow to come, wishing for him to deliver something so vicious she could be absolved. But he just kept staring at her, until she saw the glisten of tears.

He shook his head, slowly, almost imperceptibly.

"Say something, Shep," she pleaded.

"Like what?" he demanded. "Do I have a choice? Can I say, no, you can't leave me for him? Can I say that?"

When she didn't answer, he got up and left the house, letting the screen door smack the jamb so hard the pots on the stove trembled. Jill rose and turned off the oven, then sat in the silence for a long time afterward, her eyes fixed on that same pile of junk mail, waiting for someone to return, but the house remained empty and finally she walked numbly back out into the night—which seemed crisper and colder than it had when she'd walked in, as if the seasons had shifted while she'd sat.

Two hours later, Foster found her on the back porch. His lip was cracked; he'd let Shep hit him.

"It's done," Foster said as she cleaned the blood from his jaw, as if the hurt they caused was that easy to move on from, that simple, the contents of a dustpan brushed into the trash, the trash knotted and put to the curb.

*L*ies and secrets were everywhere; Jill understood that now. Everything boxed or slid into a drawer was a secret, a signal of danger. If something couldn't live out in the open, on a shelf or a countertop, then it was to be feared. When she came into the living room and saw the two strange boxes on the couch, she stopped. The front door flew open; Luke stepped inside, carrying a stack of photo albums. Jill watched him lower the pile to the couch, settling it beside the boxes. What had remained from their morning's work. Pieces of his father.

She sniffed back tears, refusing to let her emotions derail her. She wanted to speak to him while Shep was gone. Her pleading that morning had been only marginally successful; Luke had agreed to ride home with them, but he'd refused to temper his glare. All day he'd stayed outdoors, missing lunch, missing dinner. Now he was back.

"Luke, baby . . ." She stepped into his path as he moved for the door. "We need to talk about today."

"Yeah, we do." He nodded firmly, his fierce expression strange to her, the look of an adult, not a young man. "I think I've changed my mind too. About the fall. About school."

"What about school?" she asked carefully.

"I'm not going," he said matter-of-factly. "I want to help Grams reopen the shop and run it."

Panic skidded down her arms. Jill held herself to keep from shaking.

"Luke, baby, listen to me. I know this morning was hard—but your grandma can't just start over. She hasn't thought this through."

"What's to think through?" Luke demanded. "You weren't there today, Ma. You should have seen Grams going through Dad's old stuff. Her whole face lit up! I can't remember the last time I saw her so happy. You don't understand what that was like."

Had her son forgotten the day she, Jill, had sorted through her *own* room of ghosts? She knew how emotional it was to revisit so much, how it made you feel hopeful, how it made you feel invincible—and how neither feeling remained the minute those same boxes were emptied out or stored away again.

"I'm sure it did," she said gently, "but one afternoon doesn't make—"

"It wasn't just today," Luke said. "Claire and I even talked about it when I went to see her at the hotel."

Jill blinked. "You went to see Claire? When?"

"Two nights ago."

"You said you were with Amy." She stared at him, trying to wrap her head around the simple fact: her son had lied to her.

"What was I supposed to do? You and Shep made it

clear you didn't want to see her again while she was here, and I had stuff I wanted to ask her, stuff I wanted to know."

"What kind of stuff?"

"What difference does it make? *Stuff.*"

Jill looked away, torn. Her son was right to want to know as much as he could about his father, so why did she feel such outrage that he'd gone to Claire—and what had Claire told him?

It didn't matter now. She'd been right to worry from the beginning. That nagging dread she'd harbored—it was this. This moment. This panic. The fear that Claire's return would spark the past in Ivy that no one else could and cloud her thoughts with memories of the old days. Even worse, Claire had pulled Luke into their fantasy, confusing him.

"There's no way you're skipping college to help your grandmother run a failed surf shop, Luke. We won't allow it." It was an absurd thing to say—he was almost eighteen. She would have no control of his choices. Did she even at this moment?

He leveled a look of determination at her that answered her question.

"I'm doing what I want, Ma. Maybe Dad didn't want the shop, but I do." He swept up his sweatshirt from the couch and moved for the door.

Jill followed him outside. A sliver of moon softened the blackness, but the sea wind was sharp. "Where are you going?" she called.

"To the shop," Luke said, lugging his bike down the steps.

"But it's late. It's dark." Her voice was shaky, panicked. Her heart thundered behind her ribs.

"Grams said I could stay there anytime I wanted, and I think tonight I want to."

"Luke, wait!"

But in the next instant he was on his bike, a blur under the streetlight, and gone.

26

*M*orning. . . ." Claire woke to Gus's voice sliding into her thoughts, and the gentle pressure of movement against her body. She opened her eyes and smiled up at him. He was already in his board shorts, his gray eyes stormy with anticipation. "Some great breaks out there. Better get 'em while they're good."

In the kitchen, with only a thin ribbon of dawn pink for light, Gus made them coffee and filled two travel mugs while she dressed. They carried their coffees and their boards down the steps to the walkway, Margot on their heels. The beach was busy with early surfers. A few dogs rushed to greet Margot, the pets chasing one another into the surf and back up the sand, scattering shorebirds in their path. The air was crisp and tangy, full of promise and the delicious possibility that came with morning. Claire felt ageless, unstoppable.

They screwed the bottoms of their mugs into the sand and walked into the water. Their leashes snug, they paddled out, the spray startlingly cold.

They were in the water only a few minutes, beautiful, blissful minutes when the world floated away, before they saw the smoke. It bloomed in the sky to their left, a dangerous gray against the soft lavender of sunrise.

The surfers around them began toward the shore, pointing and calling out.

There were mostly houses in that direction, but there were a handful of stores too.

Claire looked across the water at Gus.

He said it before she could.

"Ivy."

*I*t was Shep who thought to get dressed and walk down to see what all the commotion was about. He and Jill had been asleep when they heard the first sirens, their thoughts swimming in that pool of just before waking, when dream and reality blend for a strange instant.

"It's probably just an abandoned bonfire," Jill said, her voice still scratchy with sleep as she sat up to watch Shep shrug into a T-shirt and zip up his shorts.

"Probably," Shep echoed, but when the second fire truck sailed past the house, Jill rose and followed him downstairs and out to the porch. They could smell the smoke now.

"I should drive," Shep said, an unmistakable edge of panic deepening his voice.

"Wait." Jill turned back to the house, needing a bra. Shoes. "I'm coming with you."

*T*he fire had started in the back of the shop.

By the time Shep and Jill arrived, the blaze had been put out, but not before it had scorched nearly half the building, crumpling one corner of the roof and leaving vicious black streaks above the store's street-facing windows. They could only get as close as the sidewalk, but Jill didn't wait for Shep to stop the van before she pushed out the door and raced up the hill.

"Luke!" she screamed to anyone who could hear. "My son's in there!"

Edgar Lawson, a volunteer fireman and friend, pressed through the crowd of officers and waved her down, stopping her a few feet short of the tape line. She rushed to meet him, breathless, her heart thundering in her ears. *God, please let my baby be okay.*

"Luke's fine. He's fine, Jill," Edgar said even before she'd reached him. "He was already out by the time the trucks got here."

"Oh, thank you, God." Jill searched the lot, frantic. "Where is he?"

"He went to the hospital to see Ivy," Edgar said, just as Shep caught up to them. "She got out too, but they took her in as a precaution. He left with that old friend of y'all's, just a few minutes ago. They went in Barry's patrol car."

Shep took Jill's hand. "Which hospital, Ed?"

. . .

*C*laire reached across the seat and touched Luke's arm where it was wedged under his other one. From the minute they'd climbed into the police car, he kept his gaze on the window, his jaw grinding with worry, his eyes unblinking on the road.

"She's going to be fine, Luke. You heard what the EMT said."

"Then why did he turn the sirens on?" Luke demanded. "If she's so fine, then why are we going so frigging fast to get there?"

"Because Deputy Abrams knows you're worried," Claire said gently.

Luke shook his head. "I should have been the one to get her out. I woke up and I couldn't see anything and I just ran out—I was half-asleep! I wanted to go back in for her, but they wouldn't let me." He pressed a fist into his forehead, his face crumpling with anguish.

"Shh. . . ." Claire rubbed his back. "We should call your mother. She must be worried sick."

It had all happened so fast. Gus had driven her into the chaos and Claire had leaped out of the truck without waiting for him to catch up to her. Within minutes of searching, she'd found Luke wandering the embankment, looking as adrift as a lost toddler in a crowded mall. Luke had seen her and rushed through the thicket of EMTs and onlookers to reach her, begging her to help him find out where they'd taken Ivy. When Barry Abrams, a deputy Claire knew from the old days, offered to give them a ride to the hospital in his police car, she didn't hesitate. Only when they were speeding down Ashley, sirens wailing, did it occur to Claire that she hadn't seen Jill.

Claire tugged open her purse to find her phone, but there wasn't time; they'd reached the hospital. The call could wait until they got inside, she thought, looking back to find Luke had already moved to the edge of his seat, ready to fly out the minute the car stopped and the door opened.

It was okay, Claire decided. Luke was with her, he was safe, and now he had to see Ivy. That was all that mattered. Jill would understand.

*S*till no answer," Jill said as she followed Shep through the hospital's automatic front doors. They'd been calling Claire's cell from the moment they got in the van but got her voice mail every time. Jill just wanted to see her son, to stop the incessant shaking of her entire body that made her feel like a propeller plane warming up. If Shep hadn't kept hold of her hand as they sprinted down the corridor to Ivy's room, Jill was certain she'd have spun out into the atmosphere.

Stepping into the room, Jill saw Luke and Claire, still in her rash guard and board shorts, flanking the sides of Ivy's bed like bookends, their hands on the guardrails.

For a strange and terrible second, Jill felt as if she were intruding on a private moment.

"Luke." She rushed across the room and pressed her

face against her son's chest, tears of relief swimming behind her closed eyes.

Luke hugged her. "I'm fine, Ma. I'm okay."

She leaned back and cleared her eyes to see Ivy. *The
bed is swallowing her*, Jill thought, stifling a startled gasp.
Foster's mother looked shrunken, fragile. Ivy's hair, usually
pulled back, lay around her face on the pillow like a gray fan.

Shep arrived beside them, pulling Luke in for a fierce hug.

"What did the doctor say?" Shep asked, turning to Ivy.

Her voice was watery and thin. "They want to keep me
here for some tests. At least a day, two at the most." Ivy
squinted to her left, where Claire stood. "Isn't that what he
said, Pepper?"

Jill shifted her gaze to Claire, feeling the awful pang of
exclusion again.

"That's right," Claire said.

"Pepper brought Luke to me in Barry Abrams's squad
car," Ivy said proudly, patting Claire's hand for emphasis.
"Made him turn on the sirens and everything to get here."

"I can't take credit for the sirens," Claire said, smiling
down at Ivy. "That was all Barry's doing."

But she'd take credit for bringing Luke, Jill thought
sourly, the quiet accusation harsh but reflexive. Jill knew
she must have worn her indignation on her face, because
when she met Claire's gaze, Claire's smile thinned.

Jill looked away, shame and anger merging hot in her
throat. This wasn't the time.

"We're just glad no one was hurt," Jill said, taking

Luke's hand from the guardrail and closing both of hers around it.

Claire leaned in closer to Ivy. "Can I get you anything? Are you hungry? How about something to drink?"

The words rushed out, sharp and quick, before Jill could soften them. "We can get her whatever she needs now, Claire. I'm sure you'd like to get back to Folly and change out of that outfit. Shep would be glad to give you a ride."

"It's fine. I don't mind," said Claire. "I used to spend whole days in this outfit. Remember?"

You know I do, Claire. You know I can't ever forget. Is that what you want me to say?

Jill felt Shep's hand close around hers and squeeze, as if he'd sensed her teetering near the edge she'd been walking toward for days now.

She squeezed back.

Shep said, "Maybe we should all go and let you get your rest, Ivy."

"I'll stay," Claire offered. "Y'all must want to get Luke home." She reached across Ivy to touch Luke's hand. "You should get some sleep."

Jill watched the interaction between her son and Claire, her gaze catching briefly on Ivy in the middle. A rush of discomfort propelled her forward. "*I'll* stay," she announced.

"They're right, Luke," Ivy whispered. "You need to get home, honey. You need sleep." But before Luke could contest, Ivy became overcome with a fit of coughs.

Jill frowned. "That cough is terrible. Where's the doctor?"

"I'm okay . . . really . . . ," Ivy managed. "The doctor isn't worried."

"Maybe he should be," said Jill. "I want to talk to him. I'll go find him."

"Let me," said Claire.

No, Jill thought, her patience at an end. "I said I'll go." She walked to the door and pushed through, her cheeks hot with nerves and irritation.

"Jill, wait!"

She could hear Claire's voice behind her as she marched down the hall, but Jill refused to slow her pace to the elevator. This wasn't just about finding the doctor. She needed air, she needed space.

She reached the metal doors and pressed the DOWN arrow.

Claire arrived beside her. "You don't even know her doctor's name."

"I'll find out."

"By going to another floor?"

"I'm going to the reception desk downstairs where we came in." Jill pressed the arrow again, harder this time. "Why don't you let Shep and Luke take you back to the house? You're welcome to stay with us until you can make new flight arrangements—"

"I'm not leaving," Claire said firmly. "Not now. Not after this."

"You don't have to worry about her, Claire. We've been taking care of Ivy for a long time now. We plan to keep taking care of her."

"I'm just trying to help."

Jill glared up at the light board, willing the floor numbers to start flashing and signal the motion of the car.

This was ridiculous. She'd take the stairs.

She scanned the hall and saw the door. Try as she did to outpace her, Claire still followed her into the stairwell. The smell of disinfectant was strong now. Jill worried she might be sick.

"Jill, wait."

She hurried down the stairs, refusing to slow. "Claire, please. Just go back to the room."

"Dammit, Jill, can you stand still for five seconds and talk to me?"

Jill stopped and let out an exasperated breath. "You want to talk? Okay, let's talk."

Claire took a step back, visibly surprised by Jill's burst of challenge.

Jill shook her head. "You had no right."

"No right to what?" said Claire. "To care about Ivy? To help her move through something painful?"

"If you cared so much about helping her move through something painful, you should have been here for the funeral."

"Is this because I brought Luke to the hospital? Are you angry with me because we didn't wait for you?"

Jill squeezed the railing. "You have a child of your own to take care of. It was obvious at dinner that you and your daughter are struggling right now, but that doesn't give you the right to come in here and try to mother my child. He's my son, not yours."

It was a wicked thing to say, a vicious thing, and Jill regretted it as soon as the words hit the air, but it was too late. She lowered her eyes, instantly ashamed.

Claire's voice was tight. "I know I'm not Luke's mother. You made sure there was no chance of that happening, didn't you?"

"Ma?"

Both women looked up to see Luke on the landing above them, staring down. "We've been looking for you guys. Y'all okay?"

"Sorry, baby. Everything's fine." Jill hurried up the stairs to meet him, feeling shaky and raw. How much had he overheard?

"Shep went to the cafeteria," Luke said. "Did y'all find the doctor?"

"I'm still looking." Jill reached up to kiss his cheek. "See you back in the room."

She felt Claire's expectant gaze follow her past her son and out the door, their conversation painfully unfinished, but Jill couldn't bear another moment in her company.

And it scared the daylights out of her to think what she might say next if she didn't leave.

*C*laire waited until the heavy stairwell door groaned closed before she walked up to meet Luke on the landing.

His eyes pooled with trepidation, with sympathy, with question.

He swallowed. "I heard what she said. About me not being your son."

Claire looked up at the flights above them and sighed. "I'm sorry you heard that. I swear I didn't mean to make things worse."

"You didn't. My mom and Shep did that. Your being here was the best thing to happen to my grams in a long time."

Claire's eyes filled. God, he was so beautiful. He was everything perfect about this place. Everything right. "No," she said. "The best thing to happen to her is *you*."

Luke smiled sadly. "I keep thinking about yesterday. How good it was we did that, huh? It's kinda like fate. Like we knew we were running out of time. You think?"

"Maybe so," she said.

"You coming up? My mom's probably not back in the room yet."

Speaking of mothers . . . have you seen yours yet?

Ivy's reminder flickered through her thoughts. Claire had put the visit off long enough.

"Tell Ivy I'll call her later, okay?" she said to Luke, giving his hand a quick squeeze before she reached for the door. "And tell her I love her."

27

*W*hen Foster walked Claire down to the beach that final night, the moon had been resplendent: a flawless ivory, untouched, untouchable. He'd stopped them at the edge of the surf and she could see when he turned that he was fighting back tears. For one splendid moment, Claire believed it was because love had overwhelmed him. Then he spoke, and it was as if someone had pried apart her ribs and reached in.

"People change, Pepper. Even when they don't mean to . . ."

That night, and for many nights afterward, Claire would wonder: Had there been other clues over the years, other warning lights that Claire had ignored, hinting that Foster was slipping away from her? It was the shock and confusion of biting into a shiny apple and finding the inside browned. Had the rot been there the whole time? Had it all been a lie? The day Foster had introduced Claire to Jill at the Crab Trap, had he loved Jill Weber even then? When he said he wanted a girl who could surf, a girl who could share his dream of running In the Curl, was that a lie too?

Shep had spilled the second awful truth when Claire fled to his house later that night—the Creamsicle orange cottage he'd shared, until a few hours before, with Jill. They'd sat outside on the porch swing, too stunned and spent to do much pushing, because neither one had wanted to go inside. Shep had said he wasn't sure he could ever go inside the house again. But then they'd emptied their beers and he'd gone back in for more.

He'd brought out the cold pizza they'd never eaten, but Claire couldn't stomach a slice. Just the smell of the caramelized onions, so luscious a few hours earlier when they were hot and sweet and promising a night of laughter and friends, now sickened her.

"A—*baby*?" Claire had nearly choked on the word.

"Foss didn't tell you?"

Claire had bent at the waist, worried she'd throw up. Shep rubbed her back; she rubbed his. They embraced; they broke apart. Dancers whose dates had abandoned them during the final song. He'd offered her the couch for the night, implored her to stay, to keep talking, but she declined, promising him she wouldn't go farther than Charleston, that she'd be back in a day or two to find a new place. For a few hours she'd believed she could still live in Folly, still live near them. Shep wasn't sure that he could.

"Will you go to your folks'?" he asked.

"Eventually," Claire said.

She'd wanted a night to collect herself before exposing the fullness of her failure to her parents, especially her father, to let the swollen crescents above and below her eyes from crying go down, so she drove to a hotel and lay awake watching television and emptying a tub of pimento cheese, her car in the parking lot two floors below, stuffed with everything she could pack.

It would be hard going back to her parents. But what else could she do? Ivy would gladly take her in—but how could she? Foster would need her more, and as his mother, Ivy would have to side with him. Claire didn't have enough money to rent a place on her own. Her salary from giving lessons had been barely enough to cover her expenses, minimal as they were. Foster had encouraged her to get other work, but she'd refused, knowing Ivy depended on her too much, knowing nowhere would be as much fun as the shop. Now here she was, broke. In every possible way. The last seven years of her life had been beaded on a thin thread, meant to last forever; until that night, she'd never had to question the strength of the clasp.

The next morning, she'd pulled in to her childhood home and taken the stairs to the front door. She knocked and waited, watching the peephole pane for signs of life beyond it. Movement and sound: her mother's heels clicking across the polished wood. Then her mother in view, slowing only a moment when she saw who had arrived. Her steps hastened. When she opened the door, her face seemed pale, her eyes startled.

"Hi, Mom."

Her mother glanced past her to the driveway. "You drove?"

Claire smiled weakly. "I left."

*H*er mother had their housekeeper fix Claire a sandwich, even though Claire had informed her mother that she hadn't had an appetite for days. They waited in the sunroom, her mother boasting at the health of her prized orchids. Nearly ten minutes inside the house, her father still hadn't appeared.

"Is he here?" Claire asked.

Her mother pointed to the ceiling. "You know he can't hear a thing in his study."

A lie. Claire knew her father's delayed entrance had nothing to do with ignorance of her arrival. She'd expected this strategy from him.

"Wait here," said her mother. "I'll let him know."

The housekeeper stepped in with her lunch and handed it to Claire. Tuna fish dripped down the side of a sesame seed roll, runny from too much mayonnaise. Her stomach turned; she set the plate down on a side table.

Claire knew exactly what would happen next. Her

father, wishing to prove himself the victor in this ages-old war, would continue to make her wait. Maybe even up to an hour. Time enough that she might understand the weight of his grudge and the cost of her return. She'd endure it. She didn't care anymore. She just wanted a real bed tonight, a quiet place to gather her thoughts and a clean pillow to cry on.

But her mother's face was strained when she returned.

"He says . . ." Her mother sat down carefully. "He says unless you are willing to come upstairs and apologize that I'm to pack up your meal and send you out with it."

"Apologize?" Claire stared at her. "For what?"

"Just do it, sweetheart. Just do it so we can get on with settling you back in and putting all this behind you."

Claire glared past her mother to the stairs that led to her father's study. She'd expected some resistance, a dash of crow sprinkled on her food, which she'd already decided she would swallow. But this was unimaginable to her. Her own father.

She'd suffered enough humiliation these past few hours; she had reached her fill.

Claire gripped her bag with both hands and squeezed as she rose to keep from crying. She wouldn't allow him a tear. "Thanks for the sandwich, Mom."

"Claire, please." Her mother followed after her to the door. "Just do this one little thing."

This one little thing? Was that what her mother thought this was? Had she considered her father's affairs little things too?

No wonder she'd never left him.

At the door, her mother's eyes filled. "Do you need money?"

"No," Claire lied. "I've got plenty."

"Let me have Adele wrap up more food. She can pack you as much as you need."

"I don't want it," said Claire. "Please thank her."

"Come back tomorrow. Promise. Let me talk to him. Come back tomorrow and we'll all sit down together and work this out, all right? Promise?"

Claire nodded, but only to comfort her mother.

She wouldn't come back the next day, or the next. Her father would never alter the terms of his contract, and Claire wouldn't see him again for another two years, and only then at his funeral.

*T*oday the azaleas looked parched. Claire stood on the wide cement steps and considered the bush's muted purple and red petals as she waited at the front door of her mother's home. It was a handsome building, so much more modern than the house Claire had grown up in. After her mother remarried, she'd craved something fresh, something new. "Like all brides do," Maura had gushed after the ceremony. "Some want new silver. I wanted a new house."

And so she had gotten one, and on the Battery, no less—one of the most desirable locations in all of Charleston, and she'd promptly filled it with new furniture. When

Claire had finally come for a visit, the only thing she'd recognized in the entire house was a cast-iron doorstop in the
parlor. She hadn't known whether to be pleased or unsettled.

The front door shuddered, signaling its impending
sweep.

"Claire?" Her mother wore a puzzled expression as she
leaned out.

"Hi, Mom."

"This is . . ." Maura blinked. "Good grief, this is really
such a surprise."

"I know."

"What on earth are you *wearing*?"

Claire met her mother's bewildered eyes. "It's a long
story."

Maura peered past her to the street. "Is Lizzie . . . ?"

"No," said Claire. "She was here, but then she had to go
home. I've been in Folly for an ESPN documentary. Like I
said . . ." Claire smiled wearily. "It's a long story."

"Well, come in, come in."

Claire followed her mother through the kitchen to the
parlor. A woman Claire's own age stood at the counter preparing a roast as they passed. The tangy smell of freshly cut
rosemary tickled the air. Her stomach clenched with hunger.

"Where's Pierce?" Claire asked, looking around

"Playing golf, where else?" her mother answered. "He'll
be home any minute. You will stay for dinner, won't you?
Better yet, stay the night. I'll have Dottie make up the
guest room for you."

Stay the night? Claire considered all the excuses she could make for why she should decline her mother's offer, but they all seemed to pale against the hard fact that her accommodations—the shop's apartment—were now gone. She could stay with Gus—*Gus!* In all the chaos of the morning, she'd lost touch with him. He'd dropped her off at the shop and been directed away from the scene by police before they could reconnect. She'd call him now. Let him know she was all right. Let him know other things—like how much she wished he were here to sweep her into the curl of his smile, his laugh, his bed.

Her mother stared at her, waiting.

"Dinner sounds great," Claire consented.

"Why don't you go on up and help yourself to a shower while I let Dottie know? Laura left a few things here from their last visit. I'm sure she wouldn't mind if you used them while you're here."

"Great," Claire said, moving to the stairs, knowing there was little use in pointing out that Warren's wife was easily three sizes smaller than Claire.

*D*espite Claire's earlier comment to Jill, getting out of her rash guard and surf shorts and into real clothes felt wonderful—even if it was one of Laura's obscenely expensive boutique dresses that, much to Claire's delight, didn't fit nearly as snugly as she'd feared.

She pulled her phone from her purse and saw three missed messages from Gus.

He picked up right away, the noise of the shop in the background. "Where are you?"

"In Charleston," Claire said, looking around the room. "At my mother's."

"How's Ivy? I've been asking around, but no one seems to have a straight answer."

"She's fine. Well . . ." Claire sat on the bed. "She's as fine as can be expected. The doctor's keeping her at the hospital overnight for observation."

"What about you?"

"He said I could leave whenever I wanted to."

"Very funny." But his chuckle seemed halfhearted and she regretted making the joke. "Seriously . . . are you okay?"

Claire ran her hand along the edge of the footboard. "I'm worried, Gus. What's Ivy going to do now? God, hasn't she lost enough?"

"Ivy's tough. She'll get through this."

"How do you know?"

"I don't; I'm just stupidly optimistic." She could hear the smile return to his voice. "You should try it sometime."

She liked that she could envision his surroundings in her mind: the busyness of the store floor, the excitement of the customers rushing to pay for their gear.

She looked at the door. "I feel like I'm twelve and everyone's waiting for me to start dinner."

"Then go," he said. "Call me when you're back, okay?"

"It won't be until tomorrow."

"I think I can wait."

"You *think*?"

"Go eat, will you? Before I come over there with a bowl of mac and cheese and feed you myself."

*P*ierce Danvers waited for her at the bottom of the stairs.

"Claire, darlin'!"

He took both of her hands and dipped down to kiss her cheek, his breath smelling faintly of gin. Claire obliged him the kiss and the squeezing of hands. Done, he straightened and took her in. While his gray hair had thinned and his hard jaw softened with age, his teasing eyes hadn't changed. Even now he looked at her with the same bemusement, the same curiosity he'd delivered when she was a teenager and he was trying his best to match her with his son, Warren. His marriage to her mother in the wake of their respective spouses' parting—Harp dying suddenly of a heart attack, Bibi leaving in divorce—had shocked no one, except Claire. Far away in Colorado, Claire hadn't been privy to any of the courtship, though from what she learned at the wedding, there had hardly been one to know about. According to the other guests, Maura had sought to comfort Pierce in the wake of Bibi's demands for a separation. Pierce had been touched; her mother, apparently, had been relentless. A year later, they were married. Claire had wondered: Had her mother taken some kind of vengeful pleasure in marrying Bibi's husband? Had it been the ultimate act of retribution? An eye for an eye? A lover for a lover?

Maura emerged from the kitchen, holding a glass of white wine.

"That looks lovely on you, Claire. You always looked so good in floral prints."

They ate in the dining room, overlooking the court-yard. The strong sunlight of day had paled to a creamy pink, making the lawn look like a blanket of velvet beyond the room's tall windows.

Pierce squinted at Claire as he worked to soften a bite of meat. "ESPN, you say?"

Claire nodded. "It wasn't as big of a deal as I'd hoped."

"And Elizabeth was here with you?" asked her mother.

"Briefly. Now she's back in Colorado with Nick."

"And that woman he took up with? She's still in the picture?"

"Nina."

"I can't really call her a woman, can I?" her mother asked, rolling her eyes. "She's a child, for goodness' sake. But work is going well?"

"It was a good year," said Claire. "I had some strong students. I can't complain."

Pierce gestured to her with his glass. "They're lucky to have you."

Claire smiled. "I don't know about that."

"And the town house in Boulder?" asked her mother.

"Golden, actually," Claire corrected gently.

"Oh, that's right. *Golden.*"

"It's fine," said Claire. "Still comfortable."

"Oh, I'm so glad."

Claire reached for her wine and took a long sip, letting the room fall into a comfortable quiet, a safe and all-too-familiar silence. The same one she'd tried vainly for so many years to explode. Why had she wasted so much time on the fight?

*W*e'll have our dessert and coffee in the court-yard," her mother announced when they'd finished. Pierce excused himself to his office and Claire followed her mother through the French doors and down into the gardens.

"Terrible news about the surfing shop," her mother said as they took their seats. "Just fortunate no one was hurt. What will she do now, Foster's mother?"

"I'm not sure," Claire said.

Maura's expression turned wistful. "I'm sure she was happy to see you. I remember you and she always had a close relationship."

So much closer than ours. That was what her mother was implying. All these years it had never occurred to Claire that her mother might have been jealous of her bond with Ivy. Now Claire swore she saw the faintest flicker of hurt pass over her mother's face, and a pang of regret sparked within her, flashing and then fading, having nowhere to go.

Claire let the subject drift off into the cool evening air and added cream to her coffee.

"Elizabeth is doing well?" her mother asked.

Claire wasn't sure how to answer. She and her mother had never shared notes on the subject of raising children—doing so now felt unnatural. Her mother's world was built on an appreciation for all things veiled and unsaid; who was Claire to demand honesty from her now? Yet as she blew across the top of her coffee, the need to press and dig and confess tugged on Claire intently. If she had gained anything from these past few days, it was that life was too short to pretend things didn't matter. Everything mattered. Just that morning at the hospital, Claire had purged more in a few hours than she had been able to do in three times as many years. It had felt good, freeing. Maybe even terrifying.

Why stop now?

"Why did you let him get away with it all those years, Mom?"

Her mother's calm expression remained so untouched that for a moment Claire wasn't sure she'd heard her. Then came a deep and heavy sigh.

"Oh, Claire." Her mother looked pained, disappointed. "We were having such a lovely visit. Is this really necessary?"

"Both of them," Claire said, undaunted. "You let *both* of them get away with it for so long. Why?"

Her mother lifted her coffee and took a slow sip, her hand steady, even as Claire felt her own fingers tremble so badly she didn't dare lower her cup for fear of soaking herself. "No one got away with anything," Maura said calmly. "I knew. We all knew. What's more, we all knew we all knew."

"But you pretended you didn't."

"You think so?"

Claire frowned. "Didn't you hate him for it? Didn't you hate *her*? Bibi was your friend once. You trusted her."

Her mother tilted her gaze to consider the speckled bloom of a potted moth orchid at their feet. The glow of dusk now completely gone, they'd had to turn on the outdoor lights to see each other. Under the harsh light of the courtyard's bulbs, her mother looked especially tired, Claire thought. Not so pinched. Not so fraught. Just tired.

A burst of sympathy filled her.

Her mother shook her head gently. "You always wanted to make it harder than it had to be."

"No," defended Claire. "I wanted things to be real. To be honest."

"You wanted fantasy."

"I wanted to be happy."

A door creaked open behind them; Pierce waved out. "Y'all need anything?" he called.

"We're fine, darling. You off to bed?"

"I'm afraid so. It's late for this old man. You ladies enjoy yourselves."

"I'll be up soon, love," her mother said, waving back.

Claire watched the brief but tender exchange with

wonder, the look of peace on her mother's face lingering even after Pierce had returned inside.

"You seem happy, Mom."

"Does that surprise you?"

"No." Claire smiled. "It's just nice to see, that's all."

"What about you, Claire Louise?" Her mother's gaze was searching. "Are *you* happy?"

Tears rose before Claire could slow them. Try as she did to pretend otherwise, there was something primal in returning to one's home, one's parent. Even if you imagined you'd moved far away. A plant given too much water, the soil unable to absorb it all in time; the excess will always spill over.

"Things are hard right now," Claire confessed. "Lizzie's angry with me. She thinks I'm trying to keep her from having a life of her own." She turned to face her mother, struck by the simplicity of her thoughts. "I just wanted it to be different between her and me."

"Different than what?" Maura asked.

"Than us," Claire said.

A glimmer of hurt washed her mother's features, then disappeared. "Of course you would." Claire couldn't be sure if her mother meant to agree or argue her point. "So, is it?"

Claire lowered her head, the clarity of her thoughts clouding again.

Maura set down her cup. "I was proud of you for your accomplishments on the water, you know. And I was quite sad for you when you stopped surfing."

Claire looked over at her mother. It was an unprece-
dented confession.

Her mother smiled. "You look shocked."

"I am. You never said anything."

"You were so busy steeling yourself for criticism you
never gave me the chance."

Was that true?

"You were sad for me?" Claire asked.

"Yes," said her mother, "because I could never understand, and I still can't, why you loved surfing so much that
you threw away everything else to have it, only to give it up
because someone broke your heart."

Claire shrugged. "I didn't have a choice, Mom. After
Foster, I couldn't make it work anymore. I wanted to but
I couldn't. Every time I got up on the board, it felt wrong.
Off."

Her mother considered her a long moment without
speaking, and then she drew in a deep breath. "I know you
don't want to hear this from me, Claire, but I'm telling you
anyway: You blame everyone for the outcome of your own
choices. You always have."

"Only the choices I didn't get to make."

"When you let someone else choose for you, that's still
your choice," said her mother. "At some point, you have to
own your part."

Claire turned in her chair. "And what about Dad? What
about his part? He refused to even see me until I apologized—
and for what? Living my life? He sent me away, his only
child. What kind of person does that?"

"Someone who isn't used to being rejected."

"That's pathetic," said Claire. "He was supposed to be my father. Not my friend."

"And yet you want your daughter to see you as her friend?"

"I want her to see me, period."

Her mother rolled her lips together slowly, an all too familiar gesture of quiet disagreement.

"I know your father broke your heart, Claire. Most days, he broke mine too. But we all make the choices that suit us at that moment in time, and eventually our hearts heal. And after enough excuses for why you can't make your life the way you want it, maybe it stops being everyone else's fault and becomes your own."

*C*laire closed the guest room door and fell against it. Her stomach ached from their too-rich dinner; her head ached from too much wine; her muscles ached from all she'd asked of them. And her heart just ached. All evening, she'd kept her phone at her side, sure Lizzie would finally return her call, but still no word came. And in its absence, the truth thundered: For all her trying, Claire hadn't managed to have a better relationship with Lizzie than she, Claire, had had with her own mother. But it wasn't too late. Despite her mother's advice, Claire was going to do things differently with her daughter. She, Claire, wouldn't let her daughter drift away.

She left another message. She'd leave a thousand if it took that.

Alone, in an unfamiliar setting, Claire felt the morning's disaster returning with full force, the uncertainty of tomorrow's plan coming with it. What exactly was she going back to, and where? The shop was lost, her few belongings lost with it, but more important, what would become of Ivy now? Despite Jill's insistence that Claire's purpose for being there was gone, Claire felt more committed than ever to staying on. Ivy would need support, understanding, patience.

Jill.

Claire undressed, replaying her fight with Jill in the stairwell, the biting words they'd spat at each other, the ones that had been simmering for such a long time, just waiting for the snap of a gate to let them finally race out.

Jill daring to question Claire's reasons for coming back, for staying to help Ivy, for encouraging her to reopen the shop.

"If you cared so much about helping her move through something painful, you should have been here for the funeral."

Claire glared up at the ceiling, wishing she'd had a better retort.

"You blame everyone for the outcome of your own choices. You always have. . . ."

She rolled onto her side, her head throbbing.

The clock blinked at her: Was it really just nine thirty?

Claire stared at it, thinking she hadn't gone to bed this early since she was, well, twelve.

She climbed under the sheet and yanked it over herself, over her head.

Over everything.

28

*J*ill ran a brush through her ponytail one more time before stepping out of the van into the hospital parking lot. Above her, the sky churned with stubborn clouds that remained from the morning's sprinkling of rain, and the air felt tight with moisture. How she wished for sun to help her wake up, to help her feel energized for what further emotional toll lay ahead. The previous night had been long and unsettled, she, Luke, and Shep nibbling at leftovers in silence, Luke finally rising from the table and closing himself in his room. Just before midnight, he'd emerged only to ask her to wake him in time so he could go with her to the hospital to see Ivy, but this morning Jill had let him sleep on instead. He'd wake and be angry—angrier—but he'd looked so peaceful when she cracked open his door at nine. He needed rest. Ivy and she didn't agree on much, but on that Jill had no doubt their opinions would align.

The hospital seemed quieter than it had the day before, or maybe it was she who was quieter, her heart having finally slowed its frantic beat after her not knowing Luke's whereabouts after the fire. Jill would swear she hadn't stopped shaking until she finally drifted off to sleep last night.

She wasn't sure why she'd wanted to come alone. Usually she feared Ivy's company without the safety of Shep or Luke, fearful of the tension between them, but today she'd been determined to face Ivy by herself. Ivy's cough hadn't improved and the doctor wished to keep her on a third day. Tomorrow, if everything checked out, Ivy would move in with them and hope the condo complex could move her into a unit earlier than planned. Ivy had been less than enthused with the plan when she thought she had time to spare. Under this kind of urgency, Jill worried her son's grandmother would refuse the plan altogether.

At the door to Ivy's room, Jill peeked in enough to see Ivy turned away, her body unmoving. She had to be asleep. Certain she was, Jill crept in and headed for the dresser to unpack. After unzipping the bag, she heard the rustle of movement, the sandpapery squeak of voice.

"Jill?"

"Oh." Jill looked up. "I thought you were sleeping."

"Just resting," Ivy said.

"How do you feel?"

"Tired. Hungry for real food. But I'm here, so there's that." Ivy glanced to the door. "Luke with you?"

"No, I wanted him to sleep." Jill heard the edge of defensiveness in her voice. It was reflexive; seventeen years of being made to feel like a mother with poor instincts.

"He could stand to sleep straight for a week after everything he's been through," said Ivy. "What about Pepper?"

"What about Claire?"

"Is she okay?"

"I don't know," Jill said. "She left the hospital and we haven't heard from her since."

"She isn't staying with y'all?"

"Like I said, Ivy, we haven't heard from her." Jill turned her attention back to the bag, carrying it to the end of the bed so she could explain as she unpacked. "I couldn't find the blue socks, but I brought a pair that's thick and looked warm. The tan robe seemed thin, so I brought the plaid instead. And I wasn't sure if the pillow cover was soft enough, so I brought a flannel one just in case."

"Flannel?" Ivy rolled her eyes. "Lord, I'm already sweating my life away in this place. The last thing I need is flannel."

"Fine," Jill said tightly, returning the pillowcase to the bag. Lord give her patience. Ivy had been through a lot. Now was not the time to draw swords.

"You need to get in touch with Pepper, Jill. She was staying with me—now she has no place to hang her hat. Where could she have stayed last night?"

"I have no idea, Ivy. Claire's an adult. She knows where we are if she needs to reach us, but I'm sure she can fend for herself. Her mother's still in Charleston. I'm sure she has plenty of room."

"They don't get along, you know that."

"That's her business."

Jill yanked the zipper closed. This was a mistake. She could just as easily have asked Shep to make the trip, to bring the clothes, to see the doctor. She lifted the bag off the dresser and crossed for the door.

She was nearly there when she heard Ivy's voice behind her.

"You should be the one to reach out, you know. After everything. It really should be *you*."

Maybe it was the lack of sleep; maybe it was the lack of sun. Whatever the reason, Jill felt the last bit of her reserve crumble away.

She let the bag drop to the floor and turned slowly back to Ivy. "I never had a chance with you, did I?"

Ivy frowned at her. "What are you talking about?"

Jill kept her gaze leveled with Ivy's, undeterred. No, ma'am. She wouldn't come this far and let Ivy deny the elephant that had been filling their rooms for nearly twenty years.

She pulled in a fortifying breath and crossed back to the bed.

"All I ever did was love your son with my whole heart, but I was never going to be good enough for him, was I?"

"I never said that, Jill."

"You never had to *say* it. It was in everything you did. The way you looked down at me, the way you criticized my every move, my every word." Jill swallowed, trying vainly to hold back the tears of frustration that threatened to well up. When the first few fell, she caught them on her thumbs and brushed them off. "I think after twenty years of being dismissed, I'm entitled to know why."

Ivy looked away, as if she'd seen a bird fly past the window.

Jill stared at her profile, waiting for some sign of understanding, of regret, of anything.

But Ivy remained unmoving, and silent.

I told you she would blame me, Foss.

Jill lowered her eyes, defeated. Taking up the bag, she turned once again to leave and said as she walked, "We'll have the extra room ready for you tomorrow."

"Jill."

Her hand against the door, Jill stopped. As much as she wanted to fling it open and let it slam loudly and deliciously behind her as she marched off down the hall, she remained.

When Ivy began again, her voice was smooth, resigned. Soft. "I'm sorry."

"I didn't ask for an apology," Jill said without turning. "I asked for a reason."

"Maybe it was because you were everything I wasn't," Ivy said, her voice so quiet Jill wasn't sure she even meant the words to be heard. But Jill turned and hung on every one. Ivy's face was tilted to her, her eyes watery. "And if my son loved you, if he wanted *you*, then that meant there was something wrong with *me*. That he wanted to get as far away from the person I was for him as he could. Can you understand that?"

Jill stared, speechless, the confession too painful.

Ivy sniffed. "Don't look so shocked. I didn't say it made sense."

"I always thought it was because of Claire," Jill said quietly. "Because you loved her first."

"No," Ivy said firmly. "I loved my son first."

Jill looked away, admonished, and not even sure Ivy meant her to be.

The room quieted again, but this time it was a silence Jill could bear.

"I lost him too, Ivy," she whispered. "I lost him too."

Ivy lifted her eyes to Jill's, just long enough for a flicker of understanding to pass between them, brief but true, before Ivy closed her eyes and rolled her face back to the window.

It was enough, Jill decided. A start.

And this time when she returned to the door, she walked through it.

*A*s she'd promised, Claire called Gus the minute the cab crossed the bridge into Folly the next morning. Her mother and Pierce had insisted on driving her back, but she'd demurred, telling them she wasn't sure where she was headed, which hadn't been a lie. Much to her amazement, Claire realized it might have been the first time she *hadn't* lied to her mother in a very long while.

After they enjoyed a cup of strong coffee in Gus's office at the store, he gave her a ride to his house and left her there to relax. Claire had made herself toast and shared the crusts with Margot. Now it was almost noon, a perfectly reasonable time to call someone in the hospital, she decided.

She stepped out onto the deck with her phone and asked for Ivy's room.

"Pepper?"

Claire dropped into the closest deck chair, collapsing with relief. "God, it's good to hear your voice. I called the front desk to get an update yesterday, but they wouldn't tell me anything because I'm not family."

"First of all, you *are* family," Ivy said. "Second, as to how I am: I'm drowning in fruit punch, they tuck me in so tightly I look like a spring roll, and the only channel that comes in is an infomercial for a motorized cane. There. Consider yourself updated."

Claire laughed helplessly, deeply, grateful for the levity. Even in a hospital bed, her beloved shop charred and collapsed, all her belongings gone, Ivy could still find the joke.

Claire squeezed her eyes shut to quiet her grief, not wanting to alarm her.

She might have known Ivy's hearing had never aged. "Everything okay, honey?"

Margot arrived at her feet. Claire reached to pat her. "I

keep thinking this is all my fault. If I hadn't pushed you to take the shop off the market . . ."

"Hush," Ivy ordered, firmly but gently. "You didn't push me to do anything. We both know it was a pipe dream. Even before the damn thing burst into flames."

Ivy's resignation broke Claire's heart. As she'd made the call, Claire had imagined buoying Ivy with talk of how to proceed with the repairs, that maybe the damage wasn't as bad as they feared, that it didn't have to mean the end of their plan.

But Ivy never did need anyone to soften life's blows.

"Luke was so excited," Claire whispered. "He'll be crushed."

"He'll live. He'll get on with it. Now it's your turn."

Claire glanced around the deck, letting Ivy's advice settle over her. She recalled Gus's words out here the other night. How he believed he'd come to Folly to face his problems when really he'd been avoiding them. Hiding out. Had she been doing the same? Throwing herself into Ivy's life, into the shop, into that world again to avoid having to go back to her own, the one so fraught with problems she couldn't seem to solve?

"It's been such a gift to see you, Pepper," Ivy said. "I can't begin to tell you, having you back here, taking me back to so much joy. But you have a home that needs you. A daughter who needs you."

Sadness swept over her again. "She *doesn't* need me," Claire said with a teary laugh. "That's the problem."

"Oh, you bet she does. Even if she doesn't know it right now."

"Then when?" asked Claire. "When will she know?"

"Who can say? Time is one hell of a brat that way. She takes as long as she takes, honey. There's no pushing her. Believe me, I've tried."

There was such comfort in Ivy's words. Claire wrapped herself in them like a bedspread and raised her face to the sky.

The air seemed warmer when Jill climbed out of the van and took the steps to the porch. Walking into her house, she felt different somehow. Lighter. Newer. As if someone had opened all the windows and blown every surface clean of dust.

She found Luke in the living room, reading on the couch, and she smiled before he saw her arrive, grateful just to see him, to find him home. She'd been so careful to hide pieces of her hurt from him, so sure she could reinvent the truth to spare his tender heart.

Now she moved to her son without hesitation, wanting him to see the evidence of her tears, the proof of her heartache and her apology and her fears. A parent's love was all these things, every minute. Her mother had taught her that.

Maybe, in very different ways, Ivy had taught her that too.

"Mom?" Worry flashed across Luke's face when he looked up and saw her approach. She took a seat beside him. "Is everything okay? Did something happen to Grams?"

"No, she's fine. I'm sorry I didn't wake you this morning."

"It's okay. I guess I was more tired than I realized." He looked at her a moment, his eyes fraught. "Can I ask you something?"

"Anything."

"Are you glad it's gone? Maybe not glad. Maybe relieved," he decided. "So, are you?"

"I think I'm relieved it's over," she admitted, speaking slowly, carefully—not because she feared her own honesty but because she wanted to embrace it. "I think sometimes we get stuck and we need life to tow us out, but no," she said, "I'm not glad. I'm relieved and I'm sad. Because it *is* gone. Because it's really gone."

Luke frowned. "I don't know what to feel," he said. "The way Grams was these past few days, happier than ever, excited again. I wanted her to keep that. But then a part of me knew opening the shop back up was never going to happen. And then I feel bad for thinking that way, because it's like Dad still lived there and as long as it was here, *he* was still here too. . . ." He squinted. "Does that make any sense?"

"All the sense in the world."

His eyes glistened. "Some days I can't remember what his voice sounded like." She reached for him. He took her hand and held it. "It's been hard for you, hasn't it?"

"Sometimes," Jill said. "Only sometimes."

Luke looked at her and smiled. "I'm glad she came, Ma. Your old friend. I'm glad I met her."

Tears flooded her eyes. "Me too, baby," Jill said. "I'm glad I met her too."

29

*I*t had been an aimless afternoon, hours lost without responsibility. Claire couldn't recall the last time she'd whiled away a whole afternoon with no greater purpose than being on the beach. No, she could: The four of them used to do that regularly, without consequence, without guilt.

Like then, today she truly had nowhere to be.

Now the beach was winding down with the day, the crowds thinning, the surfers losing their breaks and emptying out of the water, their wet boards and bodies reflecting the rosy glow of the setting sun.

They'd loved this time of day best of all. The four of them making sure to schedule one night a week when they would meet on the beach with dinner and beer packed, build a raging bonfire, and then unload their work horror stories around its crackling, climbing flames. They'd design grand plans for the weekend ahead, ambitious plans that would always be derailed by the discovery of no more beer after sunset, when Foster and Shep would make a run to Bert's. In their absence, Claire and Jill would inhale whatever decadent dessert Jill had packed and get high on sugar.

It was rare for Jill to drink too much—that had always been Claire's forte. But one night, to celebrate Shep and Jill's recent engagement (Claire and Foster couldn't be far behind!), Jill had joined them all by getting thoroughly drunk on rum and Cokes.

One and a half Solo cups in, Jill was weaving like a palmetto frond.

By the time they'd gotten the bonfire roaring, the liquor was nearly drained. Refusing to sit around a bonfire without beer, Foster and Shep had charged up the beach for reserves. For Claire, the lapping, snapping flames of the fire were like a hypnotist's swinging watch, settling her excitement down to a relaxed level. She and Jill had sprawled out beside the warmth and stared up at the sky until the stars revealed themselves through the veil of smoke.

"It won't always be like this, you know," Jill said.

Claire turned her head in the sand and searched Jill's profile in the fire's brightness, a strange panic piercing the cozy walls of her buzz. Moments ago, they'd been in hysterics, light as the sparks that rose to the sky. Now the air seemed colder, blacker. Claire wanted Jill to take the words back.

Claire sat up. "Don't say that," she ordered. "We'll always

make time for each other. We'll always make sure to have nights like this."

"Not after we have kids, we won't."

Claire waved her hand impatiently. "That's a long way away."

"It only seems like it," said Jill.

Dizzy from her speedy rise, Claire lay back down, twisting herself again into the groove she'd carved out with her rear and shoulders in the sand. "I hope we never change," she said, looking up.

"You don't mean that." Now it was Jill who sat up. "You would honestly want this forever? The four of us living like kids at sleepover camp? Never growing up?"

Claire smiled dreamily. "It has its moments."

"But it's not real life."

"What's real life?" Claire asked. "Marriages that turn ugly and combust? Jobs that make us miserable and fat? Houses we can't afford?"

Jill grabbed a handful of sand and let it sift through her fingers. "It's not all bad, you know. Growing up. Settling down."

"We are settled down," Claire said. "Look at the four of us. We have jobs, furniture, bills. We're already practically married."

"It's not the same thing. It's not real."

"Of course it is. It's real enough."

"Not for me," said Jill, looking longingly toward the dunes.

"This conversation is turning depressing." Claire rolled

over and reached for the Thermos. "We need to keep drinking."

So they did. And in spite of the lingering weight of Jill's words, the palpable sense that something permanent had shifted between them to forever break the magic spell of their world, they'd laughed the whole way home, laughed until they'd dropped into their beds, dizzy and spinning and ready to dream.

In so many ways, Claire realized, it had all just been one long dream.

"Somehow I thought I'd find you here."

Startled out of her memories, Claire turned at the man's voice and saw Shep walking down the beach toward her. For a strange second, her brain still stuck in memory, he was old Shep, returned from Bert's with more beer.

And for a beautiful, fleeting moment, the past few days and all their drama didn't exist.

"Mind if I join you?" he asked.

Claire smiled. "Not at all."

He lowered himself beside her on the sand. They stared in silence at the water, watching a sandpiper skitter up and down the shore.

"Foss was so tired that day."

Claire turned to Shep at the admission. So many times this visit she'd wanted to ask the details of Foster's death, but how could she?

She studied Shep's profile as he squinted out into the distance, grateful for the information, hoping for more.

"He only went in because I was having a shitty day,

you know. He hadn't surfed in months before that—maybe a year. Then I ran into him filling up at Red's and he could see I was having a bad time of it, so he figured why not take a ride, for old times' sake. That was Foss for you. Always wanting to make someone feel better about himself." Shep's smile thinned; his eyes darkened. "The chop was fierce and he was exhausted, I could see it." A wash of tears filled his eyes, mottled the skin of his neck. He swallowed hard. "I never should have let him go in."

Claire touched Shep's hand. "It wasn't your fault."

Shep wiped his eyes harshly with the sleeve of his sweatshirt, but he didn't concur.

"You never hated him for loving her, did you?" she asked.

"Are you kidding?" Shep smiled through his tears. "You couldn't hate Foss. That was the lousiest part of it all. You *wanted* to hate him, but you couldn't. And man, I tried; believe me."

"I know," Claire admitted. "So did I."

Shep reached down for a shell and pried it out of the sand.

"It had to be hard for you," Claire said. "Staying here afterward. Seeing them everywhere. You never wanted to leave?"

"Every day."

"So why didn't you?"

"My life was here," he said. "My family. My house. My friends. Where was I gonna go?" He studied the un-earthed shell a minute longer, then hurled it toward the surf. "Honestly, it always surprised me that you left, Claire. I always thought, no matter what, you'd never leave your waves."

Her waves. Claire felt tears of regret rise again and she shifted her gaze to the sea.

"Shep, the things I said the other day—about you being weak . . . I'm sorry. It's not true."

He sniffed. "Yeah, it is," he said. "I'm weak as hell. But I love her, Claire. I never stopped. I've always loved Jill and I always will. So if that makes me weak, so be it. I'd rather be weak with her than strong without her."

"She's stronger with you."

"Maybe. But it's not like before. I stupidly thought it could be, but of course it couldn't. In some ways, it's better. Little stuff. Knowing that thing you're so afraid of is behind you. Nothing seems scary—nothing seems untouchable either," he added with a sad smile, "but there's peace in that too."

Peace. Claire stared out at the water, hanging on that word, thinking how remarkable it was, how simple.

"I'm leaving tomorrow," she said.

"Are you sure?" Shep frowned. "You don't have to rush out."

She nodded. "This time I do. Jill was right. You both were. I had no business staying on here in the first place, pretending I'm still part of all this. I've been hiding, making excuses so I wouldn't have to fix what's broken in my own home. I've got a lot of work to do."

"If you need a place to stay tonight, you can stay at the house."

"I've got a place," she said. "I'll be fine."

"Then at least come back to say good-bye. At least something before you go away again."

Claire searched his face, the confession so close to the surface, so nearly ready to come out.

Or maybe it did without her knowing.

"Don't worry." Shep smiled. "She's missed you too."

*J*ill was in the kitchen when Shep led Claire inside, the smell of roasting chicken growing more fragrant with each step. Claire had waited while Shep called Jill from the beach, telling her that they were on their way home and that Claire was coming to say good-bye, giving Jill time to prepare.

So when Jill turned from the stove and saw Claire in the doorway, her face was relaxed.

Claire hoped hers looked the same.

Jill wiped her hands on a dish towel and threaded it through the fridge's handle. "Can I get you a glass of wine?" she asked. "Some sweet tea?"

Claire shook her head. "I'm fine."

Shep touched Claire on the shoulder. "I have a few things to catch up on in the garage," he said, walking off. "Give me a holler when you're ready to go and I'll give you a ride to Gus's house."

Jill looked startled. "Gus who owns Fins, Gus?"

"Turns out he's the one who suggested me for the documentary in the first place."

"Oh. I don't really know him, but he's well liked. And he's definitely attractive."

Claire smiled. "That he is."

The two women regarded each other a long moment. Twenty years ago, news like this would have brought their worlds to a halt. Whatever they'd been doing, they would have stopped immediately, slid into chairs around the table with a bottle of wine, and not risen until it was empty and Claire had spilled every last juicy detail of her new romance.

For a second, Claire believed she saw the same thought flash across Jill's face before she looked away.

"You can stay here tonight, you know," Jill said.

"It's okay. I have an early flight. And I know you need to get that room ready for Ivy."

Jill nodded, but it wasn't an impatient gesture. Her eyes were soft again, the way they used to be when she and Claire would confer alone, when they were closer than Claire had ever been to a friend.

Jill's voice was soft again too. The hard, defensive edge it had possessed for the last few days, gone.

"We'll take good care of her, Claire."

"I know you will." Claire saw Jill's glass of wine on the counter and wished she hadn't declined one so quickly. "It hasn't been easy, has it?"

Jill smiled sadly. "Which part?"

This should have been the moment, Claire thought as they stood there, the moment when they would apologize to each other, or burst into tears, even embrace.

But what had taken years to tangle might take years to unravel.

Neither moved; neither spoke.

She takes as long as she takes.

"I should get going," Claire said.

"You sure you don't want to wait for Luke? He should be back any minute."

"That's okay. Tell him good-bye for me." She smiled. "And tell him I feel very lucky to have gotten to know him."

"You'll see him again and you can tell him yourself," Jill said.

When they reached the front door, Claire slowed, feeling a jolt of sadness again, reminded of the days when good-byes and hellos had never been strained between them, never forced, never premeditated. In time, maybe they wouldn't be again.

Claire picked up her purse from the bench in the entry and turned to Jill, struggling to decide what to say next, when a shudder of thought passed over Jill's face. Her eyes rounded.

"Can you wait just a second?" Jill asked.

Claire watched her dash up the stairs, listened to a quick pattering of feet, and then Jill was back, carrying an envelope.

When she reached Claire, she held it out. "This belongs to you."

"What is it?"

Jill shrugged. "I don't know. I never opened it."

Claire turned it over and read the impossible names on the front, hers, Foster's. She looked up at Jill.

"Foss tried to mail it to you the year before he died," Jill said. "He never knew it didn't reach you."

"You didn't throw it away?"

"Oh no, I did," Jill said flatly. "For two whole days. Then guilt kicked in and I raced out to the garbage can in the middle of the night, tore open the bag, and rescued it." Jill pointed to a dried brown stain along one edge. "Coffee grinds."

Claire smiled. It was almost funny. "Thanks. I think."

"Just do me a favor, okay?" said Jill. "Don't open it here. And don't tell me what it says, because I don't want to know."

"Maybe I don't want to know either."

"Then *you* throw it away," said Jill. "Whatever is inside is yours."

Claire stared down at the letter, struck at the irony of it. All those months she'd pleaded for Foster to send her a letter, just one for every ten that she was sending him.

He finally did.

*T*he hammock creaked under the weight of their reclining bodies, the crackle of the aged braided ropes comforting, lulling as it matched the rhythm of the surf in the distance. Claire and Gus passed a beer back and forth, taking long, lazy sips. Above, the sky was a field of pinpricks surrounding the slivered moon. Claire smiled up at it.

"Ever made love in a hammock?" she asked.

Gus chuckled, took his swig. "Is that a challenge?"

She laughed and stole the bottle from him. "Maybe."

The breeze picked up. Claire could smell someone grilling fish several houses away, smoky and tangy.

"Suddenly I'm starving," she said.

"We could take a drive up to the Trap. Bring back a Captain's Platter and eat it on the beach."

"We could. But that would mean leaving this hammock."

He grinned, taking the beer back from her. "Then what do you suggest?"

"Fasting, of course."

"Sounds good." Gus lowered his foot to the deck to give them a push. Margot wandered by, her tail brushing Claire's toes.

"Ever get out to Colorado?" she asked him.

"As a matter of fact, I have an old friend who teaches skiing out there."

Claire closed her eyes and smiled. "Maybe you should visit him."

"Maybe I should visit you instead."

Her eyes still closed, Claire felt the hammock shift as Gus lowered the bottle to the deck.

"You should know I can't cook," she said, feeling the brief slack of the ropes as his body came over hers.

"*Now* you tell me."

September 5, 2003

Claire,

I hope this letter makes its way to you. I'm
sure if you see the name on the envelope,
you'll have mixed feelings about opening
it. I won't blame you if you tear it up un-
opened, if you burn it, if you send it back. I
debated for weeks on whether or not to
send it. Before that, I debated just as long
on whether or not to address it to Claire or
Pepper. Apparently I've grown indecisive
in my old age.

Not a day goes by that I don't think
about how it was for all of us here in Folly.
No matter the season, someone rides the
waves here to remind me of all we shared,
and I'm back there in my head every time.
Just the other day, I saw a woman on her
board and I swear it could have been
you. She looked so happy out there, and I
know it sounds crazy, but I believed it was
a sign. Proof that life had brought you to a
good place, a joyful place. I'm writing because I want to believe it's true. Because I
know that what we all shared on this
beach, all those years, made us who we are
today.

I know I hurt you and I let you down

and I know I can't ever make that right.
But I hope with all my heart that life has
been good to you and that you've carved a
wave worthy of your gifts, Pepper.

F.

30

*S*omewhere between the start of classes and endless faculty meetings, fall had arrived.

Standing on her deck with a mug of coffee, Claire mar-
veled at the fact. The air was crisper. The aspen leaves had
ripened into their autumn gold. The forecast was even pre-
dicting snow—snow!—in the next week.

Claire would be glad to see it. The first snowfall always
made her happy, made her believe that fresh starts were
possible, like a blank sheet of paper. This year, she looked
forward to the clean slate of the season's first storm more
than ever. When she'd returned from Folly, she buried herself in schoolwork and class lessons, trying to give Lizzie
the space to find her way back to her. Then, remarkably,

Lizzie had discovered that Colin had been seeing another girl—a fellow senior whose father, it turned out, had been the one to call into the school and report Colin, a series of revelations that had resulted in Lizzie arriving unexpectedly at Claire's door, red-eyed and despondent. After a marathon night of movies and Ben & Jerry's pints, Claire wished her daughter a good night and slept deeply, for the first time in months. What a difference a few weeks made. Claire looked forward to more changes in the weeks to come. She had plenty of her own to make too.

The front door lock clicked. Lizzie was home. Claire stepped back into the apartment and smiled to see her daughter come inside. A downtown gallery had advertised an internship at the start of school; Lizzie had shocked Claire by applying, then announced that she'd won it. Four weeks in, her daughter had fallen in love with the work.

"How did they say the opening went last night?" Claire asked.

"Isla said it was incredible." Lizzie swung off her scarf, then her teal beanie cap. "They sold eight pieces."

"What about the *Heron*?"

"Sold!" said Lizzie proudly. "I knew that one would go right away. I told Isla. She said I have a good eye."

"She would know." Claire noticed the package on the counter as she walked to the carafe. "What's that?"

"I don't know. It was on the steps," said Lizzie. "It's for you."

Claire picked up the padded envelope and scanned the

return address, her heart lifting. *G. Gallagher. Fins, Folly Beach, SC.*

She tore it open like a Christmas present. Reaching in, she pulled out a DVD, a bright red rash guard, and a folded piece of lined paper. She fell against the counter and read the letter hungrily.

> Hi, Hot Stuff . . . I got a copy of the show's rough cut today and I thought you'd enjoy seeing it. Despite all the crap they put you through, they must have smartened up on their way to the editing room, because your segment is fantastic. They tell me the show should air sometime in March, but who knows? All I know is the waves have been great, and there's a short board here I've been getting into shape with your name on it. (I'm serious: I've painted your name on it.) A supplier sent new samples to the store yesterday. This red one made me think of you. Swells are good right now, but I predict next summer they'll be even better, so make sure to bring the rash guard with you when you come back. I can imagine how amazing you look in it, but I'd rather not have to.
>
> I hope you're well. Margot does too.
>
> Gus

"What is this thing?" Lizzie arrived beside her, picking up the red spandex.

"It's a rash guard," Claire said, tucking the letter safely back into the empty package. "People wear them surfing to protect their skin from rubbing against the board."

"*You* would wear this?"

"Yes, I would," Claire said proudly. "And I will. Next summer, as a matter of fact."

"Next summer? What's happening next summer?"

Claire shrugged, grinned. "A lot, hopefully."

Lizzie held up the case. "So, what's on the DVD?"

"My interview."

"Wait—" Lizzie's eyes rounded. "You mean the one we went to South Carolina for?"

Claire nodded.

"Well, aren't you going to watch it?"

"I'm sure I will eventually," Claire said.

"Why not right now?"

Claire stared at her daughter, startled at the genuine interest on her face. "You really want to watch it now?"

Lizzie was already snapping the DVD out of its case and sliding it into her opened computer. "Is there any of that cheesecake left?"

Claire smiled. "Tons."

While Lizzie carried her laptop to the coffee table and scrolled to the DVD's menu, Claire cut them fat slices of cherry cheesecake and delivered them with generous swirls of whipped cream. Lizzie dragged her finger through the white cloud and grinned.

They settled back into the couch. The film began.

"Don't feel like you have to watch the whole thing," Claire said. "We can just skip the slow parts."

"No way," said Lizzie, already halfway through her slice. "I want to see all of it."

"You're sure?"

"Absolutely. I've got plenty of time."

Claire looked over at her daughter and smiled.

Maybe today they did.

ACKNOWLEDGMENTS

Writing about the bond between parents and children always reminds me what a fascinating, fierce and fragile thing it can be. I was fortunate to have parents who let me follow my heart far more often than my head. To my mother and father, I hope you both know how grateful I am for your faith in this dreamer and her relentless dreaming.

My warmest thanks to Richard Harris and Ben Constable for letting me pepper you with questions on surfing, and your tireless answers that kept me from looking like a "kook" on the page. Wishing you both continued joy in the curl.

To my editor, Danielle Perez, for encouraging me to dig deeper—this story is so much richer because of your insights and I'm very grateful. And my thanks to everyone at New American Library, especially Christina Brower, Caitlin Valenziano, Jessica Butler, and Mimi Bark for the gorgeous cover.

Acknowledgments

To my agent, Rebecca Gradinger, thank you for everything on this journey. Here's to the roads and the stories still ahead.

My gratitude to the booksellers whose stores and infectious love of books inspire us to keep reading, writing and imagining. Your support means the world.

And a very special thank-you to the readers who love the stories of our collective hearts as much as I do. In today's busy world, I know how hard it can be to find a moment to ourselves, so I'm honored that you have given your time to my books. I hope I continue to earn a place on your reading shelf.

A native New Englander who was raised in Maine, **Erika Marks** has worked as an illustrator, an art director, a cake decorator, and a carpenter. She currently lives in Charlotte, North Carolina, with her husband, a native New Orleanian, and their two daughters. This is her fourth novel.

CONNECT ONLINE

erikamarksauthor.com
facebook.com/erikamarksauthor
twitter.com/erikamarksauthr

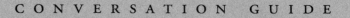

It
Comes
in Waves
Erika Marks

This Conversation Guide is intended to enrich the

individual reading experience, as well as encourage us

to explore these topics together—because books,

and life, are meant for sharing.

A Conversation Between
Erika Marks and Her Editor

Editor: The culture of surfing plays a significant role, as many of the characters are shaped and defined by their relation to it. What drew you to write about the world of surfing? Were you ever a surfer? What kinds of research did you do to draw such an accurate and vivid picture?

Erika: I have always been fascinated by the sport of surfing, but I don't think I really appreciated how much until I moved to California after college and lived among the surfing culture. Now that I live in North Carolina, we are just three hours from the water and great surfing, and many of the friends we've made here in Charlotte are accomplished surfers who regularly ride along the Carolina coast, so I was fortunate for this novel to have access to expert surfers who helped make my characters look like they knew what they were doing—even if *I'm* still learning!

Editor: You do a wonderful job evoking an intimate, atmospheric portrait of Folly Beach, South Carolina. What is your relationship to this town? Have you visited there often? Do you have any specific memories that inspired you to write about this place? How did your experiences help shape your fictional portrayal of the town?

Erika: I adore Folly Beach and have been there many times. My family and I discovered it when we first moved to North Carolina and have been hooked ever since. Part of what I love about it is that it feels very authentic and community-oriented. As always when I write about real places, I hope my affection shines through and that I do justice to the landscape in a way that pleases its residents as well as encourages the interest of those readers who might not have known about the place previously and will now want to visit.

Editor: The relationship between mothers and their children, and the different ways a mother's choices can impact their children, plays an important role in the novel. As a mother, was it easier or harder to write about the problems of parenthood? Were any of the relationships (or frictions in those relationships) informed by your own experiences?

Erika: There's no question that for me, writing about relationships—be they romantic, familial, friendship—is my favorite part of creating a story. And like writing romantic relationships, I think relationships between parents and children have the remarkable condition of being both wholly universal and yet infinitely unique to the individuals. I've explored mother-daughter bonds in my earlier novels but in those stories—for the most part—the bonds were strong and the relationships solid and healthy. For this novel, I wanted to look into a more strained mother-daughter relationship and how the struggles within that can impact further generations of mothering.

As a mother, I very much related to Claire's raw need to belong to her child, to be needed by her, and to fear the inevitable fragility that comes with watching that bond grow and age and ultimately, necessarily, thin. At a certain point, children have to be independent in a truly severing way, and so often I think it is far scarier for parents to watch their children take flight than it is for the child leaving the nest. My daughters are still young, but even so I am acutely aware of my own challenge to balance those instincts. I was a fiercely independent child and yet, I sometimes struggle to imagine my daughters showing that same independence, even though I know it is vital to their evolution and their sense of self.

Along those lines, it was important to me to show the nuances of Maura, Claire's mother. Clearly, Maura's mothering differed from Claire's with her daughter, Lizzie, but like any relationship, the layers are thick and what we see isn't always what is. Part of Claire's growth in the novel comes from her gaining a better understanding of who her mother was and is—and coming to peace with that knowledge in order to move forward in her own life and her relationship with her own daughter.

Editor: Did you find it more difficult to write about Claire or Jill? Do you feel more sympathy for one of these characters? Why?

Erika: I love this question. Initially, in early drafts of the novel, I felt my sympathies were very one-sided toward Claire, but as I worked through the revision process, Jill's character changed and became much more sympathetic, and I began to find myself torn, caring deeply for both women. Part of what I love about the revision process is that it offers the opportunity to flesh out characters we as writers think we know, but we don't, not yet. It is during those subsequent drafts that I find I really understand what makes my characters tick and with that understanding comes deep compassion and concern for their well-being.

Both Claire and Jill have suffered great loss in their lives—not just the loss of their mutual love, Foster, but also the loss of their friendship. There are qualities to both women that I love and admire and cause me to have great sympathy for them. Claire, for example, is highly emotional and utterly unapologetic for it, which, not surprisingly, has driven her to make many bad choices over the years. But still she is who she is—and that honesty, that vulnerability makes her relatable. Jill, by contrast, is stable and nurturing, a real caretaker—yet she too struggles to balance that in the face of heartache. At their core, they are both good and loving women just trying to do the best they can, and I wanted them to find peace, not just with each other, but with themselves, by the book's end. I like to think they did.

Editor: There are a lot of tough, emotional moments in the novel as friends and lovers deal with lies, betrayal, and the consequences of their actions. Which scene was the hardest for you to write?

Erika: I knew when I set out to write this novel, and I began to piece together the relationships, the emotional stakes within the story would be high, and there would be many scenes revealing the buildup and fallout of those intense emotions. For me, there is nothing more exciting than writing those scenes. But that said, the challenge can be great to get them right.

Without giving anything away, I would say the first hardest scene to write was the one of Foster and Claire in the shower, the night before he confesses his love for Jill, because Foster is trying to prepare Claire—without explicitly telling her—that he will be breaking her heart. I think we've all been on both sides of that conversation. So writing it, I wanted badly to have Claire see what Foster was trying to say, to spare her the heartache, all the while knowing that her devoted heart wouldn't allow her to read between the lines, and that I couldn't write it any other way and keep her character authentic.

Another scene that was difficult to write was the first time Claire and Jill see each other when Claire returns to Folly. It is a group scene—the estranged best friends reunite in the kitchen of a house they all used to share—and Jill's and Claire's children are there too, as is Shep, so the emotional energy is somewhat defused, but more than that, I struggled to decide how that first moment would go. If they would hug, if they would smile, what they would say—or would they not say anything? I rewrote that scene many, many times, exploring all the possibilities until it felt right to me—or better yet, right to Claire and Jill.

Editor: One of the most enduring images of the book is Claire's bright red swimsuit. Was there a reason you chose to use the color red?

Erika: I loved the idea of Claire shocking Foster and his friends both with her surfing skills and by donning a color that would startle them, even if she chooses the color somewhat offhandedly. It becomes her trademark and inspires her nickname. I find color a fascinating element in stories, and I know I always pick up on color when I read, so I am always drawn to assigning colors to certain characters or plot elements in my own novels— sometimes without even being aware in the moment that I'm giving significance to a certain color, which can make the association even richer.

QUESTIONS FOR DISCUSSION

1. At the outset of her trip, Claire is going back to Folly Beach with the goal of repairing her relationship with her daughter, but over the course of the visit, her focus shifts, especially when she learns that Shep and Jill have convinced Ivy to put the surf shop up for sale. Do you think it was Claire's place to step in and encourage Ivy to keep the shop, or was she overstepping her bounds, as Shep and Jill claimed?

2. Claire has a very complicated relationship with her mother, Maura. Do you think that Claire's desire to belong to Foster and be a part of his life was just about being in love with him, or did she also crave the sense of belonging and acceptance she felt with his mother, Ivy? Do you feel by the story's end Claire has come to terms with that question? Do you feel hopeful for her relationship with her mother going forward?

3. Not surprisingly, Claire and Jill's friendship suffered from the fallout of Jill and Foster's love. By the novel's end, do you feel Jill and Claire have a chance for reconciliation? Do you think it's ever possible to move beyond this kind of disruption/betrayal in a friendship?

4. While back in Folly, Claire voices to Ivy her worry that Foster loved only her, Claire, because Ivy approved of her. Do you agree with that assessment?

5. While Foster loved Claire, he found himself falling for Jill, even though, by all appearances, Claire was a more likely match for him. What about Jill appeals so strongly to Foster? Conversely, why does Jill fall in love with Foster?

6. Claire feels a new betrayal when she learns that Shep has taken Jill back. What do you think about his choice to resume his relationship with Jill after everything that happened between them? Do you think you could you take back a lover who had left you under similar circumstances and after so many years apart?

7. Clearly, Jill and Foster delayed acknowledging their love to each other, let alone to their partners, for so long because the confession would tear everything apart. Do you think Jill and Foster should have fought their attraction and spared their lovers the pain, or do you think their feelings would have come to light eventually, despite their attempts at hiding their love?

8. Claire's mother, Maura, asserts that Claire doesn't take responsibility for her own choices, but rather blames everyone else and sees herself as a victim—do you agree? Discuss examples in Claire's life where that may have been the case, such as her divorce, and her eventual moving away from surfing.

9. Gus arrives in Claire's life at a time when she is most vulnerable and needing a sense of peace and self-worth. How does he help her find that? Were you happy with the way things stood for Claire and Gus at the novel's end?

10. Ivy has long held to a belief that it was Jill's fault that Foster moved away from the surfing life and the shop Ivy always imagined him inheriting. By the story's end, do you feel that Ivy has come to see a different view? Do you think this will change her relationship with Jill in the future? If yes, how?

11. Claire is struggling to connect with her teenage daughter, Lizzie, who claims she feels suffocated by Claire. How do you think Claire's strained relationship with her own mother has impacted Claire and Lizzie's relationship? Do you see any parallels between Claire and Lizzie's relationship and the dynamics between Jill and her teenage son, Luke? If so, what are they?

12. Even though she is desperately curious as to the contents, Jill can't bring herself to read Foster's lost letter to

Claire, but the reader finally learns the truth of its words. Were you glad about the letter's sentiments or did you hope for a different outcome? Would you have had Jill's resolve not to read it, or would your curiosity have gotten the best of you over time? The author doesn't make it clear whether Claire eventually reads the letter, or if the letter is only there for the reader's viewing—do you like to imagine Claire did read it, or would you rather think she, like Jill, had come to a place of peace never knowing?